MEANS TO AN END

MEANS TO AN END

A NOVEL BY

JOHNNY JOHN HEINZ

TF
CP

Cover photograph by Evelyn Piechoczek: The Replica of Captain Cook's Endeavour. (Not a pirate but a discovery ship)

A catalogue record of this book is available from the British Library

First Edition: May 2002

ISBN: 1-84375-008-2

To order additional copies of this book please visit: http://www.upso.co.uk/johnny.htm

Published by: Twenty First Century Publishers Limited. in association with UPSO (Universal Publishing Solutions Online)

Printed and bound in Great Britain

TABLE OF CONTENTS

THE BEGINNING

The South Downs, UK, October 1987

Julian Vermouth strode next to Suleiman over the wet grass of the South Downs. To the left at the foot of steep cliffs lay the sea, above streamed grey clouds with a dimly lit sky behind, and in front were squalls blowing off the sea, checking their progress. Vermouth's concern was developing. If the wind strength continued to increase, it could prove tough to return to Birling Gap where they had lunched, and where their transport awaited them, Suleiman's Japanese motorbike.

They had just passed Beachy Head, having climbed up steeply from Eastbourne. They were on the Seven Sisters, the seven white chalk cliffs where the South Downs join battle with the English Channel. Each of the cliffs represents a triumph for the sea, Vermouth thought, as they passed a sign warning them to keep clear of the crumbling cliff edge; and the sea held the advantage with the weather today. From up here you could not see the height of the waves eating at the cliffs, but you could guess their power from the plumes of spray, rising up the cliff face further along. Right here, all you saw was a stretch of open grass running to the left with no visible clue that there was a vertical drop of a few hundred feet just a few steps away. Beachy Head had become a popular spot for suicides since the fifties: you simply drive your car over the edge.

Vermouth turned to Suleiman, shouting above the roar of the wind, "I think this is becoming a bit more than the afternoon stroll you expected. Is it time I enquired why you invited me, I mean, other than for the stroll?"

Suleiman laughed. "Julian, since I am moving into the business world now, I thought I must adopt some principles, a rule book. How am I going to stay fit and healthy, spending my days in offices, in airports and on aeroplanes?"

"Go to the gym."

"Easily said, Julian, but not so easy where I operate. No, the rule about business meetings is, whenever possible, to hold them outside taking exercise, where we can talk just as well as across a conference table. And another rule: always be ready for the unexpected. This rule is perhaps being tested right now."

"I can't fault that," said Vermouth.

"So I'm changing the game plan," Suleiman continued. "I thought we'd pump ourselves with a little exercise after that heavy – but very delicious, Julian, thank you – lunch of steak, potatoes and boiled vegetables."

"OK, OK, I get the point," Vermouth interrupted.

"No, I did enjoy it, beautiful taste, excellent fuel, just right for the weather. I was going to launch into my proposal now, on the way back, but with this wind, well, I would have to shout at you. Of course, we do that all the time in the military, but with even my limited experience of business I have recognised that we do not achieve our objectives by shouting at people, Jawohl." His posture shifted, in an instant, from that of a man, bent into the wind on the Sussex Downs, to the erect form of a World War I German officer, with a sharp click of the heels and forward inclination of the upper body.

"I can see why you need a rule book," Vermouth said, laughing at the incongruous gesture. Suleiman knew how to use humour to take the edge off a situation, and he had caught Vermouth's concern at the worsening weather.

"Now you will have to wait until we get back to the hotel."

Vermouth was not used to riding on the back of motorbikes. If the ride down had been bad, the ride back was horrendous. It was a heavy bike, but that did not help much in these weather conditions. It was already seven thirty by the time they turned into the driveway of Victoria House. The wind pushed hard against the bike as they made the turn. The gardens were obscured in the blackness of the storm, as they came up the driveway. They rode past the car park on the right up to the main entrance, parking on the gravel to the right.

"Sorry we had to stop a couple of times. I've done many things in my life, but motorcycling's not one of them. Just got my licence." Suleiman was pulling off his gauntlets and stashing them in the pannier. Vermouth said nothing, but wished he had known earlier, when he could have done something about it. "Why don't we go up to our rooms and change," Suleiman continued, "you do what ever phone calls you need to, and then let's meet in the bar in an hour. I'll book dinner for nine."

After Suleiman had made the dinner booking, the waiter came across to the girl at reception.

"So who's the Pasternak character?" he asked with a laugh.

"Sorry?" She did not know what he was on about.

"I thought I just saw the good doctor come in with his English butler," He explained.

"Oh, Mr Suleiman," she smiled. "He's often here. So much old world charm. I get your point: when those deep brown eyes look at me so questioningly, I do quiver. But I'm not so sure about the butler."

"I just meant the accent," he replied, returning to the bar.

The Victoria House Hotel is a beautiful country mansion, set in its own grounds. Gatwick Airport is just a few minutes away, which is why Suleiman had chosen it, convenient for him and convenient for Vermouth, who had flown in from Boston. The hotel has few bedrooms, but the public rooms have been restored to more than their original splendour. Vermouth was ready in ten minutes and came down to reception at the main entrance, to check if he had any messages, as there had been none in his room. There were none, so he had better find the bar. He looked into the doorway across from the reception desk, a large room with high ceilings, an ornate plant motif on the walls and large mirrors at either end. High windows, now curtained for the night, obviously gave onto the gardens. Beautiful, he thought, but no bar.

The receptionist watched him. She enjoyed examining the guests, categorising them. A lot of suppressed energy there, she thought. Very alert, especially the eyes. It is as if he has to check the place out, know where everything is, be ready, be in control. Vermouth saw her looking and smiled. A touch impassive in the face, though, was her final assessment as he turned and went back down the corridor. Sure enough a small bar was tucked away in a room to the right, but no Suleiman yet. He walked further down the corridor and into what was obviously the library. Books lined the walls, a chess table in one corner, various groups of chairs and an open fire blazing, everything traditional, warm, welcoming. I think we'll get our drinks and come in here, he decided.

Vermouth selected a table in the corner of the bar. It took just a couple of sips from the second spicy Bloody Mary to recover from the motorcycle ride, and on the dot of eight thirty Suleiman was there.

"Before we go in to dinner," he said, "I want to give you an overview. I'm establishing a non-profit making organisation, but with a strong business base; that is to say, the individual businesses are intended to make profits, but these will be channelled into the organisation's central pool. So let's talk about the goal. The world is changing, Julian. It's 1987; we're approaching the end of the decade. The whole political landscape is going to change, and this time I want the Arab world to have its fair share. Last time round, with the oil price hike, we won the petrodollars but lost on the investments. The West changed the goal posts with high inflation."

"This time I plan to work behind the scenes, to work commercially. I'm nearly forty, I have modest seed capital, and I want to achieve something. But, Julian, I have profile in our world, and I am thinking big. I am thinking very big. I've established my team, in particular my finance man, but I need what I would call a commercial director. It has to be someone totally familiar with the world's financial centres, someone who speaks the language of international finance. And then it has to be someone who is on my side, our side, Julian. You understand why I have come to you: you are Julian Vermouth. I know it's a long shot. You have your career, and it's worse, because you will have to move to the Gulf; neither New York nor London will do."

"I appreciate your confidence in me. However, this is not a long shot it's a non-starter," was Vermouth's immediate response.

"I expected no other reaction, but let us talk further."

Suleiman then launched into his world geopolitical views, which continued over dinner. His arguments were based on the linking of all kinds of minor events, from which he deduced impending political change. Much of it convinced Vermouth; some was more outlandish. Completely off the wall was Suleiman's view that Russia was loosing it's grip over the Soviet Union, with the likely consequence that power, industrial assets and property would be up for grabs as early as next year. Vermouth was not surprised: he was used to the views of conspiracy theorists, mostly directed against the US.

Suleiman had decided to go up to London after dinner, despite very high winds, heavy rain and his limited motorcycling experience. After all, he had claimed, it's just a quick zip up the M23. After he had left, Vermouth mulled over what they had discussed. No way could he join Suleiman. Just four years ago he had been a bank credit officer in London on forty thousand pounds a year, worried about the cost of his season ticket. In the last three years he had made several times that in New York, and if his current bet on the stock market worked, he would be home and dry financially. He did not need to go to the Gulf.

He was very conservative when it came to markets, so if he took a big stock market position, he would always place a time limit on his exposure, and he would talk everything through with his wife. It so happened that he had just taken by far the biggest punt of his life, and his wife had suggested the deadline: the beginning of carnival, she had said. She was German, so for her this meant the eleventh minute of the eleventh hour of the eleventh day of the eleventh month, eleven eleven on the eleventh of November. He was already sitting on a huge profit, which by early November should have doubled, the way things were going. He went upstairs to his room.

In the early hours of the morning Vermouth was awakened by a flashing light coming through the curtains. He crossed to the window and looked out. Wind was raging, trees bent almost to the ground, grey clouds were streaking through the sky at incredible speed and along the line of the horizon were flashes of light (shorted power lines torn down by the storm he was later to learn). He was fascinated but also fearful of the scale of the storm. Wide-awake by now, his anxiety prompted him to put a call through to New York, late evening there. He did not like what he heard about the state of the New York Stock Market today. He would check the market reaction in London on opening, but he was firmly resolved to close out his position and take his profit. I have made a killing and that is good enough, he thought.

After a fitful night, he finally woke at ten, which was five in the morning according to New York time and consequently to his body clock. Good timing, he thought, we'll know the state of the market by now, and he spent the next fifteen minutes failing to get through to anyone at all in the City of London. This is ridiculous; I'm going up to town, he decided. He dressed, grabbed his bag and headed down to reception.

"I'd like to check out, and could you order a taxi, please?"

"Yes to the first, but no to the second, I'm afraid. No taxis."

"What?"

"They've been out with chain saws since the early hours of the morning to clear the roads for the emergency services, but they're still blocked. Railways are out. Planes have landed but aren't taking off. You're in the middle of a hurricane zone. Take a look outside."

And so it was that Vermouth made the most of a weekend in the country, witnessing a level of devastation from which the countryside would take years to recover. It was the trees that had borne the brunt. Whole forested slopes flattened if they faced the wrong direction. Tree-lined roads now carpeted with trunks. Some of the shots on television showed acres of flattened forest, and this part of the country seemed to have been the worst hit. He would be well set for dinner party anecdotes, when he arrived back in New York on Tuesday night. He would spend Monday in the City, probably close out his investment position taking the profits, and then head out Tuesday lunchtime back to New York.

There is no doubt that the Great Storm of 1987 prevented a stock market collapse in the UK that Friday. There was no Black Friday. Instead there was a Black Monday, the next business day after the weekend. The reason is simply that insufficient stockbrokers made it to work that Friday to furnish the level of "sell" orders that a Black Friday would have required. This was just another case of Mother Nature flagrantly disregarding market sentiment.

By the time Vermouth took Suleiman's call on Monday night, Vermouth had been more than wiped out. He had entered the negative equity zone in a big way.

"Hello, Julian. Quite a day, but before we get into that, any positive thoughts on my proposal?"

"Suleiman, this is for you alone, and only because I owe you an honest answer. I have been wiped out, more than wiped out. If the bank doesn't bail me out, and I don't think they will, I won't even keep my job. I'm gone, Suleiman, so forget it. Just let me say, I have appreciated knowing you."

"Where are you, Julian?"

"Park Lane, the usual place."

"So am I. Meet me in the lobby now."

Vermouth slung his Vodafone onto the bed, the battery was nearly flat anyway, grabbed his jacket and headed for the door. He took the lift down and walked out to see Suleiman, dressed in a grey pinstripe. They moved across to a quiet corner of the foyer.

"You look devastated, Julian."

"I am. I stick to the safest investments. I keep the tightest of risk profiles. In this case, I was sitting on a profits cushion that allowed me to take a position way above my normal limits. I could have closed out and taken the profit at any time. And I always set a strict deadline to avoid being caught be a falling market and losing out with the price dropping before I can sell my shares. In this case I simply couldn't deal on Friday, sell shares, no one answered the phone, and on Monday it was all just too quick."

"It's my fault," Suleiman replied. "If I hadn't petrified you on the back of the bike, you would have come up on Thursday night. Like me, you would have been one of the few to get into the City. *God helps those who help themselves* is from the Bible, isn't it?" Suleiman took his religion seriously, but he still liked to add a light-hearted tone to show he was in touch with the twentieth century.

"I decided that if it was the will of Allah to change the English countryside on such a scale, maybe he wanted me to do something too. I thought, if I'm gonna do it, I'm gonna do it, bet the ranch, the whole caboodle." For the last couple of phrases he had tried out his Texan. "I was able to liquidate my seed capital, turn it all into cash and use the cash to bet on the index, *he who dares wins.* I remember that quote from my previous association with the SAS. So that's what I did on Friday, and today I closed out. I bet everything on the index, on the market going down on Monday, today. I bet just like on the horse races. And the result: my seed capital has a crop yield beyond the wildest dreams of any Texan oilman turned corn baron. So do you want to hear my new proposal, Julian?"

"Shoot."

"Tell me your loss. I will cover it twice over, and that's your *golden hello* for joining me."

***

Mankind has divided the world into "squares" bounded by lines of longitude and latitude, like a giant spherical chessboard except that the "squares" are not square and diminish in size as you approach the poles. From London, go three squares down and five across, and you reach southern India and the City of Bangalore.

Dressed in an ornate green sari, she stood before her elder brother, red hair flowing across her shoulders. In her hand she held a letter, the envelope discarded on the Kashan rug, set off against a pale grey marble floor. Her eyes gleamed. Just seventeen years old and she had the chance to go to university in Moscow. The decision lay with her brother. He was thoughtful, but he would not deny her this. By the time she had graduated he would probably have married, and the next generation would be well on the way. She had her life. It was for him to continue the family line, which had reduced to just the two of them in their generation since the family left Iran in the 1979 revolution.

"We should not wait," he said. "Go now, and then your Russian will be fluent by the time your studies begin." And her excitement surged through him, as she hugged him with gratitude.

CHAPTER ONE - FRANK

Tunbridge Wells, UK, 2 December 2000

The weirdest things happen on a day like any other.

"I'm off running," I shouted to my wife, as I opened the front door and ran down the steps, slipping my wallet into my tracksuit pocket. I shall pick up eggs for breakfast at the shop on the way back, I thought.

"See you later, Frank." I heard from Mrs Chardonnay, wife and mother.

It was eight in the morning on a clear December Saturday. The sun was low, but the sky blue and the temperature a little above zero. I ran up the hill to Forest Road and crossed it, to take Benhall Mill Road out into the country. It is a steady downhill incline for about a mile, before descending sharply to the millstream and then cutting up steeply along a sunken lane overhung by trees. No ice today, so I could keep to an energetic pace, warming up nicely before hitting the hill. For me running is a time to think through what is happening on deals I am doing at the bank, and to plan – this is good. Bad is when a merciless jingle insists on repeating itself in your head, at your running pace, however you vary the pace.

At the top of the hill, I cut left to take me across to Hawkenbury, where another left would take me back to start a second lap. Two laps would give me six miles, but the trouble with laps is that as you are nearing the end of them the human body has a habit of raising minor issues with muscles and tendons, suggesting they might prefer to rest now – experience shows that, once into the second lap, these little goblins disappear, only to return when you are thinking of a third or a fourth lap. Today I felt energetic.

As I reached the Red Eagle pub, a group of people was standing in the car park.

"He'll do." I heard a voice, laughing.

"Yeah, we need another for the match. Come on, mate."

I have never quite worked out why you sometimes stop and get involved, when mostly you just wave or make some humorous (usually trite) remark that you regret afterwards. But I found myself in a discussion about the bus being late and two of the Rugby fifteen not having showed. Hamid was a tall muscular prop-forward, weighing a good hundred kilos. He spoke with a slight sub-continental lilt, and was very persuasive about my taking the one-and-a-half hour trip from Tunbridge Wells to Windsor for the match, not to forget the booze-up afterwards.

"Just a second," I say. "I tell my wife I'm out for a forty-five minute run and turn up ten hours later from a Rugby match in Windsor, *in which I've taken part?*" I look at Hamid, but obviously not with the appearance of total conviction that this is such a bad thing to do on a Saturday morning in December. What else beckoned? Christmas shopping?

Zoë, a female supporter, looked me square on, shaking a mass of red hair across her shoulders. "Why don't you come? It'll be great fun. It always is. Do you live up the way you were running? Jimmy here is going back to the clubhouse at the end of Forest Road. He can drop off a note at your place, for your wife." She graced me with an open smile.

Hamid suggested: "We've got some size ten boots spare. If that's your size, we're in business. Shirt's no problem."

So that's the way it was. My house *was* just up the road; I *do* take size ten; and maybe, just *maybe*, the forceful invitation of a gracefully built, thirty-year-old redhead influenced my decision.

***

The match *was* fun. I had not played for years, but that is not so important for Rugby. I have stamina from my running, and as long as you do not mind whacking into people, getting bruised in the ribs, risking your femurs and taking skull-numbing blows, you can have a good time.

As to the journey back from Windsor, Zoë was off on a trip, so a friend was dropping her at Heathrow. Hamid and I were invited to join them in the car back to Tunbridge Wells, rather than waiting for the others, still in action in the bar and probably later on the bus.

We pulled into the short-term parking of Terminal Three at Heathrow, ascended a flight of stairs and crossed via the walkway into the terminal. Not much had been spoken in the car. I guess it was a pretty weird situation. I did not know any of these people before nine this morning, but here we were in the afternoon, having played Rugby together, dropping off Zoë at Heathrow for her holidays. As we stepped into the terminal we were greeted effusively with loud remonstrations by two dark men in their twenties, who had taken it upon themselves to stop us dead in our tracks.

"Azhar," Zoë said, "this is Frank. You won't believe it. We picked him up off the street in Tunbridge Wells this morning for the match, let him get pummelled a bit on the pitch, and here he is."

"Well, nice to meet you, Colonel Frank," said Azhar. "Tunbridge Wells *is* populated by retired colonels, no? You should change your tailor though." He was eyeing my ill-fitting jeans that I had just borrowed after the match. "Anyway, let's get Zoë through quickly. Give me your tickets, Zoë, and we'll let these guys be on their way once we've got you sorted out."

Zoë told me that Azhar worked for the airline. It made it all so easy. He would just bring us straight out to the plane.

"Where are we going?" I asked, as we all set off in the direction of Departures?"

"Frank, surely you are not the type to let a lady walk home on her own. You're taking me to the plane."

"We can't. There's passport control." Azhar was just clipping a badge in a plastic holder onto each of us.

"Leave it to me," he said. "My father, you know, is an international businessman and he's over fifty years old. Every time he flies in or out of Karachi where we live my grandfather is there, right there on the concourse. That's our custom, and with a little help from our airline we do the same here."

"Come on, Frank! It will be fun!" Zoë said. "You'll even get some Champagne."

One moment we were landside and then we passed through security and, without passport control, next moment we were airside. I was used to passing through without showing a passport for European flights and it occurred to me that I did not actually know where Zoë was going. Sure enough, after the few standard kilometres of corridors, there we were, and I mean all of us, on the upper deck of a 747, like passengers on the Titanic waiting for the announcement that those not sailing should disembark.

"Isn't this airline dry?" I asked, thinking about the promised Champagne, and they all laughed.

"We bring our own Champagne, Frank."

***

Sometimes you awaken from a dream, and it still seems to continue as you lie dozing in bed. If it is a pleasant dream, maybe you even encourage it to stay on a bit, as you stretch warm limbs under the covers and think, Sunday, no need to move yet.

And this was a pleasant dream, as an elegant female, clad in a colourful green robe, moved towards me.

In the background I heard, "It's a high class Parisian fashion statement."

"Sorry?" I mumbled.

"I thought your were admiring the stewardess. They commissioned a French fashion house to design their livery years ago"

Now I *knew* I was still dreaming. This was Zoë speaking to me. As the pleasant sensation of the dream was replaced by confusion, I began to feel a stiffness in my limbs and bruising around the ribcage. So I was obviously dreaming about the Rugby match. Or was the Rugby match part of the dream? Suddenly I had an urgent and angry need to check this dream out right now. Eyes wide open, I turned to Zoë in the full expectation she would turn into my dog, a TV screen, or just be a portal to another part of the dream, whatever happens in dreams. But no, there she sat, with a faint smile, prompting my perfectly reasonable question or questions: "What are you doing here? Where am I? What is going on? I think I had better wake up now."

"You are awake, Frank. We're an hour outside Karachi."

Panic immediately set in, the way it does in dreams. You want to move, but you are powerless. You want to struggle and then the vision changes and it gets worse, the nightmare grips. But I could move, I was not powerless, and Zoë still sat there, half smiling, and the panic was still there, no the panic was surging, and I wanted to wake up now.

The voice came from across the aisle. Hamid: "I think we have some explaining to do, Frank."

I swung round and there was Hamid. I looked back and forward: a few rows of empty seats, the hostess now gliding down the spiral stairs, a door to the cockpit. I had a sense of complete disorientation: this was definitely worse than shopping in the supermarket.

"It's just us on the upper deck. They don't get heavily booked these days, even though no one else flies this route non-stop anymore." Hamid said.

I looked at Hamid. Although I was fully aware that the only reasonable explanation was that I was still in the dream, a string of thoughts ran through my head as time stopped for a moment, the way it does at the acute moment of a car crash. Was I in a coma? Had I been kidnapped? Was this some kind of theatre? This wasn't a birthday treat, like a kissogram, was it? Well, it wasn't my birthday. My thoughts coalesced into a question. "Where on earth does my wife think I am?"

"She'll think you're with Jeremy," Hamid responded.

" With Jeremy?"

"Yes, Jeremy from Windsor."

This was getting to be strange. "How do you know that I know anyone called Jeremy in Windsor?"

"Well," Hamid questioned, "how do you think you happen to be on a plane to Karachi? We've been studying you. As to your first question, we told your wife that you had taken a knock in the game, nothing serious, but an X-ray was in order and it was the usual four hour plus NHS queue. We told her that if it got too late, you would stay with Jeremy (who by the way is on holiday), and she thought that sounded sensible in the circumstances."

"OK," I interrupted, still not sure if I was in a dream, a plane or elsewhere, but willing to play along for the moment, "but that still doesn't tell me how I got on a plane at Heathrow without a ticket. Airports have security, you know."

Zoë leant across. "Frank, calm down. We bought your ticket. Azhar simply checked you in with your passport, and us too, before we got to the terminal. Our airline can be quite passenger-friendly compared to many European carriers. You didn't really believe that nonsense about seeing me off from the cabin did you? That doesn't happen these days." Her smile was still as sweet as ever, but I felt rage building within me. As I stood up from my seat, she said, "Frank, we haven't kidnapped you. You came willingly. There was no duress. OK, I admit you didn't know we had your passport. It must have been an oversight on my part not to mention it, and I don't think anyone down there will be interested anyway." She pointed to the stairs. I could see a certain logic in that. It would be futile to accost another passenger: *excuse me, sir, I think I may have been kidnapped;* or, *could you tell me where this plane is headed?*

I had to clear my thoughts and work out what was going on, and more importantly, why. So let's say this was real, and they were telling the truth. I had somehow been lured by a Rugby match (improbable but true) and tricked into going to the airport (probable and true), only to board a plane in the belief of seeing off someone I did not know, on an international flight, to I knew not where, apparently without passport and ticket (improbable and, from my current perspective, apparently true). They must have drugged me. Why me?

Zoë obviously had sympathy for my confusion, as if reading my thoughts. "Yes, you did seem a bit drowsy from that glass of *Champagne,*" giving a little knowing smile, "when we boarded. The point is that you fitted our profile very well. We got to know a little about you, and thought we would like to know you better. We'll be landing in Karachi soon, so why not have some late supper. Be fresh. You'll learn more then."

"Who are you?"

"You know. We met earlier. I'm Zoë."

" No, not "*you*", "*you plural*"."

I looked left and right to Zoë and Hamid, and left again to Zoë, only to see a wall. My panic had subsided. No one was threatening me. They would simply have to put me on the first plane back. Supper.

***

Karachi airport is an ultra-modern, marble clad complex, less than ten years old, designed to high specifications by the French. This is not the third world: this is just a refreshing stroll through the air-conditioned arrival zone. I expect many aid workers think they must have taken the wrong plane or missed their stop. We passed straight through passport control with a wave from the booth before I even had a chance to start my questions. I was relieved because it would be problematic to deal with a junior officer at this point, before even entering the country. In the customs hall a group of a dozen smart white uniformed officers stood to one side of the hall. Three of them broke away towards us, and this was the first time in my life that I felt a real sense of relief to see customs officers moving towards me. I would be able to explain everything to someone of authority in the group.

Some people may experience intimidation from customs officers in these countries, but business travel had taught me a few tricks of the trade. Anyway, I could pull out a business card from my wallet and establish my credentials as a banker. So it may be awkward and unusual but the airline would have to take me back to the UK, that is the procedure if they land you anywhere without a valid visa. I had even seen it happen to colleagues with expired passports, to their embarrassment

Considering that only an hour ago I was not sure whether I was awake and this was real, I now felt confident and up to it. In the worst case I was going to spend Sunday in Karachi, before boarding an evening flight, that is if I could not get on a flight right now. There ought to be a few planes landing and turning round over the next couple of hours. I could even be back for work on Monday. Strange, how normal you can feel in the most inexplicable of circumstances; how you think you will just sort it out with an: *"excuse me sir, I think I should not have been on this plane. Could you let me know which plane to take now for my return flight to London?"*

At this point I learnt that Zoë was really a "Zara", as she introduced me to the senior of the three officers and apparently the Controller of Customs. He was very affable and welcoming. His assistant, Javed, would take care of our every need, and he, the Controller, was always there if needed. The first thing Javed did was to produce the visiting card of his cousin.

"He's just qualified with an MBA from the Lahore University of Management Sciences. He has vast experience of the business world, would be of greatest value to an international institution. I would be most grateful, if you could recommend him to officials within banking institutions with which you are acquainted."

Things seemed to be going my way: I would express great interest in helping Javed's cousin, and Javed would help me, though I was still not quite sure of what to do about Hamid and Zoë/Zara, who were still hanging around, as if they were part of the proceedings. Javed ushered us through a well-camouflaged door and seated us across from him at a rosewood table.

"Tea-coffee, green tea?" Javed enquired politely. "Excuse me Mr…", looking at my passport, "…Francis Chardonnay. I assure you this is the merest formality. I must ask if you have goods to declare to me in your luggage. Certain luxuries must be taxed. Do you have alcohol?"

I looked at him; time to get the ball rolling. "As far as I know, I have no baggage."

"He has nothing to declare." Hamid cut in.

And this is when I launched into my story, somewhat mystified, as I set out my demands (if necessary to be met by higher authority), by Javed's continued equanimity and lack of either surprise or concern.

"You wish to leave?" He reached into a draw. "The next available flight out is via Frankfurt. They are scheduled to land shortly and will then take off for Germany. This is a ticket in your name, your boarding card and your baggage checks."

I sat back, looked across at Javed, a dim suspicion in the back of my mind. "I am relieved. Nonetheless, how did you know that I was arriving, let alone that I would want to depart on the next flight out?"

"Actually, we would prefer you to stay," Zara cut in. "We do have a more interesting proposition."

I did not want to hear her proposition. "Tonight sounds great." I reached for the tickets.

"I would just point out the baggage checks," Hamid said.

"What do you mean?"

"Well, you said you have no baggage, but your air ticket has checked baggage for loading."

"So it can't be mine. I shall simply have them leave it."

Javed resumed, "That will not be possible. I have checked it for you."

Doubt spread across my face as I looked at him. "How do I know you are an assistant to the Collector of Customs, or, indeed, that he was the Controller of Customs?"

"In light of your strange circumstance, Sir, I take no offence. He is the Collector, but no matter for you. You are here, and I am here. You want to leave, and I have your ticket, which I will give you. You will land in Frankfurt. Unfortunately, you will have to pass through customs at Frankfurt, unusually, because it is the booking that I have made for you. On leaving through the "nothing to declare" channel, you will be met, relieved of your twenty five kilo suitcase and permitted to proceed to London, with the ticket you will be given in Frankfurt, that is to say if you have not been examined by the German Zoll, customs. My uncle has just returned from a day trip that ended up lasting seven years. He was very unhappy: all he needed was a little extra money to complete his hotel construction. Alternatively, I am satisfied that you have no contraband or dutiable goods with you, and I am happy that you should proceed with your friends into Karachi."

Nothing about the room suggested anything sinister. The pleasant smiling faces of my new friends and Javed should have lent warmth to the atmosphere. Yet, I felt a sickening curdling of the spirit, defying even the best of skills to retain equanimity and negotiate, learnt at endless management seminars.

"This is not entrapment," said Zara, or was it Zoë. My mind floated free. "Listen. We are offering you an alternative, a proposition. It will be good for your career." Some chance, I thought. I'm finished, trapped in a drug smuggling set-up.

"This is not a smuggling exercise," I heard Zara say from three thousand miles away. "This is just our way of encouraging you to listen to our plans." Hamid smiled encouragingly.

"You can be home by Sunday afternoon, and no one will even have the slightest suspicion you came to Karachi. There isn't even a visa in your passport. Most people would anyway think it impossible that you could have been in Karachi, what with the alibi of the Rugby match, but the flights work – as long as you have the stamina, or sleep, like you did, on the way over. We'll get you on a flight to Gatwick and have one of the Rugby team drop you home, as if nothing happened."

This was obviously meant to bring me back to the real world, which it appeared I had vacated for a few seconds, and settle this very simple innocuous conundrum I faced. It did settle it. I stayed.

***

Yellow taxis lined up outside the airport, awaiting passengers from the incoming international flights despite the late night hour. We were ahead of the game flying non-stop from London. Karachi used to be a hub many years ago. Today it is cheaper to refuel where the oil is, across the Gulf, and a stopover in the Gulf allows the airlines to include passengers for Dubai, Abu Dhabi, Bahrain or Muscat, wherever they stop, to improve seat occupancy. In front of us was a sizeable parking area. We did not take a taxi, for a black Landcruiser materialised as soon as we stepped out of the building, very VIP.

Not every city has its unique smell, but Karachi has. You might not notice it the moment you step out of the airport, but in certain areas of town it grows on you about as quickly as salmonella flourish in under-cooked chicken, while in other parts there is the scent of sub-tropical vegetation, and then the salt breeze off the sea. The highway into the city has another unique advantage over a city like, say, Vienna: you do not seem to have to stop when the traffic lights turn red, at least not during the night, and that is irrespective of what the other traffic may be doing.

"We don't have much time," Hamid said, "but now that we are out here, I am going to propose that we win an extra day. You can take the flight first thing on Monday. Then, if you take the Gatwick

Express up to town, you'll be in the office before lunch. I'm on the same flight. Your cover story won't change really. We'll just fix the extension for you. Don't worry. It's all planned like that anyway. I just thought you would be more comfortable coming with us if you knew you could still get out today. And apart from that, why not take a look at Karachi!" A heavily ornamented truck without lights rolled across the intersection in front of us, heavily skewed to one side, with an unbalanced load and dud springs. Seconds later we flew through, as if oblivious to the danger.

" First, give me a clue," I suggested.

This was Zara's cue. "Before we reach the hotel, you will know why you are here and what we think you can do for us. As far as we are concerned, this is all above board, if a touch unusual. Then we will have twenty four hours to discuss the groundwork for the practical implementation of this project." This was beginning to sound less and less like a Rugby excursion.

"I shall introduce us a bit better, rather than the simple exchange of names in Tunbridge Wells. We are not an organisation: I think I would best describe us as business people, but we have a kind of extra dimension, let's say. Hamid is in finance, like you, but more accountancy. He is originally from Karachi, a Mohajir, meaning his family moved here in 1949 when Pakistan was founded by Jinnah, Indian Muslims. Me, our family is really spread through Iran, Afghanistan and northern Pakistan, hence the red hair, but they don't call me Zoë here. Hamid, I and a few others have worked together for a while now."

"Let me make a point now about banking. In the West you join a bank, and traditionally you work for that bank, a loyal employee. OK, you'll say it's changing, but you get the point. Here we are part of a community, and the community wants to have its people in the bank, to serve it. That's the difference in the East. You want a loan; you go to NatWest and fill in a form. We want a loan; we go to our man in the bank who puts us in touch with his friend in the bank etc. We all owe one another favours. Look just over there to the right. Just up the road there is the Agha Khan Hospital. When you went to have your X-ray yesterday, (OK I know you didn't really), but if you had, you would have felt you have a right to go to casualty and demand attention. If we go to hospital, we look for the guy from our community (maybe we have pre-arranged it), but certainly if we are a villager, we seek out the guy from our village, who passes us on through his system of contacts."

" So where is this leading? Well, we think you have an interesting profile to be our man in your bank. Stop, hear me out." I was opening my lips in objection. She leant in closer and the Landcruiser maintained the outer lane.

"You have an interesting scope of business, and this is a great chance to enhance your banking career. Your job requires you to work with clients in your bank's geographical region comprising Europe, the Middle East and Asia, to help clients raise funds and organise their projects. We, that is to say friends of ours, have projects of this type, and we are going to bring them to you and your bank. As far as your bank is concerned, you will be working on bona fide projects with us. You will travel the region on this business. Your bank will earn fees. Your career will be enhanced." And she added incongruously, " Money breeds money."

"May I interrupt?" I cut in. "Back at the airport it looked as if one option was for me to smuggle drugs for you. I don't think this is the basis for a business discussion, and yes, I think I should take the flight today."

"I don't disagree," Hamid said. "Those weren't our drugs, by the way. How do you expect us to get you through immigration and customs without a visa, if there's no prospect for them (sorry, I mean for certain individuals, just like in customs anywhere) to make a buck? We'll come back to that, but don't jump to conclusions. We'll go through the details during the course of the day, and night if you like, and then you can tell me. After all, having bothered to come all the way here, why not check it out?"

His logic seemed irrefutable to a UK banker, stuck in a speeding Landcruiser, violating every known western traffic convention, on a December night in Karachi, with no visa, no stamped passport, no real sense of why he was here, how he was going to get out, and with the occasional but distinct sound of automatic gunfire in the background. At least I had some new Rugby pals.

***

We arrived at our hotel to the remnants of an airline's annual event in gardens leading down to the waterfront.

"Get your key at reception. They have your name. Breakfast at nine." Chirped Zara as she slipped away in a swirl of red hair.

Even in the most extraordinary circumstances, we still act as we normally do. It is only in an emergency, when the adrenalin flows, that our breathing shortens and our behaviour becomes unpredictable. Well, I was breathing normally, so I would do what I normally do – I strolled into the gardens to see if I could get a beer. The band had long since departed, but a few clusters of revellers were standing among the round tables, set up by the open air dance floor, others seated in twos and threes at tables, one big noisy group over in the corner. The lawns led down to a kind of jetty at the waterfront, at the end of which a barge was moored. The water was still and black, clearly not the ocean, but beyond the ornamental lighting of the barge was darkness, limiting my view. Drinks were still being served at a table to the side, and it truly was German beer flown in for the event.

I took a beer and wandered into the palms. I looked at my watch: it was just over thirteen hours since the match ended, just gone one in the morning at home. I thought of my wife and daughters back there, my son, but it all seemed so distant, another world. Yet I did not feel threatened, I was not locked up, handcuffed. I was just left free to do what I wanted. Maybe I was being watched. I did not know. I felt as if I were having a nice cool beer on a pleasant summer's evening outside after dark, and I suppose I was, except that it was winter. I cannot say my mind was in turmoil. It just seemed I would have to wait and see what it was they wanted. I had not done anything wrong, had I?

"This is by invitation only. Still I guess you look as if you could be eligible." I turned to see a tall blond man in his late forties on his own at a table a few feet away. I moved across and sat down a couple of chairs around the curve of the table.

"I thought there'd be a few pilots here. I'm Sid, by the way, from down under. It's really for local businessmen and expats, only the hard core left now, who'll probably stay till breakfast. Still, where else do you get a free beer in Karachi? I fly out of the Gulf by the way. A lot of us Aussies ended up in the Gulf, after we went on strike and the government sacked us all, and put the air force pilots in. You look like you just got in, and your not an expat. You wouldn't stay at this hotel if you were. It had its heyday many years ago."

"Hi." I wasn't sure if I should say my name. This was the first interaction with the real world since the UK, I mean, assuming I really was here.

"When I stop over in places like this, I just sit and drink beer," Sid continued. "Just make sure I stop drinking six hours before I'm due to fly the plane. We have very strict alcohol rules. Who are you flying with?"

"Not sure yet," I said. "The Monday morning flight, probably. Breakfast time. London via Dubai."

"Hey, that's mine. We leave at six, so if you catch me drinking after midnight tomorrow, I guess that's tonight now, warn me!" He chuckled. "I'll get us another couple of cold ones."

I watched him move across to the bar. Several others were now leaving through the arch to the side of the hotel. He came back with four beers.

"Right. They were closing down, so I thought we had better get a couple in."

I'd missed out on most of the Rugby booze-up, slept on the plane, why not?

"Hang on." I said. In all of ninety seconds I was back with another four beers. A few other tables were still sparsely populated. Ours was the only table supporting eight beers, but then, to give the others their due, it was almost breakfast time.

After an active day's sport, flying all afternoon/evening, virtually nothing to eat, it does not take long to drink four beers, but at least I had a touch of normality before heading off to my room, and Sid had a bit of company, albeit still non-pilot company. Sid was right about the hotel. My room looked as if it had been updated in 1956: clean, but paper and paint peeling, gaps around a window-mounted air conditioning unit. It had a phone but whom was I going to call? I took off my Rugby-club-borrowed jeans and shirt, and noticed an open canvas bag in the corner with some clothes and toiletries in it. Must be mine, I thought.

I awoke to a phone ringing by my bed.

"John Stanley here." A polite English voice, well to do.

"Who?"

"I shall expect you here at 8 a.m. Two doors down to the left, 609." And he had rung off.

If I was going, I had ten minutes.

I knocked and the door opened to a powerfully built young man with almost coal black skin.

"I'm here to see John Stanley."

"This is he. Do come in." In cultivated English tones. "I do tend to surprise people. Anglo-Indian. It's legendary that just a couple of hundred English ruled the entire Indian sub-continent, the District Commissioners. They had rather more extended and more scattered families, than might have been the case, had they stayed at home. I'm one. My great grandfather's fault. Some of us were recognised; hence my middle name, Saint John (pronounced Sanjun, frenchified), so I go back to William the Conqueror." His dark brown eyes smiled. "Bit of a joke really John Saint John. Do sit over here at the table. Excuse the state of the décor." His introduction had given me a moment to get my bearings, and this suite was certainly no more elaborate than my room.

"You may wonder why you're here."

"Not at all," I broke in, but he was not perturbed by my tone.

"We have forty-five minutes to get down to business. I am expected to brief you, and that is all. You may ask me questions for clarification, which I will answer. No commitment is expected from you, nor decision. You may relax, but I suggest you stay alert and listen to what I have to say. Let's go."

Sanjun proceeded to explain to me how a banker of my profile had been chosen. Still in my thirties, experience of business across cultures, including the Middle East, slotted into the right kind of position in the right type of international bank. According to him, my profile dovetailed into their plans. He talked at length about the multi-faceted business interests they represented; they were not planning illegal operations, he insisted, merely endeavouring to ensure that they had their own people, on their side, in the banks that would be assisting them and representing their financial interests. I should regard it as an informal arrangement that would ensure that interesting and lucrative propositions would be directed with first right of refusal to me and my bank. This would be good for the bank and, of course, for my career.

The assignments would be varied, so it would not be clear to my bank that they would be in any way linked, which would make me look even better as someone who brought in new business for the bank from various sources. This would be "our little secret". From their side, they would expect from me frank and open lines of communication, and given that I would be working substantially on their transactions, they would expect me to take a very pro-active advisory role, and to be available to travel with them on their business on a regular basis. All transactions would be proposed on an arm's length basis, meaning I could reject any particular deal that did not look right for my bank, and they would be subject to the normal processes of evaluation and approval of my bank.

"Not unlike what you are doing at present," he summarised.

"And if I don't?"

"That's not part of this discussion. Breakfast is downstairs at nine. Thank you for joining me this morning." He stood up, donned his jacket, opened the door and left. I never saw him again.

I returned to my room to ponder this proposition. What was there to ponder? Despite hardly an hour's sleep, I felt fresh. The sleep on the plane had sufficed, I suppose. Apparently, I was not being asked to do anything, at least not right now, so I might as well get through the day and hop on the plane tomorrow morning, return to normality, steer clear of impromptu Rugby match invitations in future, and *maybe*, just maybe, I would be OK. Not a convincing train of thought.

Sure enough, at nine, Hamid and Zara were ensconced at a table near the buffet, he in casual, she in the local shalwar kameez, light baggy trousers and a tunic, combining colours with a translucent sheen, a scarf over the left shoulder. She looked across, gaily waving an invitation to an old Rugby team chum, I suppose, me. I looked around the room. Clearly my Australian buddy from last night was either still drinking beer somewhere, to get enough in before the self-imposed pre-take-off dry spell, or else taking a snooze, so I joined their table.

"My programme started at eight. It seems we are squeezing in breakfast. What's next? Or should I make my own plans today?" I asked.

"You're looking good this morning," Zara chirped, showing greater American flair than I anticipated from the hotel buffet, eggs maybe, but no doubt light on the bacon.

"We have a good hour to kill before things open up around here, so let's have a really good breakfast. Then, since you *are* here after all," she said, turning her head towards me with a smile, "you might like to start your Christmas shopping early. Rugs, silver, jewellery, you name it; we've got it here, like nowhere else. Get your wife some gold necklaces. You simply pay by weight. The workmanship, which by the way can be exquisite, is virtually free. Take a look at the leather goods."

"So the formal programme is over is it? What about my passport and tickets? I thought we had twenty four hours *to lay the groundwork*, as you put it in the car last night."

Hamid handed a packet to me. "John seemed happy that he had achieved all that in forty-five minutes. He is a very capable young man. We do have a dinner you can join this evening, but otherwise it's for you to decide what you do with or without us. We are here to help."

I checked the packet. Sure enough, passport and a ticket to Gatwick via Dubai. I looked at the passport, checked old visas, and could tell it really was mine. What now? Hightail it to the British High Commission and explain the story. It would not work, would it? Too implausible. Anyway, what about the implications for my job, any future job: *did you hear about Frank Chardonnay? Some cock'n bull story about alien abduction to Karachi for the weekend.* No, since I now had a way back, let me assume it to be real, take it, take stock back in the safety of the UK and not upset the apple cart here.

" So what?" Zara was appraising me.

"Yeah, Christmas shopping this morning, since I *am* here, after all."

In daylight, I could see that we were located on a creek of fairly turgid looking water, bounded by what appeared to be mangrove swamps.

"Is this Karachi's holiday hot spot, sub-tropical paradise?" I enquired, as we pulled out of the hotel.

Zara laughed. " Karachi's not a holiday spot. It's a commercial city and port, but it has great bazaars. Actually, the beach is quite nice. Maybe you'll see next time." No way, I thought. We sat in the back of the Landcruiser, a good choice of vehicle as it turned out. We weaved between trucks, camels, buses with people hanging off the roof, motorised rickshaws, motorcycles individually transporting entire families, heading for the centre of town.

"Lovely day," I said.

"It always is this time of year, mid November to April, blue skies and sunshine, but we need you in the UK for the time-being, Frank."

"Just as my spirits were reviving, you have to bring that up. Well, I guess, I'll just treat this as our honeymoon then." One up to me. Maybe shopping could be fun after all.

So many events piled into such a short space of time. I realised I had not really - how should I put it? - noticed who these people were who had brought me here, other than immediate appearances and impressions, certainly not their persona. I glanced at Zara, who might just as well be a photograph in a magazine for all that I knew of her; or in her case I revised this to the cover of the leading women's magazines. Following her along the crowded street, the breeze catching her clothes and hair, as she weaved her way, I perceived an advantage over the more traditional Muslim practice of the female following four steps behind, but still I had no idea of who she was. I admired the confidence and charm with which she deflected the shopkeepers' practiced skill of selling unwanted goods to outsiders at prices over the odds. But then she did not seem to be an outsider: cheerful greetings and chats punctuating our progress through the bustling shopping streets. She showed no hesitation in meeting my Christmas shopping needs in a jewellery store at prices that even I could accept, although it did strike me later that I should not have left an audit trail with my credit card.

"I'll take you down to Clifton Beach. It's just ten minutes. It will be beautiful today. Let's get out of the crush here. Come on. Look the driver's just over here." He pulled up to us, and we boarded.

"Zara, I shouldn't have used my credit card, should I?"

"Frank, why's anyone going to check your credit card? Though I admit you might not want your wife to see the statement, before you tell her where you've been."

"Tell her where I've been?"

"Why not? In due course, once you've got used to the idea. You haven't done anything wrong. At least, not that I know about. OK, it might make you look a bit stupid, but I guess she knows you well enough. She did marry you. I mean, I wouldn't have joined some crazy Rugby trip like you did. But no harm done. I'd leave out the bit about the Frankfurt suitcase, if I were you."

"You're full of good advice, Zara. I wish you'd told me when we first met. What are those pillars?" We were approaching a roundabout.

"Those are the three swords of Islam. Impressive, huh? You see how this crazy traffic is moving in all directions, weaving over all three lanes on this side and over the three across the concrete barrier. Listen to this. A few years ago there's this man, totally blind, gets on his motorcycle, sitting facing backwards. Blindfolds himself for good measure. He starts back there, at the three swords roundabout we've just passed, and rides through the traffic up to the roundabout we are approaching and back again, using only his sense of hearing. Can you believe that? Sitting backwards? Blind?" Frankly, I found it hard to believe that our Landcruiser was left unscathed through this medley of Highway Code violations. It struck me that the blind man might actually have used his sense of smell, fragrant vegetation occasionally punctuated by the result of blocked drains, but I decided against raising this for the moment, as I was beginning to enjoy Zara's company. We took the next roundabout, two swords at this one, something vaguely naval or maybe cotton spinning at the next.

"We are in Clifton. On the right is the British High Commission. I'm sure the idea of a visit occurred to you last night, but good sense prevailed. I admire your resourcefulness, finding not only beer but also a drinking partner on your first night in Karachi. My room overlooked the gardens. I was watching you, Frank. He was a nice looking guy, I thought."

We stopped on the promenade at the beach and walked down to the sand. The beach stretched out in a wide bay and was scattered with people and camels. A few kids were playing in the water, and there were whole families, full clothed, in as deep as their knees and way out to sea, obviously a very shallow shelving beach, all sand.

"Isn't this unusual. I mean, you and me on the beach, unchaperoned." I asked.

"No, I love it, Frank. Isn't it great to be out of the grey UK?" The sun glinted in her hair, a sense of fun emanating from her.

"You up for a run?" And we set off up the beach, a light following wind, sand heavy underfoot.

"Why did you go into banking, Frank? I mean, it's not like the kind of philosophical and medieval stuff you did at Cambridge – sorry, I've seen your CV."

"You'd be surprised at the weird stuff some of my banking colleagues studied. Or then again maybe not, since you've probably seen their CVs too." I was being defensive, erecting barriers, and instantly regretted it, so I continued. "But no, banking was my plan all along. It seems that mostly when you choose, you cut out all the other possible choices. You know; if you're a lawyer, you do law; if you're a doctor, you do medicine. It seemed to me that if you do international banking, you get involved with all kinds of activities, and often with a view from the top. And that's pretty much how I've found it to be, but it's changing, as the focus switches to markets and financial instruments. We don't really look at the real business any more in the way we used to. What about you?"

"I'm your pro forma young professional, suitable to fill any slot in the organisation." She turned towards me and spoke with her eyes, behind the words that came out. "When the European Community expands far enough eastwards, they'll take me on at the European Investment Bank; or I might end up in Central Asia for the Asian Development Bank, when *they* expand west. I'm happy where I am for the time-being."

"And where's that?"

"Here, on Clifton Beach with you, but only for the moment." She looked up to where the driver was coasting along the road beside the beach, waving to her from the open window of the Landcruiser.

CHAPTER TWO - DUBAI

London, 4 December 2000

I landed at Gatwick well ahead of schedule. Hamid and I had sat apart: there was nothing to discuss. Straight off the plane and onto the Gatwick Express, and I was in the office before lunch. Jill, our child secretary, right out of university, slim tall and blonde, greeted me with a quip about where I could have found the sun in December. I had the feeling she was jealous of my tan, but I did not think she would have accepted an invitation to join me next time. I was not her type, approaching middle age in my early thirties, passable but not striking of appearance, slightly balding. She was more interested in the young guys in computer support. She said she had seen my note about the external meeting this morning (did this surprise me, even though I hadn't left her one?), and now I was at my desk. I called home, but the answer phone was on, so I said "Hi" and hung up. I felt safe, a return of normalcy, but who were these people from the Rugby trip?

As Zara had bid me farewell last night in Karachi, I had asked, "Zara, what would have happened, if I had done the normal thing and ignored the *invitation* to join your Rugby trip?" She had looked me in the eyes and replied, "Frank, you have blue-grey eyes, like mine, we go well together," turned with an elegant swirl and left.

Right. No reminiscing. Let's get on the Internet. Where shall I start? Facts. The screen came up. Heathrow departures. No, it's got arrivals; where are departures? OK, Google search. Let me find the flight I was on. Gradually I worked my way through a few billion artificial synapses, so familiar to us users of the modern electronic world, in one billionth of one second. I don't believe it: when our flight was scheduled to depart we were still in the Rugby club bar in Windsor. So the flight was late. But we had tickets for this flight. The timing could never have worked if the plane had left on time. Who were these people? Could they really have delayed a flight? For me? I felt 100% less relaxed about the whole thing than I had been on getting back to the office.

How could they have known that I would join the Rugby trip? What if they didn't? Let's think. I agreed to join the Rugby trip. The bus arrived at that moment and I boarded. What about the missing two players? In fact Hamid had not played, and yet we had been a full team of fifteen. This means that there had been no missing players. Sitting back, thinking this through, it gradually dawned on me that they had never intended me to join the trip.

My impromptu decision had nearly scuppered their plans, most likely. Their plan was to intercept me in Tunbridge Wells, and then, somehow or other, to get me on the flight to Karachi. So when I got on the Rugby club bus they would have had to rethink their plans. Maybe Hamid was never intended to fly with us, but this became a necessary ruse to get me to accompany them to the point where we boarded the plane. They must have cleared me through security on some other ticket, and then taken me to the Karachi plane. I still could not work out how: it was all so implausible, but it had happened.

Then the other mystery: they had had my passport. I keep it in the safe at home, but no, I had sent it last week to the Romanian consular office for a visa. Did I get it back? After all that had happened, I could not remember for the moment. Had they intercepted my passport? Let me think about this. I would have given the passport to my secretary, who would have sent it by internal mail to the in-house travel office. They would have used a courier to send it to the Romanians and to retrieve it with the visa. So that process has three possible weak links: my secretary, internal office mail and the travel office, given that neither the Romanians nor the courier service seemed likely. But then whoever stole my passport would also have needed the information that I was applying for a Romanian visa. If that limits the field, then it had to be the travel office or my secretary, and the latter I really could not believe. I was admiring my talents as a sleuth when Jill popped her head around the door with a secretarial prompt.

"Frank, it's the two o'clock meeting." The Monday afternoon meeting. Great!

I was among the first to enter the boardroom, evidencing that to say no one really rushed for these meetings would be an understatement.

A trite: "Hi, Frank. Good weekend?" greeted me.

"Yeah. Got roped into a Rugby match actually. Still a bit sore." As always I was telling the truth, at least to the extent required by the circumstances. I sat at the middle of the table, fake mahogany with space for fourteen, or more at a pinch, as others filed in. I looked around: Derek, looking through his notes, getting ready to tell everyone about all the wonderful things he had done, which everyone knew was crap; Jonathan, about to tell us success stories, others' successes, claimed for himself; Jennifer, ready to rap anyone's knuckles, with her sickly smile; Mike, already preparing for next weekend, once the inconvenience of being in the office was out of the way; Bill from compliance acting as if he was everybody's best friend and was there to smooth the bureaucracy for us; and no one was quite sure who was going to try and grab the meeting chairmanship today.

I have often wondered, as I sit through all the nefarious little games and stratagems being played, whether the others are sitting back and looking at me in the same way as I am looking at them. I snapped out of my reverie: it was my turn. As I reached the end of my recital about how many millions of dollars I had almost earned last week and how surely the deal flow would translate into hard cash maybe even as early as tomorrow, our Illustrious Leader, as he did not know himself to be known, who had unusually turned up to chair the meeting today, slid a fax across the table to me.

"You remember Julian Vermouth. Worked for us, years ago," he said. "Well, obviously he's turned up in the Gulf with a bank out there. Wants you to give them a call. Some kind of joint deal with them. Let me know what happens. And, Frank, cut the crap next time." The meeting exploded into laughter to the satisfaction of our leader. The message was clear: it was my turn to "shape up or ship out", which is the terminology he had used in this very meeting to address the last guy who had "left" the bank. Such a subtle way this buzzard had.

"Vermouth, hello. I said, hello." I heard on the end of the line I had just dialled.

"Oh, hello. This is Frank Chardonnay. We did meet up once when you worked with us. I was referring..."

"Frank. Yes, I certainly do remember. We had a fair bit of correspondence, one way or another. How are things doing over there? Give my regards to everyone. OK. Hang on; I'm just bringing in my colleague. I'll put you on the speaker. Hello, can you hear? Frank? This is Danny Malbeque. Danny, this is Frank Chardonnay. Wants to hear about our deal. So over to you, Danny. Bye, Frank, and do give my regards. Nice to speak to you."

"Frank, this is Danny, and by the way before you say it, *snap*, I mean on the grape varieties. I have your email address, so I shall put a couple of files through to you right away." There was an Australian twang to his voice. "We have a Powerpoint presentation, which is a kind of executive summary of the transaction, and an Excel spreadsheet with the numbers. Take a look at those when you get them. I won't go into detail over the phone, but here's the rationale. We are already mandated to do this deal but we don't have the expertise to carry it out on our own. First call, you might think, would be one of the biggies, a bank or accounting firm, but realistically, they would simply endeavour to take over the mandate to all intents and purposes. Cut us out. We would not look good in the eyes of our client. We think we could work on a much more co-operative basis with someone like you, your bank. We manage the client relationship; you bring product expertise and a window onto the international market out of London. You get it."

"Danny, this sounds exactly like the kind of role we can fulfil, especially given the existing relationship between our two banks. What we need to do is go over the scope and identify roles."

"That's right. Are you free to travel? Have you got a bike?"

"Have I got a what, Danny?"

"A bike, a mountain bike."

"Well, yes."

"OK, Frank, here's the deal. You look over the email. I have box loads of documentation here that you will need to see. If it looks like a flier, book yourself a flight to get in on Thursday night. Friday is our day off here, so bring your cycling gear. I'll pick you up at 9 a.m. at the Jamilla Beach Resort - we'll get you a booking there - and we'll head for the hills. If you want to make a weekend of it, bring your wife. Sorry about the short notice, but it's the usual story. It's all happening now. I could have been talking to you three weeks ago and we would have been way down the line, if the client had only signed the mandate, instead of poncing around, like they always do. Get back to me to confirm your flights."

So this was it. Maybe I was going to get a major assignment. It would take my mind off this last crazy weekend in Karachi. Business-wise I could get ship-shape.

It is the case that bankers' wives, certainly where international business is concerned, grow accustomed to their husbands disappearing at short notice for a couple of days. Usually this does not carry over into the conduct of their private lives, as was the case with my impromptu weekend in Karachi, but the groundwork is laid, so it's not such a desperately difficult situation. My wife seemed to have been busy anyway that weekend, so after the standard interrogation on how Jeremy was, and I confess that I was probably as well apprised of that as if I had actually seen him, things were back to normal. By Tuesday the whole story was out, suitably modified and edited, and the prospect of a weekend in Dubai laid to rest any thoughts of retribution that she might otherwise have harboured.

***

The Jamilla Beach Resort stands on the long sandy beaches which run to the southwest of Dubai. You sweep up to the lobby in your limousine, if you have one, and it seems everyone else does, step out into the balmy evening air, displaying your jewellery if you have any of value, and move through into the atrium. To the back of the hotel, gardens interspersed with pool and bars lead down to the beach and the tranquil waters of the Gulf. It took us all of two and half minutes to see that a posting with the bank here ranked several grades above London in December, except for the cocktail parties perhaps. And standing right there in the sea is the seven star edifice of the New Arabian Tower Hotel, a mecca for Middle Eastern hotel *aficionados*: one of the few hotels in the world where you have to pay just to go inside, unless you are, to hazard a guess, one of those who turns up with three or four Russian dancers gracing his arm.

On the dot of nine I was downstairs in the lobby, wondering how I would recognise Danny. I need not have worried. A tall thin Australian dressed in cut-off denim shorts and a white shirt came up to me. "Frank?"

"Yes, hello. You must be Danny."

"Right. I've got everything we need in the car." He looked me over. "Good, I'm glad you have your helmet with you, what with the stony ground and the sun. Let's go."

We turned left out of the foyer and walked beneath the palms through manicured gardens to a dark green Landcruiser in the hotel car park. The temperature was a beautiful twenty odd degrees and the sky was blue.

Once in the vehicle, Danny passed across a notebook computer from the back seat. I opened it, hit the enter button, as he suggested, and it sprang to life.

"It's the route for today. I downloaded it from the GPS last time I did this ride. You have to get to know the rides around here. We did this route as a group. With the GPS I can do it on my own safely. Otherwise you risk getting lost. This time of year that's OK, but I tell you, in the summer, no way Hosé, you're a gonner, no chance, vulture fodder."

"You have GPS on your bike!" I exclaimed, having not come across this.

"I sure do. This is it. Mounts on a bracket. Afterwards you download it to the PC." He pointed at a 5 cm black box on the dashboard. "Just check it out. We're going up a wadi, you know, a dry river. But just look at the route out and back. On the computer screen you can see both the way out and the way back, but sometimes the track's just three or four feet wide. Incredible accuracy this GPS has. They have it on cruise missiles, you know, CNN and all that, so why not on my bike?" Sure enough I could see the bicycle's spidery progress up the track with a few loops and deviations which were probably natural obstacles.

We drove up north and then across towards the hills which

separate Dubai from Oman. Mostly the terrain was undulating desert with scrub, but as we approached the hills, the landscape became rugged and totally dry, I mean, absolutely totally dry.

"OK. Before we get on the bikes, click on the icon that says "mandate.doc". Danny instructed me. This I did and spent a few minutes reading the letter, which set out the relationship to be agreed between our two banks. I looked closely at the paragraph labelled "fees", since this would contain the ridiculously large sums of money payable to my bank for my paltry efforts. This is the most important clause in the letter to any banker worth his salt, and I have always counted myself in that category, even if my Illustrious Leader does not.

"I've reviewed the material," I said, thinking exclusively of the fees, "and it looks good. Also you've been very precise in this letter, right down to fees."

"As we ride, I'll flesh it out for you," Danny said, "put some meat on the bones, give you the background about how we come to be where we are and so on. In the meantime, let's get these bikes sorted out. We're here." We parked next to what looked like heaps of natural shale. We unloaded and mounted the bikes. At first the going was tough, as I tried not to slide on the shale and crash ignominiously before we had even started. Danny set the pace riding ahead, twitching the GPS every now and then. We crossed the brow of a hill and descended to a small farming village. The school and mosque were new, everything was bright white, and there seemed to be some sort of minor commercial development with a few new houses. A group of villagers chatted next to a general store, where we stopped for a couple of bottles of water, an additional reserve just in case. From there, we headed up through the Wadi, with a steadily increasing gradient. The track become stonier and the size of the stones increased, suggesting a huge torrent hurling boulders down with it. Round each bend the track rose further to a new horizon and the gradient steepened.

"You have to watch out if it starts to rain. It can be very quick. Most years it doesn't, but these wadis can turn into death traps with flash floods. Anyway, let's talk. We're out of range of everything, mobiles included. This is the type of place we like to talk. You know why you're here, don't you?"

I had thought I knew, but this sinister undertone suggested a connection I had not even dreamt of.

"You mean…"

He broke in: "They briefed you, I assume. We went through your boss to make this an institutional contact, rather than your personal contact. That way you work for us in the bank on a bank deal rather than bringing your deal to the bank. You understand? I'm going to fill you in on the detail, or your bit of it."

So there I was, back where I had started, just when I thought I was getting out of the mess. Now I was sinking fast in a morass which was dragging me down. Those were my thoughts as I realised I was into my first deal. The generosity of the fees in the mandate letter began to make sense, as well as the rather peculiar invitation to go mountain biking. Where else are you guaranteed freedom from eavesdroppers these days?

Danny gave me the works. A holding company was established, which was going to pull together various private power projects, get involved in distribution of electricity, restructure and float various parts on different stock exchanges. The principals, the big guys, behind all this were only mentioned in general terms. My bank's role was to be primarily advisory in nature, which meant they did not have to provide money themselves but raise it from other banks, i.e. earn fees from lending other banks' money. I realised now that there would be no difficulty in getting this kind of deal signed up with my bank. The bank's money would not be at risk and we would simply rake in fees.

An hour into the wadi, Danny had brought me up to speed. There, among the rugged hills, we had reached a farm, just a few hundred square metres of date palms surrounded by stone walls and wire, no doubt watered by an underground spring. He suggested we turn round. I was in favour of that: his bike had full suspension, while I had a bone jarring experience which could only become worse at higher speed on the way down. The temperature was rising, and I knew the British winter had not acclimatised me to this kind of heat. Hard exercise dispels gloom, so I quickly accustomed myself to the shock of why I was really there. Looking on the bright side, this was just another sunny weekend, the second in a row, and I still did not know what it was they wanted of me.

It was well before midday, but the sun shone high in a clear blue sky above the jagged hills. We drank from the water bottles, which were still cool from ice blocks Danny had packed into them. The reserve water, purchased at the village below, would be hot by now. Setting off back down the wadi, we sped along the rock-strewn track – not the place to take a fall. As I jolted over the rocks, Danny gradually pulled ahead, disappearing around a bend a couple of hundred yards down the track. There was no chance of taking a wrong turn here. There was just one way down the wadi to the plain below, so I slowed the pace, and I took a moment to think this through.

Again everything seemed normal despite the circumstances leading up to my being here, and the unusual location. It seemed that I was being offered a transaction that would be good for me, and good for my bank. Why were they doing this? Maybe this was a means of keeping a lucrative piece of business "in-house" from their point of view by creating an informal group of "partners". Certainly, I had not been asked to do anything illegitimate. It was decision time, and so I used standard bank procedure: *play it by ear until you know what's going on and then grab it or walk away as the case may be*.

Danny was waiting round the bend. "Great isn't it, Frank. Less than an hour outside town, and we have this incredible scene. You can't do this in London. I go out on the bike most weekends. We have some amazing rides around here, technically quite tricky. You can meet the other guys next time. They're mostly expats, so we don't get an early start, like we did today, before the heat gets up. Friday is our day off here so they are nursing their Thursday night hangovers and don't want to get up too early. Drink some water. It's heating up."

"Yeah, this is an incredible sight." I said. "These boulders look like they've been thrown down by some raging torrent, but everything's bone dry. How do these thorn bushes survive?" I surveyed the few straggly bushes on the bed of the wadi and scattered across the hills on either side.

"Beats me," he said. "I wouldn't survive this ride without at least two litres of water, and I guess the thorn bushes get nothing like that. We'll need some liquid replacement when we get back. Let's go."

As we descended, the stones on the track diminished in size until the ride became relatively smooth. Then we approached the shale, rising before us like dunes. As we rode onto the shale, the temperature rose sharply, the sun's heat radiating from the dark stones. There was no clear path, so you could ride anywhere, but it was getting tricky to stay on the bikes, as they slid over the stones, and it was not easy to choose a route that avoided your sliding down into a hollow. This was not the weather for climbing out carrying your bike. I felt light-headed and was beginning to flag, when the Landcruiser appeared behind a mound of rocks, parked a couple of hundred yards away, a very welcome Landcruiser, an air conditioned Landcruiser with cold water in the back.

We loaded the bikes, downed the water remaining on the bikes, refreshed ourselves with supplies in the vehicle and settled into the air-conditioned ride back to the city.

"We'll go to my place," Danny suggested. "Liquid replacement. Priority number one." We took the road back through the sand, dunes and thorn bushes.

It was approaching one o'clock when we reached Danny's place. We drove into a square. In the centre were lawns and palm trees that Danny's house overlooked, lying on the east side of the square. Quite a contrast to the desert we have just been through, I thought.

"The women are out in town," Danny said. "Let's get changed and get on with it."

After a refreshing shower, we established ourselves on a patio with a small pool, more of a paddling pool for kids. A maid brought a jug of chilled water, which we swallowed in approximately zero point zero seconds. Danny pulled a couple of beers out of a fridge just inside from the patio door.

"I think we need a couple of cold ones. We've earned it," he said.

We then got into a business discussion on mutual past experiences, during which the pile of empty cans grew. The conversation changed and the pile grew further.

"Hey, it's getting on for four," Danny remarked. "I arranged that we would all meet back at the hotel. It's still a bit early. Let's have a couple more cold ones and then hit the road." He laughed and pointed at the pile of empty cans. By five we were ready to go. We went outside and got into his burgundy BMW.

"You don't drink and drive here," he said. "In fact, as a Muslim you take care about even appearing on the street after any alcohol. They sling you in jail for the night. The hotel's just down the road." Clearly, the beers back at the house didn't count, I thought, but he added, "They won't expect us to have had any beers yet, not at this time of day. My wife will drive home."

As he pulled out into the road, the lights at the junction up ahead turned green. We swung left into the main road and hit 100 mph instantly, or so it seemed to me.

"I just got this BM," he said. "Fun isn't it?"

"Well," I said, "you seem to subscribe to the theory that the faster you go, the less time you spend on the road, so the less likely you are to suffer accidents or traffic fines. Has it worked?"

"Yeah, I think that's about right. They don't drive very safely here, so I minimise my time spent on the road. Though I admit, Frank, I'd never thought of it that way until you drew it to my attention just now." Another couple of turns and we were approaching the Jamilla Hotel.

"We've got here in just under three minutes," he told me, and I was glad to have arrived. He pulled into the hotel parking.

"I don't think they'll be here quite yet, the wives. Punctuality isn't known to be a female trait. Why don't you call up to the room and leave a message on the machine to say we'll be in the bar on the roof?"

We took the lift up the many storeys to the top of the hotel. From there, you look down into an atrium with an amazing modernistic display, which would qualify for the Tate Modern. We passed through into the bar, and then out to the open-air roof terrace overlooking the sea to the west and Dubai to the north. We took a table at the edge and ordered a couple of beers in the continued interests of avoiding dehydration from our bike ride, by now some five to six hours before. With Danny suitably softened by the liquid replacement therapy we had assiduously followed, I thought it an opportunity to probe a little.

"How long have you worked with these guys, Danny?"

"You might not know this, Frank. I was with your guys

originally, but that was before your time. A lot of us here in Dubai are from that stable including Vermouth. As for me, banking's my hobby now. My main thing is mountain biking, every Friday, with training sessions first thing in the morning during the week. I wouldn't take this banking stuff too seriously, Frank."

"And what we're working on now?" I pressed.

"Cheers, Frank." He raised his beer glass. "Don't take it too seriously. Everything we do is above board. Keep it that way. No one expects anything else from you."

"But who's behind all this?" I continued to probe.

"Frank, I'll let you into a secret. I know a little more about your introduction to the group, but that's only because that's the way it is in Karachi, where I do business. We talk to our friends. So the group does have a couple of, what you might call "executives", who may from your point of view appear a little unconventional in their methods, but they're just getting the job done. Take your old prime minister: she may sink South American battleships, but if she had so much as pointed a Derringer at the leader of the opposition, she'd have been put away. Well, she was put away in the end, anyway, wasn't she, out to pasture, a bloodless coup? It's different with them. Out in the countryside a feudal lord still has serfs who prostrate themselves before him. He has power of life and death over his serfs, when he presides over the tribal court, and guess who they vote for in the elections, none other than their feudal lord. In Karachi he may behave like a businessman, while in the national or local assembly he has more arrows in his quiver than your Tony does: some of them have been known to kidnap or torture opposing factions; others roam town with bands of Kalashnikov toting thugs, loaded on trucks. What I am saying is don't bother to understand it: just do deals for your bank within the terms of your mandate – and go mountain biking. Let's get a couple more beers."

Clearly this was it from Danny for the time being, but I was intrigued by what he meant with "unconventional methods".

On Saturday morning Danny picked me up at the hotel to go to the office, the first day of the working week in Dubai. They gave me a meeting room, to go through the information on the energy projects. I would need to draft a full presentation to explain what the project was and the benefits of the mandate available to my bank, but this looked little more than a formality – we had not had an opportunity like this either this year or last at the bank.

I plagiarised information on the floppy disks and within an hour had put together a package which, as far as I could see, covered just about everything, from the rationale to the timescale of implementation and the financial benefits, together with detailed cash flow analyses. The only skimpy area was the project sponsors, but I guessed we would get by on what we had and, anyway, bank references were available.

At eleven they called me in to speak to Vermouth on the phone. It was a perfunctory call. He seemed somewhat preoccupied, and excused himself for not lining anything up on the social front, but he was in London and heading back to Dubai tonight and on to Singapore the next day on a business trip.

CHAPTER THREE – THE BOARD

Singapore, 10 December 2000

Vermouth usually took a night flight to Singapore. It was one of those inconvenient six-hour flights, where by the time you have eaten dinner, you barely have time to snooze before they are serving breakfast. The advantage was that he had spent Sunday at the office in Dubai, on his return from London, and would have the full Monday in Singapore to do his banking business, before the Board convened in the evening at the Golden Grove Hotel, Board with a capital B.

He was an unusual member of the Board, the only one who was neither from the Middle East nor Asia, and he was effectively the right-hand man of Suleiman, the Chairman of the Board, at least as far as Board matters were concerned. In other spheres he had strong competition. Yet he was in some ways more "ethnic" than some of them. He had studied classical Arabic and Farsi, as spoken in Iran, at Cambridge, to which he had added the ability to speak as an Egyptian or Syrian through later travels, but always with a discernable English accent. He also had a smattering of Urdu and Hindi. It was not this that commended him to the Board, however; rather the fact that he had the experience of a Wall Street banker and had included Hebrew in his repertoire - a number of important Israelis considered him to be on their side of the fence, a window for them on the Arab world. He sat back and pondered the day ahead.

The Board meeting would be almost routine: it was the more important agenda that occupied him. He hoped to persuade

Suleiman to convene a subsequent meeting of the "core group", so that he could win them over to the new project. It represented a drastic change from the way they had operated to date, and he felt they could move into another realm of possibilities, if they could work out how to implement his plans effectively. Only he and Suleiman had an inkling of the plan. As he juggled with the final presentation on his notebook computer, he was convinced that he had a powerful argument to demonstrate that this was panacea, the cure for all their problems, including his problems.

Singapore Airport is among the most efficient for the arriving passenger. Within ten minutes of touchdown Vermouth was on the East Coast Parkway, resplendent with roadside shrubs, heading for the centre of town. He would not have taken this route, but he had long since given up educating the world's taxi drivers. The trick of international travel with a heavy schedule was to sit back and relax when you could. He would drop his bag at the hotel and then launch into the day's meetings with two local and four foreign banks to conduct his banking business. After that it would be a brief rest, and then the Board.

The taxi headed for the city centre along Orchard Road, took a left turn and after a few hundred yards swung right into the Golden Grove Hotel complex. He gave the driver twenty-five Singapore dollars and stepped out into the humidity for the few steps to the air-conditioned foyer. They call it aircon in Singapore, and he smiled at the recollection of the old joke of the French community. When questioning a new arrival settling in, they would ask, "Tu as l'air con?" These facile thoughts were interrupted by the surprise of seeing Suleiman, the Chairman, at the far end of the foyer, almost out of view, in this vast plant filled foyer.

Suleiman was in conversation with Zenap, that red haired operative. How she irritated Vermouth! Suleiman seemed to trust her to go everywhere and do everything; and these stupid aliases she was always using. She never changed her appearance, so how come no one ever recognised her for what she was. Why didn't immigration at Heathrow stop her: *Excuse me, Madam, we seem to recall having seen you pass through last week under a different name and passport. Would you mind coming with us?* But they never had.

Vermouth was one of the few with an insight into what she did, or indeed, to even know she existed.

He did not see her as a threat; it was just her manner, her sense of her own power, that drove him mad. In any interaction with him she seemed to come off best, and then she would smile at him warmly. Aggression he could have accepted: charm was tough to deal with. Still he had no time to do other than check in at the hotel reception and drop his bag, nor would he anyway have acknowledged their presence without Suleiman's invitation, which was not forthcoming.

Suleiman saw Vermouth across the foyer, but he wanted to get the story on Frank Chardonnay from his redheaded friend, Zenap.

"So," Zenap was saying, "Murphy's Law cuts in right at the start, like the lights go red but we've stuck the gear shift in reverse and go shooting off backwards."

"Tell me. It sounds fun!" Suleiman said.

"Yeah. Well I have a duty to tell you because we took a big risk. I'll come to that. We had this guy who lives near him, Hamid, on the job. Now we don't want to do a snatch in broad daylight on the street," Zenap continued.

"I agree," Suleiman concurred. "These things can easily get out of hand or be observed, scotching the whole thing."

"Anyway, Hamid has worked out when Frank will come by on his morning jog, and it clicks with him that this is right past the pick up point for Hamid's next Rugby trip, and it's Hamid who organises the bus for them."

"Is this reliable?" Suleiman asked.

"Frank's regular, and we had a fallback. So this is how it goes. Hamid told the other players he had a bit of knee trouble and had called a friend who would be along in a moment to replace him. We'd worked out a few ruses about how we could stop Frank, but as it turns out, he goes for the very first one. Now everyone thinks this is a great joke when this guy comes running up and Hamid and I act like we're picking him up off the street, because they *know* he's supposed to be joining them as Hamid's replacement. But we *know* that he'll refuse because he doesn't know the first thing about it or even who Hamid is. Then Hamid will decide to play after all, the coach will drive off and we will do the snatch as planned. It'll look as if we were just a group of people having a joke, who then break up and leave separately."

"So what went wrong?" Suleiman asked.

"You won't believe it! We're kind of playing for time to get to the point where the coach will be leaving, and Frank says OK he'll play in the match and jumps on the coach. Who in their right mind would do that? Now we don't see how to get him off the coach, and sure enough it pulls out. What's more he plays in the match!"

"So this destroyed the entire plan of how to get him out of the country and down to Karachi," Suleiman said, seeing the implications for timing of the plan that he had approved: they would miss the plane.

"It did," she said, "but this when Murphy's Law got trashed. We shifted through the gears right up into overdrive, starting with the fact that the plane was delayed two hours."

"But you still had to get him on the plane, and our plan had fallen away," Suleiman objected.

"This is exactly right," she said. "I would never have planned what we did. It was so implausible that I would have said, no way. So the Heathrow guy, Azhar, says we can get him through security etc. The problem is what is Frank going to do when he gets to the boarding gate, if we get him that far, sees the destination, last call flashing, the works. But, I think to myself, if we abort now we lose a month."

"Probably more," Suleiman added. "What with their Christmas and New Year."

"Yes. So I say, let's take the risk. If he objects vehemently, we simply abandon him. I'll be in the air, the others will evaporate, and he can explain why he's the wrong side of passport control with neither passport nor ticket."

"How did you do it then?" Suleiman asked.

"It was incredible. We all had badges like we were a group. Frank just walked straight through. OK, he'd had a few drinks after the match. Then he's on the plane. A glass of laced Champagne and he's out cold."

"And now tell me about Karachi," Suleiman said with a smile.

"That was even better." Now she really launched into it. "He was scared out of his wits by the drugs to Frankfurt routine, spent the remains of the night knocking back beers in the hotel gardens, and after the first session in the morning, pre-breakfast, we decided we had our man."

"So you just brought in the others as belt and braces," Suleiman suggested.

"No need to pull in the rest of the team and go through the whole coercion programme. I mean, the reason we chose Karachi was because we couldn't have got half those guys visas to the UK, even if we had wanted. We had five guys lined up to put the third degree on him, tighten the thumb screws, stretch him on the rack. But we didn't need them. We could have done it in Tunbridge Wells. We just took him for a walk on the beach."

Suleiman was visibly pleased: "Alls well that ends well."

"Yup, and I hear from Vermouth's guys in Dubai, that the presentation Frank drew up for his bank the day before yesterday should fly. He must have landed back in London a few hours ago. We have the right man there, Suleiman: he's easy to manipulate. I think his bank will be on board within the week."

***

Suleiman convened the Board at seven sharp. Every member would be punctual, and Suleiman would control the entire process of the meeting. A formal agenda was never circulated, but there was an established pattern. Whatever was discussed, one thing was certain, the meeting would be to the point and short. Vermouth was well aware of this, and it had taken Suleiman less than a minute before the meeting to agree to a meeting of "the core group", after the Board meeting, and at a safe house.

Suleiman surveyed the members with authority. Each member admired and trusted him, but none knew why. Physically he was just short of six foot, powerful shoulders and strong features. Despite his fifty odd years his hair and moustache were jet black. He had always been a military man and still was, trained at Sandhurst, according to rumour later running several successful commando operations.

His manner was courteous, he knew when to apply humour and his dark eyes beamed out IQ. Maybe this explained how he also happened to be a professor of economics at an Internet based distance-learning institute. Incongruous maybe, but then he was also Chairman of the Board, not a position you would fill through an advert in the Appointments Section of the newspaper. The phrase the Board had coined to describe him was "a pragmatic idealist", oxymorons being the order of the day as far as he was concerned.

As usual Vermouth sat to Suleiman's right, and his report was the first.

"In the last three months I can report that we have added three new banks to work with us, the last and most important addition being last week. This is in connection with the power generation and distribution business of which you are aware. We have started the implementation phase. I will report to you with progress and precise figures at the next meeting." Vermouth had these figure in front of him, but he did not want to undermine the impact of his presentation later to the "core group".

"As to existing commercial operations, I will address the three spheres of activity. First, in financial instruments, we have seen substantial growth in our portfolios, particularly from technology and Internet stocks, which as you know we liquidated to take our profits just before the market collapse. We have managed to use our corporate finance activities in mergers, acquisitions and public offerings, as a vehicle to move substantial sums of money to where we can use them, as you will see from the folder in front of you. Secondly, as to powder, we see no change of flows, but a 12% increase in revenues. Pretties no change."

In the jargon of the Board "pretties" referred to the jewellery trade, and "powder", well, that was the equivalent in UK Customs speak of "grade A drugs." There you have it, gems and narcotics.

Only Vanesh or Suleiman would ever question Vermouth. Today they had no questions, and Vanesh proceeded with his report as Chief Financial Officer.

"The underlying problem remains. We have money where we do not need it, and we do not have it where we need it. We have mitigated this to an extent through the operations set up by Messrs Vermouth and Co., as he just mentioned, but we need to do more. This is the most crucial question that faces our finances. We have the money, but we still cannot use it all. In the last year our revenues have grown geometrically, both from the goods we trade and our investment of surpluses. My motion, which I have discussed with the Chairman, is that we turn our full attention to the funds transfer problem for presentation at an extraordinary Board meeting next month."

The Chairman is taking me seriously, Vermouth mused. As always, Vanesh, with his Indian accent and clipped speech, had restricted himself to the only issues that counted, as brash as a any business school graduate with none of the profiling. Vermouth had always admired him and could see how he had got where he had. A small man, his piercing eyes burned with an intensity, sufficient, no doubt, to change the polarity of the magnetic pole.

Vermouth knew that Vanesh would be at the "core group" meeting. The only other of the eleven Board members, apart from himself and Suleiman, would be Jamal Ali. Jamal Ali always came on last at Board meetings, and he did today. His report would list their disbursements to "charity". This was the sweetener, the reason why they did what they did. Hearing how the money was spent was a morale boost: it held each of them to his chosen path, justified the risks he took. The "charities" were typically fronts for organisations which either feature on the US sanction lists, or would feature on them if the US knew about them. There were few exceptions on today's list.

In other words, the Board used the profits made from its businesses to support movements and groups actively engaged, whether by peaceful means or violent, in pursuing their causes and redressing what they held to be wrongs against their brethren. Some members were suspicious of how Vermouth fitted in, but none dared challenge Suleiman's judgement.

Vermouth smiled to himself at the irony that they liked to meet in Singapore because it was so safe and secure, no riots, no terrorism, little crime. He looked across at Vanesh, the finance man. Vanesh had been in Suleiman's study group at business school, both of them in their late thirties then. Despite or maybe because of their cultural differences, a south Indian and a Saudi, the two had become firm friends. Like Vermouth, Vanesh had joined Suleiman back at the beginning in '87. They were a trading house at first, and Suleiman's idea was to use his profits to support commercial enterprises in Arab countries. Well, he could do what he liked with his profits as far as

Vermouth and Vanesh were concerned. Jamal Ali had joined as their commodities man, which became their main business. The other Board members came later, usually proposed by Suleiman for a tenure of three years, but Jamal Ali had taken a growing role in these appointements in the last five years. Perhaps it was Jamal's influence that explained the shift from support of commercial enterprises to political and religious groups.

Jamal Ali who had started his report on disbursements to "charity". He could almost be a seventeenth century Italian aristocrat, Vermouth thought, with his aquiline nose, olive complexion and black hair. He had a noble look in his eyes, but then he is a pious man, Vermouth mused, and the Koran does favour trading, well certainly over banking as I do it.

Jamal also held unconventional ideas. Although he was not involved in the gem business, he had come up with the idea that customs and excise were unlawful misappropriations by the West of the profits that rightfully belonged to the producers. He had checked out tanzanite, a rare product in East Africa, and moved them into smuggling. Vermouth was sure that Suleiman had adopted similar reasoning when he had, unknown to Vermouth, sold out much of the other business and moved into narcotics.

As the meeting drew to a close, Vermouth was thinking over his position since he had first become aware of the new narcotics business. The growing cash surpluses in strange places had alerted him. At first Vermouth, who anyway held his regular banking job and now acted only at the central level of the Board's finances and not with the operating businesses, had felt there was sufficient distance from him, and that he need not be concerned. It was the need to shift cash surpluses that had finally dragged him in. He had had to bring in other banks to handle the volume, and this had brought for him a sense of personal danger. Now with Frank Chardonnay's bank, it concerned him that Frank was probably going to have to know too much, to be in a position to transcact the business. If Frank knew too much Vermouth could be incriminated. Maybe his new scheme really was the way out, giving them alternative business.

The meeting closed within forty-five minutes and broke up without formality. Socialising was neither desired nor encouraged.

Travelling to the meetings was a huge drain on busy schedules, but there was no alternative to face-to-face discussions. It was unlikely that bugging the meeting would provide value to an uninformed intruder, but video-conferencing was definitely out. It was not unknown for a participant to fly in on a long-haul flight and straight back out after the meeting. The only hard and fast rule was that there had to be a secondary route to the meeting for the eventuality that the first route was subject to delay, however inconvenient – neither absence nor unpunctuality was tolerated.

Vermouth always experienced a buzz at the Board's meetings, so he was fully hyped for the ensuing meeting at the safe house. They would each travel there separately, at least fifteen minutes apart, so the meeting was unlikely to start before nine fifteen this evening.

The safe house was actually one of four houses. Each of the houses was kept free for a different three months of the year. The rest of the time they would be rented out to companies on a short term basis for expatriate executives at the higher end of the market, in banking, oil, power and so on. The tenants would usually have a string of foreign guests, parties, other expats around, so that coming and going was the norm at the houses. In the three months of own use, the Board and visitors would blend beautifully.

The rental income and real estate values had risen dramatically over the years, so that this arrangement for safe houses had also become a valuable investment, held through their Singpaporean intermediary. It reminded Vermouth of the offices and homes his old bank had maintained around the world in the old days. These properties had gradually been sold off over the years for a pittance, usually by managers trying to meet annual profit targets by realising the value in the house through sale. The justification would be something like: "We're in the business of banking not real estate." In practice the real estate had soared in value, while these clever bankers had lost money in one crisis after another: South America, foreign exchange markets, junk bonds, South East Asia, Russia, derivatives; you name it, they were there with their bank's money, losing it. What a contrast to the clear-eyed pragmatism of the Board, Vermouth thought.

The house in Andrew Road was the best of the safe houses. It was located just opposite the Singapore television studios, which meant that people were coming and going by taxi, car and limo at all times of day and night. The house, set in its own grounds, ran down the opposite slope from the TV studios in a series of split-levels. On the right was an open storm drain which led to jungle adjoining the Chinese cemetery, which in turn adjoined jungle stretching to the north of the island of Singapore and the short stretch of water to Malaysia.

Through the jungle, crossing just two roads, you could bring contraband or humans down from the sea to virtually the centre of Singapore, up the storm drain, dry except during the daily storms, and into the house. This route had been used many times. While the drain was potentially visible, the expats had again come to the rescue. The Hash House Harriers, those weekly international jogging groups, regularly ran along railway lines, through cemeteries, up storm drains and through swamps. The mountain bikers followed suit. Whereas in the rest of the world a drainage channel may be reserved for water and rats, in Singapore they were an integral part of the expat paradise.

Vermouth was the last to arrive. He stepped out of the taxi and passed through open electronic gates to the main door. The gates swung to behind him. He entered the house through the front door, descended red tiled steps to the first level past the dining room, and down another flight of steps to the lounge. On two sides of the lounge wall-to-ceiling windows opened to the terrace, and bougainvillea clad railings gave on to the pool fifteen feet below. Someone had dropped a white garden table and four matching chairs into the deep end of the pool and set places underwater together with a Champagne bottle and four glasses. With the pool lighting on it looked surreal. Vermouth was always tempted to try a dive into the pool from the railings, but he speculated that the only Board member who would clear the twelve odd horizontal foot leap and fifteen foot drop was Suleiman.

Vermouth was due to start his presentation immediately. He set up his notebook computer to project onto a screen set up at the end of the room. The other three participants were positioned on brown leather sofas, backing onto a natural brick wall. To the right was a two-foot high recess running at chest height along the entire wall.

Set in the recess was a kind of 3D collage of Persian silver and brass jugs and vases, old musical instruments, antique Indian toys and miniature samovars, all backlit to shimmer and gleam.

The screen sprang to life with a world map, showing with multi-coloured arrows the routes taken by their merchandise.

"We have been very successful in trading," Vermouth said. "We have built substantial investments which are now inside the world financial system." He clicked a mouse and the world map broke up to reveal the New York skyline, the world financial centre.

"But mostly we are operating outside the system, and it treats us unjustly as far as our trading profits are concerned. We make money on commodities that the West wants, but they act as if we are criminals, and this is not true. We are not to blame if an Italian in Milan steals a car radio to finance his habit. It is not our fault and it is not our problem: it is Italy's problem. We meet consumer demand in the free market economy, just like any other supplier of basic commodities."

Vermouth was deliberately using arguments familiar to those in the milieu of his audience. "Yet they endeavour to confiscate our profits. They ask us where our profits arose. Even when we make money transfers which they deem legitimate, they charge us huge foreign exchange commissions. When the prophet, peace be upon him, rode through the desert, did anyone challenge him for what he owned? Did he pay out 5% on his credit card just because he was spending French francs from a dollar account? No."

Vanesh added: "It's the same with the fund managers: they charge us an up-front commission, hidden dealing charges, annual fees, and then they generate for us a profit below the stock market index, while paying themselves salaries of maybe ten million dollars a year or more." Vermouth looked around at the approving nods, and made his point.

"So what do we do? We have to get inside the system." Vermouth stated.

"I want you to really understand what I am driving at," he continued. "I shall start with a very simple example. Let's take a fictitious base metal. We'll call it "tulium" to avoid confusion with the real world. Suleiman, you are an economist, among other things. If I buy a tulium mine, how do I make money?"

Suleiman's response was immediate: "You invest in high quality equipment and extract tulium ore at the lowest possible cost, selling judiciously on world markets."

"That's equivalent to the approach we take in all our business today," Vermouth replied. "I want us to move on. Consider this alternative: we maximise our profits by extracting the least possible ore. As long as the ore is in the ground, we can continue to make money. As soon as we have sold it, it's gone. We have taken our profit just once instead of many times."

This was novel to Vanesh: "How?"

"We play both sides of the options markets. Our safety valve is to sell ore if, and only if, the market moves against us before we have been able to buy back at a lower price ore which we have sold forward earlier, or vice versa. Physical delivery we avoid at all costs; indeed, we may even take manageable losses rather than deliver. The point is that as long as the ore is in the ground, we can trade large positions in the markets with relative impunity. We can outmanoeuvre the end-users and middlemen indefinitely."

"So, you mean we sell ore at one price to deliver, say, next week," said Jamal, who had been listening intently, "but we hope that the price of ore has dropped before the week is out. Then we can buy someone else's ore at a lower price and use that ore rather than digging our own out of the ground."

"Exactly," Vermouth responded, "and as long as we have ore in the ground we can always play the market safely, because we can always deliver our own ore, if we have to. In reality we would play the market both ways. Our contracts to buy and sell will cancel one another out, leaving us with the profits. It is just as if we were selling our ore many times, instead of just once."

"But, gentlemen, I just wanted you to understand the principle. "This is where it gets complicated. We will be using other people's holdings, be they miners or end-users, rather than any product we own ourselves, and we will not be restricted to ore, but trade any product. This way we get the benefit of huge positions in the markets we choose to play for zero investment of our own." By now Vermouth could feel the atmosphere building. He clicked off the screen, preferring to move forward ad lib, addressing his audience as they reacted.

"Before we move into the plan," he continued, "I want you to consider one more angle. We are a pragmatic organisation. Mostly we deal with the doers, the people who actually get things done, at the various institutions we work with. Many of these people are highly qualified, experienced professionals. Some of them will rise to the top echelons; most will not, even though they are every bit as capable as their high-ranking colleagues. Some will rise because of their skills, commitment and the respect of their peers. Others, maybe most of those who do rise, will rise because they are willing to knife their colleagues in the back, lie, cheat and deny, all the standard procedures of corporate political life. They are motivated by ego and greed, and would probably make good politicians, present company excepted, of course. This latter group is ready to take risks and to put their self-interest above organisational goals."

He could see he was losing attention, with this commonplace statement, so he came to the point. "What we will do is match the venality and greed of these people to the new opportunities of the derivatives markets and play middle-man."

"I can't comment on the rogue trader affair that happened right here in Singapore, other than what the press speculated: namely, that huge supposed profits prompted top management to ignore warning signs, refusing to admit the limitations of their own lack of knowledge of the markets, preferring to stay on the band wagon for as long as these supposed profits rolled in. But I do know of other examples, where it is my belief that the auditors were either negligent or implicated in the rape of a company. I don't condone this, but if they are doing it, then we are going to help ourselves to the pirates' buried treasure."

Vanesh: "OK. How?"

Vermouth was ready for this one: "This needs a lot of work, but I have some ideas going with the lawyers. Let me first summarise the structure of one kind of deal and then talk about how we get it done. Let's take the big oil and energy groups. They are taking huge positions of the kind I talked about for tulium, but in their own products. Sometimes this business is more profitable than their underlying business. Some would like to take larger positions, but they can't. They would have to disclose the size of these additional commitments in their financial accounts and to the regulatory authorities. So what do we do? Well, we've come up with a limited partnership structure which takes this exposure out of their accounts. This means that they can do much more business by working with our structure. The bottom line is that they can take bigger risks and make more money."

Suleiman: "Why will they work with us?"

Vermouth: "We will cut the top officers, Chairman, Chief Executive, Chief Financial Officer, into the partnership profits personally. But let's make it even easier for ourselves. Let's look for a corporation that we can identify as already being underwater on its forward contracts. They may have hidden their losses for the moment, which is easy to achieve with some financial manipulation, but the losses will hit one day. Top management will be kicked out in disgrace, so let's give them a way out other than bankruptcy and public humiliation, at least in the interim."

The room remained silent and thoughtful, so Vermouth moved on.

"To do this we will need to use a combination of private bankers, accountants and consultants. The first two we have, the latter we will manufacture. We already have the man for the job on board."

He than presented the US dollar amounts he had in mind to a collective gasp from his audience. If this were true they would be doing the equivalent of twenty years of business in one year. Astonishing, but even better, all their profits would be right there in New York, clean, sparkling and fresh; no laundering required here. This was beautifully presented on the last slide of Vermouth's presentation, a cartoon sketch of the Board at lunch on Wall Street.

The "core group" examined the options, talked through different scenarios, and by midnight had reached a decision, a better decision than Vermouth could have hoped for: they would try to get the first deal going before the Board's next meeting, so that there would be something tangible to discuss. Vermouth was relieved. He was beginning to see a way of shifting to more legitimate business. He would not be dragged into the drug smuggling after all.

Unfortunately, Vermouth could not read the thoughts of the others. Suleiman was thinking, we'll play along and see, but it might be too big for us. Trading is what we know. Jamal was concerned by the elements of the structure which seemed to run contrary to his religious beliefs. Vanesh felt that if this scheme were to fly, then they would have to change the Board's objectives, because they could not give this kind of money to Jamal's friends. He felt that Suleiman had changed. He was entirely focused on running the business to maximise profits without regard for consequences. Suleiman is, Vanesh thought, becoming extremely proficient at doing well: it is just that he is doing the wrong thing very well.

They left the meeting as a group. It was less visible to casual onlookers.

CHAPTER FOUR - NATHAN

London, 2 December 2000

In the week preceding the Singapore Board meeting, London was grey and cold. Nathan sat, overlooking Beaufort Street below, in his first floor mansion flat in Chelsea. His mood was as grey as the December morning. Just when his career should have taken off, he was stuck in an impossible no-man's-land, outside the law and outside its protection. Six months ago he had seen himself as an up-and-coming private banker. Now he was supposed to betray his major client's confidence. How could he do this? Yet it seemed the only way out. He looked down at the dossier they had given him to study. He had studied it and still did not know where to start, or even if he should start. If he could just escape, start again, a new career, could he?

He thought back to a conversation with his first boss in private banking, when he had started in the business five years ago. Nathan, you have to understand the rules. What we do at the bank has to be entirely above board: we do not assist in illegal activity; we do not deal with illegitimate money; we do not help our clients move money out of their country in contravention of foreign exchange regulations. However, and listen carefully, when money is offshore in a legitimate account, then we want that money, we want to manage that money, that is our wealth management programme. Don't misunderstand me. We are not talking about handling a pirate's buried treasure trove: we are talking about legitimate offshore banking.

The nub of the problem was that Nathan had become aware of evidence of apparent fraudulent activity, dubious financial transactions, and maybe worse, by his major client. Not a problem in itself: the problem was that the client knew this, and might, no would, want to do something about it. The choice looked stark: either he was in his client's pocket and would sacrifice a promising career; or he was dead. His information was dynamite, or so he surmised.

My bank will step in to protect me, he had thought at the time. But then he had tried to work out whom to approach in the bank. He had looked at the procedures, the compliance process he would have to follow, the committees that would debate steps to be taken, referral to the legal department, focusing principally on how to protect the bank, and in the end he would simply be re-assigned, and remain as personally at threat as ever.

He had experienced two anguished weeks of doubt, inner turmoil, until he concluded that he must secretly contact the Fraud Squad, in flagrant breach of his employment contract, but in tune with his sense of morality. A meeting had taken place. The Fraud Squad could do nothing. There was no proven crime and certainly no connection with the UK. He was left high and dry at the mercy of the bad guys, should they wish to move in.

Since then, he had spent three months in purgatory, trying to maintain his normal role at the bank but fearful of the impending demands of his client He would check the street in the morning before stepping onto the pavement, vary his route to work and follow the most haphazard time-table which could fit his professional life, to outwit imagined pursuers. Then the call had come. There had been a bland meeting at which he was advised that a connection had been established between his client and international terrorism. His approach to the Fraud Squad had been noted, and it was considered that he might be of particular value in view of his special position. If he would be prepared to read a little background material, they would take the discussion further. There had been two further interviews at which it seemed he was vetted. He had agreed in principle to seek and provide information. He was to be an informer. Returning to the present, he looked at his watch; 11.30, time to go to the meeting. If he had been in purgatory, now he was descending into hell.

Nathan donned his Barbour hanging in the hall. He studied himself in the mirror. I feel like Jesus on the cross, he thought, but nothing shows and I still look like Nathan. Green eyes stared back at him. Maybe I am a bit pale, he thought, but it is the same dark hair; perhaps a bit serious, but no, the corners of the eyes indicate a smile, a friendly smile; I am still five eleven, seventy kilos. Yes, I do look like some guy just off to the pub. He picked up a couple of letters for posting and headed down the stairs. He turned left into Beaufort Street away from the river, dropped the letters into the post box, and headed towards the King's Road. Turning left at the corner, he came against the flow of shoppers heading east, and continued to the Devil's Retreat pub. Pretty appropriate choice of venue, he thought weakly, stepping inside.

"Nathan, Nathan, do come along." A dumpy man, wearing a priest's dog collar under a tweed jacket, greeted him as he stepped through the door.

"You must be Reverend Coulthard."

"Yes, yes. Come, take a seat over here. I'll just get us a couple of pints of bitter – so that we don't stand out too much, you know."

Nathan watched him order at the bar. A short man, thin grey hair and a round face, somehow exuding a natural friendliness and, he thought, with insignificance flowing off him in waves. The Reverend returned, slopping the two pints as he walked. His appearance contrasted with Nathan's tall slim form, dark brown hair and clear open expression.

"Let's get the formalities out of the way, or should I say informalities. Call me Peter, not Reverend, most do. Don't be too concerned about the dog collar. I was a vicar once, C of E, until they, eh, defrocked me." An ingenuous grin played across his lips. "Cheers. To our, eh, con…eh, co-operation, whoops I almost said conspiracy. Let me explain. This is the sort of place I like to meet, have a couple of pints, pretty convenient for you, just around the corner. We won't need to do any clandestine undercover stuff, when we meet. We're part of the furniture here. We'll stand out as being familiar and hence blend in. Think, even spies must have their regular habits and friends. The laundrette doesn't get taken a part every time they drop by to operate the coin machine to wash their underwear. Normality, that's the best cover. And we've known one another for years, haven't we. Come on practice. Laugh." And they both leant back with a hearty laugh, and Nathan actually felt amused, well, at least a little anaesthetised.

"Now let me fill you in on a few basic points. It's unlikely that you will see anyone other than me. Mostly we'll chat right here, and you or I will make a few pertinent points in the course of the conversation, just as I am doing right now. But let me tell you rule number one in the Reverend Coulthard's *Everything You Need to Know to Stay Alive in Espionage*: if it's serious, smile, relax, lean back and never speak in an **undertone**." He raised his voice, but no heads turned. "Well, that's basically it. I never got on to rule two, and haven't found a publisher either." The Reverend smiled, drew a long satisfying draught of beer, and his eyes invited Nathan's confidence and trust.

"You should think of me as your guardian angel. If you think things may get tough, it is I who calls the cavalry. Custer answers to me, as far as you are concerned. Whoops, maybe Custer's a bad choice, didn't go too well for him did it. No, I'll tell you what, think of me as not just your guardian angel but as an archangel, if it gives you a bit more confidence, you know, omniscient that kind of thing." Nathan drank his beer in the ensuing pause, thinking of purgatory, and now, with the Reverend's banter, seeing a dot of light at the top of the mineshaft. The Reverend downed his pint.

"Don't go away. I'll just get us another. Same again?" The Reverend jostled his way through the growing lunchtime crowd to the bar.

Ordering took a little longer this time, giving Nathan the chance to ponder what it was that they would really expect of him. He had no idea of what he was supposed to do. Yes, he had read the file, but it all seemed so, well, Middle Eastern, and he really could not see how he would fit into the pattern. He could not see his client dropping him deep insights or even hints at his nefarious activities. What he had learnt had been by freak accident - he had clearly not been supposed to know, and that is why he was so, well to put it bluntly, terrified. The Reverend was back.

"Just let me say that the situation is moving fast." A new seriousness in his tone. "You've read the file, here's the face." He passed across a photo. "Take an appreciating glance now and put it in your pocket. Later I suggest you destroy it. She's very attractive, isn't she? Just let me point out that in the Church of England we do not have regular confession, unlike the Catholic Church, so," he quipped, "on that side of things you're on your own."

"Peter, I've read the file, and I honestly don't see where I fit into this. In fact, before reading the file I thought maybe, but now, well, it's all just so convoluted, and I can't for a moment see any of these people revealing confidences to anyone like me. I mean, I'm just so *establishment.*"

"Absolutely, absolutely. Our Arabian friends race horses just like the aristocracy does here; in fact, they do much of their horse racing right here in England, hobnob with the Queen, that kind of thing, so don't worry about that side of things, old boy. In fact, your chap's even Sandhurst trained, good officers' mess material, just your type. We'll just take it in steps. Now this is it, and it's very simple. We believe this *femme fatale* in the photo is very close to the centre. She seems to have been involved in a number of what I would call recruitment operations in Europe, and is always on the look-out, and her judgement is trusted."

"We think she operates under an alias, and maybe more than one. For our purposes I have named her Jemimah. We believe they are pulling something together right now, and I will not burden you with that knowledge. She does not know this, but you are going to meet her on, we hope, Tuesday night, probably mid-evening, in a City wine bar. Don't ask me why, just turn up and get into conversation with her group. When we leave, I'm going to give you a couple of dialogue scripts to help out. If you gain her trust, she will report back. You will be immediately matched up at the centre with, well, let's say you, since they already know you through your work. And you are in."

"We'll see what happens. There is no way, I repeat, no way, that they are going for one moment to believe that this is anything other than happy coincidence, Christmas combined with Easter, triple "A" serendipity. Capito?" The Reverend seemed to enjoy the discrepancy between his manner of his speech and his priestly appearance. "So that's it, the agenda. Any other business? We'll have another pint - you're not driving this afternoon are you? – shoot the breeze for twenty minutes, our cover remember, and leave boisterously. Vindaloo!" He finished, echoing the refrain of a much played song.

On Tuesday Nathan left the office early. He thought he would have a beer or two to calm his nerves, before going over to the wine bar for his assignation. He strolled over to Leadenhall Market. The pubs were already busy in the pre-Christmas season, people meeting early after work as their workload dropped off for Christmas. He pushed his way through to the bar, and after some time managed to attract the attention of one of the chaps behind the counter to bring him a pint of lager. I know the girl's face, he thought, I have read the scripts, but how do *I* do it? I have never managed to pull girls in bars before; we get introduced by friends or family, and the Reverend had not been that much help with his boozy wit. He mused for a bit, but then he saw a couple of the dealers from his bank's dealing room crossing to the bar, and thought he had better get out of there quick, if he wanted to remain halfway sober for his assignation. He left the market, walked up Bishopsgate and turned into London Wall. It took him fifteen minutes to reach the wine bar. It was almost empty, so he took a place at the centre of the bar and ordered a bottle of Chablis. Centrally positioned, he thought, he would be able to move strategically when his target arrived.

He did not have to wait long: they entered as a group of five, three young men, the target and a girl in her early twenties. The equanimity won from two pints of lager and a glass of Chablis left him. "I don't even know her name, but hold on, I wouldn't, would I? I'm not supposed to know her. I don't know her. Will I give myself away? How? I've only seen her picture." Confusion raced through his brain. He began to flush. The five moved to towards the bar, sharing some joke, laughing, almost boisterous. She sat at the very end of the bar. He glanced across, trying not to be surreptitious and failing, as he poured a second glass of Chablis. The five continued with an animated discussion and the bar gradually filled.

He was soon on his second bottle of Chablis, wondering what he could do, as he eyed her, where she was squeezed into the corner. He could not just go over and say, *Hi, mind if I join you*, or, *Excuse me is this place free?* It manifestly was not free. He thought back to the meeting at the Devil's Retreat, the confident manner of the

Reverend. Clearly they had chosen the wrong stooge here. He was hopelessly out of his depth with this kind of thing. He, Nathan, pick up a girl in a bar, or even introduce himself and start a conversation as they had suggested. Someone squeezed into the space next to him as he poured himself another glass.

"Hello, I can read your mind, I think, maybe." A soft suggestive voice.

He turned and looked into blue-grey eyes surrounded by a mass of red hair, falling over her shoulders.

"Sorry?"

"You've been knocking back this," she twisted the bottle to her, "Chablis, and glancing down the bar in our direction, my direction, since we came in, as if, like, well, you wanted to meet me. Do you?"

"I've blown it?" he thought. Well thank goodness for that; I'll be out of this crazy situation. But her look held him, deepened and drew him. His courtesy took over and he offered her a glass.

Nathan woke late on Wednesday morning. He thought back to the evening before, to recollect what he had learned about her, and he realised it was nothing. It was he who had talked of his successes, his aspirations, at first. Then unintentionally, his true concerns had begun to voice themselves, but thankfully only in general terms. What would he say when the Reverend Peter called to debrief him? As it transpired, the Reverend didn't seem interested. He called Nathan on his cell phone on the way to work, simply uttered, "Let me know when they make contact," and hung up. But even if he had learnt little about her last night, she remained in the forefront of his mind, all Wednesday, all Thursday. Then on Friday, as he left the office after work, he saw an elegant redhead in a camel coat, walking fifty yards ahead on his side of the pavement, away from him. She cannot have seen him, but without thinking he had already quickened his pace. Too late, she hailed a taxi and was gone. Was it her?

It was gone seven by the time he was back in his flat. He had no plans tonight; somehow his mind was too unsettled. He needed something to happen, instead of living with the turmoil of these "what if" scenarios floating in circles round his brain, and they were mainly pretty nasty "ifs". At eight the phone rang. He reached for it.

"Hello."

"Hello, I'm so glad to catch you at home tonight, Nathan." A familiar female voice, which he could not place immediately."

"Yeah, no special plans tonight." He said, waiting for the clue as to who this was.

"You know, I had this incredible co-incidence. I was just mentioning our talk, and it turns out Bill Robinson knows you, or I mean, knows who you are. He was supposed to give you a call next week while he's in London, so I showed him your card, and he said we ought to give you a call now, check what you're doing tonight."

Bill Robinson, Nathan thought, still no clue. "So who does Bill work for?"

"Well, not so much for as with," the voice said. "Suleiman."

It clicked. So this was she, the redhead from the photo, from the wine bar. Suleiman was the client from whom came the threat to Nathan's existence. The Reverend's plan had worked. Nathan was in. And a cold chill settled upon him.

"Nathan?" she prompted.

"Yeah, sorry, I was just looking at my diary," he lied. "What do you propose?"

"Bill, wanted Italian, so we've got a table at Il Duce Bianco in Montpelier Street. We'll be there at eight thirty. They have valet parking if you want to drive." She said.

"Well, this is a pleasant surprise," Nathan said. "I shall certainly look forward to seeing you again, and Bill, of course. Just shows you that you should chat to people in pubs and wine bars, doesn't it?" He laughed.

"OK, see you later, bye for now."

He called the Reverend. This bubbly little chap, full of jokes in the Devil's Retreat, simply said, "Let me know what they propose," and hung up.

Sure enough, as Nathan drove up to Il Duce Bianco, a uniformed valet stepped forward to take his car keys. The restaurant had been heavily decorated for Christmas, which he felt detracted from its elegance. He was punctual, but they were there, and he was ushered across to a table near the window. Bill Robinson, about five eleven, hair greying at the edges, stood to greet him. Like Nathan, he was wearing a dark suit. She – I still don't know her name, he thought with a moment's panic – remained seated.

"Bill Robinson," he introduced himself in a moderated American tone. "Glad you could make it at such short notice. As for me, this is a flying visit, so this opportunity to meet really does work very well." He waived to the seat next to him. The round table was set for four. Nathan was next to Bill but there was a chair between Nathan and her. Maybe someone else is coming, Nathan thought, but he did not ask.

She suggested that they start Italian style with aperitifs, choosing a Campari soda, and soon she was leading an animated discussion. Nathan relaxed and found he was enjoying himself. Bill was regaling them with an anecdote about a conference he had just been to in Delhi.

"So I had to fly in from Karachi on a Pakistani plane," he was saying. "Now the fact is, as I understand it, that Pakistani air traffic control always delays the Indians and vice versa, so this has escalated to about four hours of delays. Anyway it gets worse. I've got this Pakistani client with me. So once we finally land in Delhi, we're first off the plane, and I usher this guy ahead of me to immigration, and the clerk at the desk says – sorry, special forms for Pakistani, I get them later, back of the line – and the line is by now one whole aircraft long. So I breeze through, telling my client that I'll secure transport for us. Sure enough this young Indian from the hotel is waiting outside. I've met him before. He always turns up with a rose for me, which does not have the significance it might have here in London, by the way.

"After a bit of chitchat, he points to a spot thirty yards away and says there's a bomb. This is, like, right were all the international passengers are walking by. So I ask him how he knows, and he says, they threw a red anorak over it."

"Shows great presence of mind and public concern to mark the bomb," she chipped in.

"Yeah," Bill continued. "So he goes across to take a look, while I retreat behind a concrete pillar for safety. Then this big truck arrives, stops eighty yards away and this guy, all suited up in bomb disposal gear, waddles over to take a look, so do about a hundred Indians who are waiting at the bus stops, which are also right there. They all stand round in a tight circle peering in at the bomb in the centre. Only the one guy is suited up for the occasion."

"I hope this has a happy ending." Nathan said.

"So you *do* believe in reincarnation," Bill laughed. "Then the bomb disposal guy gets out this big reel, ties it to the bomb and walks backwards, unreeling as he goes. Then he stops, gives the line a couple of tugs and reels it back in. By now the hotel guy is back, so I ask him what the reel is. He tells me it's just a bit of rope. The officer wanted to check the bomb wouldn't go off, he says, so he tied the rope on to give it a yank. It's probably not high explosives is what he told me. Great, I think of the still living onlookers in a close circle around the bomb. The truck drives up to the bomb. They unload a big container into which they drop the bomb, reload the container and leave, probably right through the centre of Delhi, or maybe they wait for rush hour."

"You know Kashmir's not so far, and a couple of bombs did explode in cafés there recently," said Nathan.

"I can tell you, I was very aware of that, as I stood behind my pillar."

"In the meantime, we call the hotel, to hear that my client was taken out of the airport the back way, and has been asleep in bed for an hour. Such consideration for me, waiting for him at the airport. So now comes the punch line. At the conference the next day, this Italian comes up to me and says he heard there was a bomb scare at the airport last night. And I tell him, I don't think so, I was there, yes, OK, there was a bomb, but no one was scared." They all laughed and Bill leaned back in his chair.

"Now to business," Bill said. "You work on the Suleiman account."

"I do," Nathan said, "but really just to kind of co-ordinate. I've met various representatives but never him, so I'm not fully apprised of his real needs." Nathan was glad of the opportunity to distance himself, maybe get the message across that he was not a threat, they need not worry about what he may have inadvertently discovered. This balloon of hope was punctured instantly.

"Mr Suleiman," Bill said, "is appreciative of your work to date and wishes to continue the relationship with your bank. However, he does have concerns about you." Nathan looked at Bill and at her, but she seemed to see nothing unusual about the direction the conversation was taking. "I have told Mr Suleiman that there is a solution, and I am going to ask you if you wish to be part of this solution, instead of being part of a rather large potential problem, which has the potential to quash your professional life for the next five years – at best." Nathan flinched at this *at best,* remembering his speculations of the last few months.

"But before I give you the solution," Bill continued, "just let me give you some advice, or tell you the way I see this. We all do our bit; we're each just a detail in the big picture. Mr Suleiman does his thing. I do my thing. He is not in my jurisdiction: he can do what he likes as far as I am concerned. You should be aware of this, as a private banker. And right now Mr Suleiman would like you to work with us. By that, I mean continue to develop the relationship with your bank. At the same time, we would like to introduce to you some new clients for your bank. This is the way Mr Suleiman operates. He likes his associates to deal with the same institutions. He sees business synergies in this. Very specifically, I plan a meeting with your boss on Monday, so I want to know your answer."

Nathan was not sure he had been asked a question or that a proposal had been made. But if this was being routed through his boss, i.e. his bank, that should be OK, and he began to feel more comfortable about the whole situation. Maybe they were heading for resolution of his problem after all.

"Compartmentalisation is the keystone of my approach to business," Nathan answered.

"Great," Bill said, standing up, "I'm sorry I have to take off like this, but I'm sure you'll appreciate that I was expecting to meet you tonight as little as you me. Got to get on. See you on Monday. No on second thoughts perhaps we don't need that meeting anymore. I'll give you a call."

Bill left, and she turned towards Nathan. "I do hope this was alright, Nathan. You see this was such a co-coincidence. The subject came up because Bill was putting the proposal to me and I just happened to mention we had met. He said he was planning to approach you anyway. You see, you and me, we're supposed to be working on the same programme." This really surprised Nathan.

Many things he may have anticipated but not this, so he reacted with the blandest of comments, in the manner of his profession.

"You know this has happened so fast, and, actually, I don't recall your telling me your name by the way." He felt somewhat awkward.

She leant across, "Howdy, partner. Shake." She reached out her hand, which he shook and released, reluctantly. Her smile seemed to know that. "Nathan, to you I am Zelda, just to you. Let this be our secret. Zelda." She held Nathan with her gaze, her lips holding a gentle smile.

"Nice to know you, Zelda," he said. "Now what's this about partners?"

"I think your bank will want to join in, when they hear about the programme," she responded, adopting a more business-like tone. "We're going to be setting up a number of private banking accounts related to the energy trading and derivatives businesses. Basically your bank will be providing account facilities, domicile for the operation, and so on, while a consulting outfit works out the appropriate structures with the lawyers. As to me, I've been asked to set up some meetings in the States, for the moment. You and I will be making the cold calls on these potential clients together."

Nathan was not sure of what she meant by "domicile for the operation", but this did not seem the best moment for a display of ignorance, so he nodded in agreement and thought he would be practical by exchanging contact numbers.

"We'll need to contact one another. What's your mobile number?"

"I don't have one: I meet people," she laughed and continued. "I'm glad Bill had to leave before the main course. If we're going to travel together, we might as well get to know one another. And just to get off on the right footing, I stake my claim to half Bill's veal when it arrives." Nathan toasted her with another glass of Bardolino, admiring her slender form and elegant style.

"You cut, I choose," he said, returning her smile.

***

"Farah! It is so wonderful to see you!" She said, as she opened the door. "I do miss you. Come in. Come in. It is very late, but I am so glad you came."

Farah's aunt had move to London three years ago. She lived in a purpose built redbrick building on the corner of Marloes Road and the Cromwell Road.

Parasites had formed an abscess in her liver and she had come for an operation at the Cromwell Hospital, a first class hospital in London with the very best liver consultants. Her doctor in Madras had trained in the UK in the fifties. As soon as he saw her problem on the ultra-sound scan he had called his friend who had established the hospital and arranged an appointment.

Farah had brought her to the hospital and rented an apartment as close as possible. When she came out of the hospital, Aunt Fatimah had loved to hear the languages in the corridors of the apartment block, so familiar to her, the cooking smells. Close to the hospital, the apartment block had become a favourite for middle eastern patients and their relatives. Life was so different from the big house in Madras: there she was important but lonely; here she would stop and talk to people coming into the building, often with relatives at the hospital. They would love to talk their languages with her in this foreign place. She had little space and no staff, but life was fun. She had stayed on.

Fatimah watched Farah's slim, elegant form as she moved through to the room overlooking the Cromwell Road, and she thought of her own youth, so different in Teheran. As Fatimah prepared tea for them both in a cubicle off the room, Farah sat and gazed into the middle distance. She felt so comfortable with her aunt, at home, a feeling she only experienced with her aunt, since the aerobatic accident when her brother had died.

Fatimah was a beautiful woman. She looked just like an older sister to Farah. Tresses of red hair hung around her shoulders. Her blue-grey eyes looked deeply into you, and her complexion came close to matching Farah's thirty years, cast in the marble used for Greek goddesses. Imagine the goddess, Diana, and you have Fatimah, and then if Diana had an identical daughter that would be Farah.

Farah always visited her aunt when she was in London, even when it was almost impossible, like tonight, close to midnight. It was her only link with her family, after her brother had died while she was in Moscow.

Fatimah brought the tea on a Persian silver tray and sat opposite her. They simply sat and gazed at one another, the mirror reflection adding years as the image of Farah came back from Fatimah.

"You know, Auntie," Farah said, "I so love what I do. I love what I want to do. I do it. And when I come to London, I see you."

"You are the only one now, Farah," Fatimah said with regret in her voice.

"You are tearful, Auntie. And so am I, but only with you."

"Farah, I remember them all when I see you," Fatimah whispered, thinking of the family in Teheran, as it was.

"I remember the harem," Farah said. "You were always there. We used to line up to see father every Saturday, in order of age. Jem was always in front of me, and she would pinch me and make me cry and get into trouble."

"She was my favourite," Fatimah said.

"But not mine. And then Zuri, in front of us, still young enough to be in the harem, would talk to father and Jem would be quiet. I would always listen to my brother Zuri as he told father what he had done during the week. I loved Zuri, Auntie. I loved Zuri."

"I loved you all, Farah," Fatimah said. She had not told Farah of that day, nor ever would, the day when she had rescued the young Farah and her eldest brother from the blaze that had destroyed their house, their servants, and - she could not bear to think of this and never did – their family, all the uncles and aunts and children, everyone they loved, in the Revolution of 1979 in Iran.

Farah was so young then. She had not known. Farah hoped she would never know. Fatimah had learnt to live with this. She did not want the next generation to suffer as she had. Farah's older brother had re-established the family in Bangalore. His death had been devastating, but also in a way a blessing, because he bridged the gap of knowledge between generations, now gone with him. With her, Fatimah, the painful memories would die.

Fatimah sipped her tea and sighed. In Farah before her she saw her father, Farah's grandfather. He had established the family, and now Farah seemed so intent on doing the same. It seemed uncanny to see this young girl, so like her father.

"Why do I see you so seldom?" Fatimah asked Farah.

"You see me every time I come to London. Even now at midnight, when it is not possible." Farah replied.

"Why not more often? Why not stay?" Fatimah asked her.

"I don't know, Auntie. I know what I must do, and I do it. Somehow I just know what I should do."

"What is that, Farah?" Fatimah melted into reminiscence of her youth, the life they had known, long gone. Farah gazed back at her.

"Auntie, I do not know. I think you know better than me. I do not know. I do it. I have no choice, Auntie. It is me." Farah slid back in the armchair, exhaling deeply. Almost dreamily, she said, "Auntie, they have taken so much from us. I just feel it. You do not tell me, but I see it in your eyes. In my heart, Auntie, deep in my heart, I must redress this, redress this before I can be who I want to be. Auntie, I met a man tonight. I could love him, but not yet."

Fatimah moved across to Farah and hugged her tight against her. And for Farah the outside world, the word in which she lived, was in retreat, but only for that moment.

***

Dubai, 21 December 2000

Vermouth had been impressed by Nathan, when he had met him in London in his role as Bill Robinson. Smartly turned out, Nathan was very clear headed, very competent, but above all upright and inspiring trust, a rare quality in such a young man. He was an excellent prototype of a private banker, Vermouth thought, who could go far. It was true that in a sense he had been "entrapped", but he was making the best of it, and clearly seeking the solution which would allow everyone to come out clean. Apart from his unfortunate glimpse behind the curtain, there was no reason why he should not undertake the programme that had been presented to him. Certainly he was a cut above that slimy slug, Frank Chardonnay, the type of guy who would slide from one disaster to the next, too weak-minded to have any semblance of control over his destiny. Maybe that was part of the penalty you paid for sticking it out in that tin pot bank where Frank worked, in Frank's case for far too long.

As to the woman, despite his mistrust of her, he had to admit, that if he were to describe her in tennis terms, it would be that she only ever ser ved aces. Where on earth had she got the information on Constexo Energy to start with? How did she manage to get their chairman, Brewster, to bite? Vermouth had worked with some pretty slick operators but this was uncanny. What was it about her that he did not like? Some visceral, some innate mistrust. The wicked witch? In fact, he thought she was more like a female Dorian Gray, charming the world, while…

The telephone interrupted his reverie. The call he was expecting, routed through from a spare line on the switchboard. "Hello."

"Hello, this is Nathan, calling from London."

"Nathan, thank you for returning my call, and thank you for meeting us in London. I was very impressed by your understanding of the programme, and I am looking forward to working together with you."

"Thank you, sir," Nathan replied.

"I'm sorry it took a while to get back to you. Travel, I'm afraid. Now Nathan, the real reason for my call is to say that the calling schedule has been set up for January and your tickets are on the way. Now that it's definitely going ahead, I want to make two points to you: the first is that this is a private banking matter and your disclosure and confidentiality requirements are exactly those in the policy of your bank; and the second is that I am running this programme, so for the purposes of this programme, save as I have just mentioned, you report to me and no one else. Don't bother to call me, however. I will ask you what I need to know and that will suffice as far as this reporting line is concerned. I know what I need to know. Is that clear?"

"That is very clear," Nathan said. He had a good feeling that this new dotted line boss knew exactly where things were at.

"As to your partner," Vermouth continued, "she has a track record of achieving every objective and more, and half the time that's before we've even worked out what the objective is. The point I am making is that you should not hesitate to use her as a resource. I wish you success."

Vermouth put down the phone and smiled. He thought he had

pulled off a pretty good Bill Robinson earlier in the month in London. What would he tell Nathan, when they met? *Yes, funny you should mention that, others have said we're very similar.*

CHAPTER FIVE - ENERGY

London, 10 December 2000

My wife and I returned home from Dubai early on Sunday evening. Daniel, the driver I use for the airport, met us when we landed at Heathrow. The travel people had booked us on a flight, emanating from Colombo. These people seem to have a mind of their own, or sometimes I wonder if they have a mind at all. So now we had to labour our way around the M25 instead of landing at Gatwick, which is where Dubai's own airline goes, and I do not even earn air miles with this flight! As if I, Frank Chardonnay, deal-maker *extaordinaire*, haven't raised this kind of issue often enough, but I am a captive client, destined to fly the world in the most inconvenient manner possible – next I can see them providing a special wooden seat at the back of the plane by the toilets, for members of my bank only by special reservation, and then they will still double book it. Lord above!

Still, my wife had had a great time. Just too short, she said. She would have loved another couple of days on the beach or under the palms by the pool, reading, drinking, eating, being waited on. She did not even seem to mind that Danny and I had consumed a month's maximum recommended alcohol intake in forty-eight hours. All in all this was a successful trip, and now for maximum effect, I would take the six eleven up to London first thing tomorrow and feed the deal of the century straight into the sausage machine and get approval to sign the mandate.

Sure enough, when I did the rounds with my deal at the bank

next morning, no one was interested in looking at my thirty-five-page report with additional appendices, but they did want to know when the fees would come in. This was good. It allowed me to say that if we faxed back the signed mandate before close of business today in Dubai (i.e. this morning in London), we would have the fees tomorrow.

Now, towards the middle of December a lot of bankers can get very interested in fees, that is to say fees in December and not fees in January. There is a very simple difference. They will be paid a bonus out of the December fees a year earlier than January fees by reason of the end of their budget year coinciding with the end of the calendar year. The fact that none of them had anything to do with these fees and would have nothing to do with doing the subsequent work, except for getting in the way every now and then, was not relevant to the bonus process. The simple principle is that the more distant you are from the deal in an upward direction in the bank hierarchy, the bigger your share of the resulting bonus.

My fees were so big that approval was guaranteed, and my acceptance of the mandate went out at eleven ten London time, and I called Danny to make sure he retrieved it from his fax machine. The fax was signed by me, as always. That way if anything went wrong, my bosses did not know about it. The fact that by the time things went wrong they might have been reporting the fee income once a month for the last eighteen months usually had no bearing on their apparent and convenient lack of recollection. Some of them could make the Irangate perpetrators look like a wimps who could not even get into the Boy Scouts. The next thing on the agenda was for my secretary, Jill, to pass an urgent message to say I could not make the weekly Monday meeting at two o'clock because I was negotiating the closure of a major deal. With that I went to lunch.

Lunch was a bit of a reunion with a couple of the guys we had done a deal for back in the eighties. Richard had been the number two in finance at the time and Neil was their in-house lawyer. Like many of the eighties deals, it had turned sour a couple of years later, but we had all made out like bandits at the time. Top management had been kicked out, which meant they got better jobs elsewhere, so that they could screw those shareholders too, and they had recruited

Richard and Neil to do the job for them, since they still had not learned how to do it themselves.

I had wanted a mandate, of course, but since our bank had led the way to have their old friends fired from the previous screw-up, this had proved difficult. We met at the Pacifique Grillade in Mayfair. I did not expect to see many bankers in there at lunchtime. As far as I knew, this was more of a media hangout in the evening. I descended the stairs to the *art nouveau* basement, at least that was my take on the décor, not being quite sure what *art nouveau* is, so maybe I have got the wrong style, I thought to myself, and maybe its *Jugendstil.* No matter, my lunch guests were already at the bar, the plan being to have a few beers before moving over to our booth for lunch.

"So where've you been, Frank, you're looking tanned," Richard, my lunch guest, said as he greeted me.

"We've just closed on a big deal. I was out in Dubai." I replied.

The conversation moved on to their various activities over the last six months and plans for the coming year. It had always been my great white hope that I would somehow resurrect our relationship with these people, and once again opportunities seemed to be there, but the fish were not biting today. In the back of my mind, I knew that I had to find a counterbalance to avoid being totally sucked in to the business of the people whose mandate I had just signed before lunch. We had a bottle of French white with the hors d'oeuvre, and by the time we had moved on to red with the main course it was abundantly clear that there was still no business here for me.

It was three thirty by the time we ascended to street level. Instead of parting on Piccadilly, Richard suggested we go somewhere for a pint, unless I had an urgent reason to race back to the office. I agreed, but then my phone rang. It was Danny and he wanted to talk, so I asked him to hold for a second while I said my goodbyes.

"Good lunch, huh. I guess you've just turned your phone back on," Danny said.

"You know how it is in London this time of year. Pretty tough for us bankers."

"I do. I can smell it from here. My guess is Margaux. So thanks for the mandate. I've talked to Vermouth in Singapore. He wants to set up the first major meeting with all parties. We need to know you will be there. It's scheduled for next Monday, one full day. Can you make it?" A combination of lager, white and red wine is not known to induce timidity, so I had no hesitation in my response.

"Sure."

"In that case, take the flight out on Saturday which stops in Dubai. I'll join you and we'll be in Colombo by lunchtime Sunday."

"Colombo?"

"Yeah, didn't I say? We're all meeting in Sri Lanka for some reason."

Back in the office, Jill was struggling with my expense claims from Dubai. It was always the modest pile of receipts that caused her the problem, when she couldn't work out why I hadn't had any meals, or why there seemed to be a bottle of red wine on the breakfast bill and nothing for the rest of the day. The idea that hotel billing times might not coincide with my consumption, or that someone might have invited me to a meal, did not seem to occur to her. But I liked the red wine at breakfast conclusion: I thought it would be good for my image when the Accounts Department came to check the expense claims.

She looked up.

"You've all got to attend a dinner on Tuesday. Chairman's in town." This was good. Not only did I have the opportunity of a trip to Sri Lanka, but I was going to be very visibly missing the chairman's dinner because I was engaged on a major deal. I think Jill quite enjoyed apprising our Illustrious Leader's secretary of this. But he still called me in to see him.

"So it seems your ticket's come up after all, Frank. You'll survive another quarter."

"It seems that way." I replied.

"You wanna watch your weight, Frank. Bit of a paunch there. When's your medical?" He asked.

"It'll keep me going longer in a nuclear winter." I advised him, but he seemed to want to develop the theme.

"Balding a bit, just under five eleven, slightly grey. Premature for someone just turned thirty."

"Is this a management technique they're teaching you now?" I quipped.

"You remember that bunch that screwed it up here?" he asked, changing the subject.

"No."

"Your ex-colleagues, Frank."

"If you mean former executives of the bank who put good business on the books, which was wrongly written down so that their successors could achieve their budgets with supposed recoveries of bad debts which were never bad to start with, rather than by doing business themselves, yes, I remember those ex-colleagues."

"Yup, I guess those are the same rats as I'm thinking of, Frank. I just wanted to make sure you knew I was serious about cleaning up around here."

"If you want to chop out the dead wood, I'll give you a list."

"Not what I had in mind, Frank."

"So what do you have in mind?" Bravado on my part.

"Give me time, Frank. I just wanted to wish you luck on your trip."

This seemed as good a point as any to stand up and leave, so I did. I had not the foggiest idea of what he was on about. He was probably fantasising about ways to secure my deal's stream of fee income, and then chop me, so that he could take the credit; but so what, he would take the credit anyway. Maybe it was just the fun of chopping me. You sometimes had to wonder if these people were committable psychopaths full time or just at work.

A full week in the office could become a bit of a drag without some careful time management on my part. Nothing to do on the deal, because as far as I could see all the work required so far had been done in Dubai, the stuff I had seen in the boxes. I was not really keen that I would be working on the coming weekend, so I decided to shoot off early today, and told Jill I would also take Friday off as well in lieu of working on Saturday, i.e. sitting on the plane eating dinner and knocking back a few cognacs. In the meantime, I would arrange to punctuate the week's lunches and cocktail parties with a few appearances in the office.

***

I did not know what to expect in Colombo, but with all the material

I had seen in Dubai, I felt well briefed if we were to be meeting the client. One thing I have always prided myself on is that I can easily assimilate and retain the complex information required for this kind of work. I recognise my shortcomings, in particular that life seems to lead me rather than me leading life, but I do seriously believe that I provide real value to my clients on the job, and at the bar when appropriate, which in the case of my clients is not infrequent.

We picked up Danny in Dubai as planned, or rather the airline did. His view of this leg of the journey was that it was time for a pre-emptive snooze. I was not sure what the *pre-emptive* meant and did not hazard a guess, in case I found out too early, but the *snooze* suited me well. We landed on schedule, grabbed our carry-on bags and were VIPed out of the terminal to a waiting Mitsubishi Pajero. Exiting the airport, we wove our way through a few portable barriers. They did not look as if they could control a football crowd, let alone Tamil Tiger suicide bombers. No wonder the Tigers had recently blown up half the local airline on the runway.

First, we drove into Colombo to pick up a couple of people at the Rinola hotel, who turned out to be secretaries. They sat on the jump seats at the back. Colombo has a smart beach and promenade which we followed, heading south. After a couple of miles the driver stopped outside a porcelain shop. It transpired that this was the works outlet for Sumitaki, the famous Japanese name, which had established a plant here years ago. We were picking up a set of porcelain for one of the conference delegates, so Danny and I took a look around. Although many of the designs were a touch ornate for my taste, there was some amazing stuff at unbelievable prices. We took off again in the Pajero and were soon at our destination, the Gardenia Hotel.

The Gardenia Hotel was a huge and very attractive, perhaps colonial style, building. At hotel reception Danny said that he had a couple of hour's work to do. I registered and then briefly checked the place out. There were a number of jewellery shops, which reminded me of my shopping expedition with Zara in Karachi a couple of weeks ago – I half expected her to emerge from one. Emeralds were high on the agenda and there seemed to be a lot of lapis lazuli. Precious stones do not hold my attention for more than about five seconds, so I went up and changed for a run and a swim. This is my standard procedure wherever I travel.

I ran along the beach barefoot, the blue sea on my right with heavy waves rolling in close to the shore. The sand was coarse and sharp. I ran for about ten minutes, which was about as much as my feet were going to take on the sharp sand, and then plunged into the waves. They were stronger than I anticipated with an undertow, so I gave up after a few minutes, returning to the hotel and my room. I read for a bit, wandered around the hotel for a bit, read a bit more. Danny had vanished. No one else seemed to be concerned about me. At eight a note was slipped under my door to advise me of a pick-up tomorrow at six in the morning, so I simply ordered the spiciest dish on the room service menu, ignored the mini-bar and sank into the soft, downy double bed for an early night.

***

The meeting started with a minimum of formality. We had been taken to a villa just over an hour south of Colombo, driving through lush vegetation with the coast to our right and villages generally to the landside on our left. The villa was set in its own gardens which you entered through twin wrought iron gates. The driveway took you past servant's quarters and then on to the main house. We stopped under a white portico, crossed through an archway and were in an internal courtyard with café tables set out under a pergola.

Once in the main house, we were offered fruit juices, coffee and pastries, but there was no time. We were almost immediately asked to move through and take our seats in the Kandy Room. It was seven thirty in the morning. We had place cards with print a touch too fine, so it took me a moment to find "Frank Chardonnay". The table and chairs were a fairly informal pastel green rattan. My seat was in the middle on the left of the chairman's seat, two down from Vermouth, who had greeted me affably on the way in. The chairman, six foot, powerful, dark haired, walked in, sat down and called the meeting to order in one fluid movement. A dozen seats were filled.

"For those of you who have not met me, my name is Suleiman,

and I look forward to meeting you all in due course (in fact, I did not get that opportunity). The purpose of this meeting is to establish our modus operandi and assign responsibilities for the very important project, which lies before us. This is the only time we shall all be together today. There is no point in wasting time having all delegates listen to issues which concern just a few." This is a sound approach, I thought, rather than the interferences of the ill-informed which I was more used to. "Each of us will deal with his own issues and liaison will be effected as required. For this reason we will break into groups. Vermouth."

Vermouth stood to address us. "I am point man today for everyone. Anything you need, come to me here. Agendas are in the folders in front of you. Let's get to work."

I opened my folder, which contained a sheet with *Cinnamon Room with Ferdinand Moon* written on it. I stood up, and sure enough, off to the left was an arrow showing a number of rooms including mine. Like good boy scouts we all followed the arrows. My interlocutor entered the room immediately behind me, a Spanish looking guy with a huge cigar stuck between his teeth, and introduced himself as Ferdie.

"Can't get these in the States, Frank. They're Havana's. Only place you do get them is in the White House." I opened my folder.

"There seems to be a mix up here, Ferdie. I don't have an agenda."

"The day there's a mix up at one of Suleiman's meetings, I'll vote Clinton back into office. No mix up. You have no agenda."

"So what do I do?"

"I have the agenda, Frank. I'm here to brief you. I'm not gonna pull any punches. You don't like anything, you tell me. You don't like me, you go do whatever it is they do in San Francisco."

"I'm all ears, Ferdie."

As Ferdie progressed, my head began to swirl, my stomach thanked me for skipping breakfast today, and my heart truly did begin to palpitate for the first time in my life. I could not believe how I had dug myself so deep in this hole. It had got off to a good start. Ferdie had intimated that keeping my bank sweet was a number one priority. If anyone above me started creating problems, they would see that he would get fired, and I had thought fondly of my Illustrious Leader.

It was the ensuing revelations that concerned me. None of what Ferdie said was new to me: it's just that virtually everything he said is what I really did not want to know about. Take the power projects. All the equipment purchased was being invoiced at 20% over the price, so that the equipment supplier could pay the extra funds received into a Swiss bank account for our group's benefit. Different companies in the group were to buy and sell from one another at bogus prices and often with no goods moving. Companies were to be bought and sold, merged, spun off, floated, delisted and usually with one of two objectives: either to shift funds around internationally or to manipulate share prices.

Then there was the big one, which I had yet to understand. Somehow they were going to use derivatives and options trading markets to achieve something which to me looked very akin to money laundering. My bank's role, which I had also not fully understood, seemed to be to run accounts for many of these entities and add an air of legitimacy. He then passed across a sheet of A4 size paper with boxes, names, numbers and arrows on it. It set out the value gained from the planned exercise for which the total box showed US$ 550 million, which seemed to be an estimate of the net profit.

"So to sum up, Frank. These are the mechanics for your bit of the operation. You don't have to know about the other aspects. I've probably phrased this a bit more bluntly than the big accounting firms do when they take this kind of consultancy role, but Mr Suleiman does not like us to beat about the bush."

It had taken four hours, which had passed in ten minutes. Four hours, or ten minutes, in which my world had changed. Either I had to do something majorly drastic or go mountain biking with Danny. I was beginning to understand Danny's point of view. The easy way was to knuckle down, do what they want, and become a mega-hero at the bank, pulling in fees like nobody's business.

As if on schedule the door behind me opened the moment Ferdie closed his folder.

"You guys coming?" A breathy female voice. Ferdie nodded. I sighed and looked down at the table, still distraught.

"Frank?" she said. Who could this be, one of the secretaries from the Rinola? I stood up and looked round.

"Zara!" I exclaimed. Ferdie was packing his stuff into his document carrier. Who is Zara? He thought. I hope Zenap doesn't take offence.

"I thought that since you did your jewellery shopping a while back, Frank, we three should go to the beach. What say you, Ferdie?"

"I want the beach with the Lion brand beer, not the Three Coins."

"Done! Let's go."

So we went out. The Pajero was waiting, and we headed further south, the three of us in the back, the driver in the front, and the beer cooler in the very back. Ferdie helped us to three Lion beers, icy to touch, and immediately launched into a string of ribald jokes that should have made Zara blush. For some reason Ferdie kept calling her some weird name like Zenap, which did not seem to faze her. In the end we drove a good couple of hours, which did not matter because we had a pretty big beer cooler in the back.

The local driving style seemed to be to follow a vehicle until you saw someone coming the other way, at which point you would pull out to overtake, hooting like mad, and then at the last moment you swerved in front of your victim, just avoiding certain death. As for me, certain death looked like a pretty good option after the session with Ferdie. By the time we reached the beach I was mellowing. Zara called the beach something like Ben Tota; whatever it was it sounded to me like some Italian mountain which had relocated to Scotland.

We tumbled out of the Pajero and headed across the beach towards the sea. Behind us were hotels opening out V-shaped towards the sea with gardens, palms, bars and pools in the V. Ahead was open sea and to the left a rocky reef running parallel to the sand just a few yards out. Local kids were doing very impressive somersaults from the beach into the sea. Scattered along the beach were a few older folk, characterised by white, or red, skins and large bellies. From the few words snatched from the wind as they passed, I guessed German pensioners.

"It's not busy this year", Zara said. "Most of the hotels have had to batten down the hatches. Blowing up airliners on the ground in Colombo is bad for tourism. It's up to the left." We walked about half a mile, passing signs advertising Sauerkraut and other German culinary delicacies, and reached Ferdie's preferred bar, where they brought us three half-litre bottles of Lion brand beer before we even asked.

"I had to give you the full gen, Frank. You can't afford to screw up with Suleiman or he'll kill you – I don't mean literally – and if you don't know what you're doing you will screw up."

Zara supported him: "You have to keep it in perspective, Frank. You are out here in Sri Lanka. To all intents and purposes you can forget what Ferdie told you, now that you know it, if you know what I mean. I'm looking forward to working with you, Frank. Two weekends together already in as many weeks, wow!" She was laughing and swaying on her chair. The sun by now dropping lower, she pulled out a pair of dark glasses and masked those seductive blue-grey eyes.

"OK, so tell me what I do." I suggested.

"You do your job, Frank, and nothing else. So it's going to be a whole lot easier now that you have some background. You will have accounts opened at your bank, you will have money transferred, you will write up projects, prepare Information Memoranda, all the things you do so well. The only difference is that you will have five hundred percent more support than you have had from any other client before, you will always get what you ask for, and your bank will earn huge fees. There *is* no catch."

"Since you put it like that."

"I do."

She stood up taking my hand. Ferdie dumped some cash on the table, and we headed back towards the Pajero.

As we walked, Zara said, "OK, Frank, let's quickly run through the list.

"One: profits are skimmed through over-invoicing. You don't know."

"Two: profits are moved out through transfer pricing. You don't know."

"Three is slightly more complicated: our foreign investment vehicle subscribes to a rights issue of our locally quoted company, we ramp up the share price by bidding for the (usually limited) free float with a local vehicle, our foreign vehicle sells to our local vehicle at the ramped up price and that's how we ship the funds out of the country. You don't know."

"Four: we won't go in to detail, but we shift the funds through an acquisition. You don't know."

"Five: our energy companies do forward trades, derivative trades etc. with each other like bets on a two horse race, but if the trade goes the wrong way, we simply tear it up and write it retrospectively the opposite way. You don't know."

"All you do, Frank, is the mechanics, and that's all you need to know, now that you know, or rather don't know. Is that clear or shall I go on?" she finished.

"I think you've made your point, Zara," I said.

Another exotic beach promenade with Zara was over.

In the Pajero I asked her about Hamid and the Rugby trip.

"He just had a bit part. Recruited for one scene," she said. "You must have realised by now, that you threw everything out of kilter when you got on that bus. We had to rejig the whole thing. Hamid was chuffed that he got to fly out to Karachi for the weekend. We were naughty, too, slipping a little something in your Champagne, when you were dumb enough to actually board the 747."

"And my passport?" I asked.

"Your passport." She laughed. "Your travel guys don't have security to match even Buck House. You remember the guy who climbed the wall and got as far as the Queen's bedroom, with her in it!" She smiled again. "You're growing on me, Frank. You make me horny. I think I'm going to need electric shock treatment to hold me back. Stop grinning, Ferdie." Well, that should give him a bit to think about over the coming weeks, she thought.

They arrived back at the Gardenia shortly before midnight, having eaten *en route*. As I was waiting for the lift, I saw Ferdie in discussion with a very attractive, but very irate lady. From what I could gather, she was his wife. She was giving him stick for coming back at midnight and being totally immersed in business deals with no time for her. I could see her point, in as far as it *was* close to midnight, but I did not think that rampaging around bars at the beach really qualified as *business*. I decided not to intervene. I guessed he might want to keep quiet about that bit, in the circumstances.

A few minutes later Suleiman heard a characteristic knock on his door. He looked up, a pool of light on the desk before him, various pieces of electronic equipment, a red LED blinking. The door was not locked. She stepped in, closed the door and leant her back against it. Why does she have to come now, he thought. During the day I can handle it, but here, now, in this suite, the door ajar to the adjoining bedroom. Over the last few months he had felt a growing electric charge between them. As if reading his mind, she stepped towards him, unbuttoning her shift from the top down. The red garment slipped down, falling to the floor around her feet, to reveal her naked form, a sight for man over the ages, unchangeable by fashion, and she took a step closer.

"Suleiman, I have only ever worked with you, not for you. Is that correct?"

"It is," he intoned in a half-voice."

"That is important for the conversation we will have later. First you may choose. You may have me for yourself, or you may have me for our cause. It is your choice. It cannot be both. If you have me for yourself, you will not allow me to do what I must for our cause." He gazed at her, taking his time, the curves of her figure glowing in the dim light.

"Zenap, twenty years ago the choice would have been as certain as it is today, but it would have been a different choice. Recover your dress." As she turned to pick up her shift, he saw her bend and he rose from the desk, seduced by what he saw. Should he reverse this choice before it was too late? But in a fluid movement she had raised the shift above her head, slipped it over her red hair and shoulders, down to her hips and below. I have trusted him with myself, she thought. This man will now trust me absolutely, forever.

"Suleiman, I was not here for this. I do not know why this happened. We must speak urgently, which is why I have come."

They had moved to the coffee table and were sipping J&B with ice.

"I have been researching the missing computer files which were hacked," she said.

"And?"

"And they're too greedy. They came back for more, and I've traced them to the UK. They could be hackers, they could be intelligence, they could be Prince Charles for all the trace tells me. Now I want to remind you that I work with you. I don't follow orders."

"OK."

"I stuck in a decoy. It washes you clean but leaves Vermouth incriminated. I know you won't like that, but we'll have to deal with that later. Better him than you as far as the Board is concerned."

"So the hacker thinks I'm not a drug baron, money launderer, whatever else, after all."

"Not the hacker, Suleiman, British intelligence."

"But you told me you can't tell from the trace."

"I can't, but I put in another decoy, incriminating me. Don't worry. I've only incriminated my alias, which I can dump any time."

"So what does that tell us?"

"It tells us nothing. At least it didn't until I met that UK private banker by contrived chance, not contrived by me."

"The guy I asked you to have checked out, because of that unfortunate slip?"

"The very one, Suleiman. I picked him up in a bar, but I know he was sent to pick me up – he couldn't keep his eyes off me." Suleiman could not help smiling.

"I don't think that's conclusive proof."

"It wouldn't be, except that the guy was pissed out of his mind by the time I reached the bar, and there were plenty of other sexier numbers to ogle. But it's what I've matched it to that counts. I have detailed notes from our watcher who was checking him over. I only downloaded them today - I've been busy and this was routine stuff – and this is why I'm talking to you now, after midnight." She drained the remains of her glass and topped up the J&B, neat without ice this time. "Just three days earlier he went into the Devil's Retreat pub and met a Church of England vicar. The watcher recorded them drinking four pints of bitter and then leaving in good spirits. He couldn't overhear any of their conversation."

"I guess they would be in good spirits after four pints of bitter, Zenap."

"I've checked and double checked three months of the watcher's records, Suleiman. The records are meticulous. This guy drinks, no doubt about that, but you know what, he drinks max two pints of beer and then moves on to wine, G and T, a Bloody Mary, you name it, but he never, I repeat never, drinks four pints of beer."

"That doesn't tell me anything, Zenap, except that he was thirsty that day."

"The devil is in the detail, Suleiman. What it says to me, plain as day, is that the vicar doesn't know the habits of his bosom chum he's meeting in the Devil's Retreat, because it was the vicar who bought all the drinks. And you tell me who goes out to meet a vicar he doesn't know and drinks four pints of beer. You know what that tells me? It tells me that the vicar is not a vicar. And you know what the next question is? You tell me who runs around pubs, masquerading as a vicar, knocking back pints of beer with people they are only pretending to know, but greet as old pals at the door. Suleiman, there is no coincidence in espionage. QED."

"You would not be Zenap, if you had no game plan."

"There's not much I can do. I just wanted you to know that a channel is open for passing deceptive information."

"What about our friend the banker?"

"We are going to use him and I hope turn him at some point. As regards the vicar, well, he already knows that his mole believes in your guilt, so he's not going to ask him about you again. In fact, the vicar's going to turn his attentions to Vermouth, and since the vicar now believes that you are innocent, he's not going to be interested in what his mole says about you, which anyway will be nothing, since he won't ask him about you. Sorry if that sounds a bit convoluted, but that's the way I read it. So that's it. I'm off to bed, and I'm sure you appreciate that the earlier thing has to have been a one-off, Suleiman."

"I do. Thank you, thank you twice, and good night."

CHAPTER SIX - BREWSTER

Upper Peninsula, Michigan, 15 January 2001

Brewster was a big man, but neither his ample girth nor tall stature came anywhere near to matching the size of his ego. He had headed Constexo Energy for a decade, during which time it had grown from its base of oil and power to become a diversified energy supplier and trader, a leading player in a new and burgeoning market. Constexo had started out in pharmaceuticals as an early pioneer, before moving into oil in the sixties and taking its present name. Unlike his peers, Brewster felt no need to sit at the epicentre: everyone else could come to him. Hunting and fishing was his scene, particularly in the winter, so he had located himself well north of Milwaukee in the Upper Peninsula of Michigan.

Built in a hexagon, his lakeside "cabin" had three faces towards the lake, and on the land side two wings attached to the hexagon's sides created a v-shaped entry to the main door. Set back in the woods was a series of outbuildings containing all the essentials for lakeside living: various boats; a cabin cruiser; a Yukon off-roader; snow mobiles; dump trucks; a couple of limousines and a full scale automatic car wash. Fishing tackle and guns were kept in the cellar of the main house – you can't be too careful. Any kind of intrusion alarm was deemed superfluous – who would dare intrude on Brewster?

Sitting with Brewster was Lorenson, in all respects as weedy as Brewster was big. He had been made up to Chief Financial Officer two years ago.

"So what this guy says," Brewster was saying, "is that he'll set up limited partnerships to ship the problem out, AND, they'll cut us in on the profits. Now I don't see a conflict of interest. We've got a quarter of a billion dollar problem. This will solve it. That's good for the corporation. So we benefit too. OK, I admit we do. But look at it this way: I've already added five billion dollars of value to the shareholders this last couple of years, and that compares to less than two hundred million paid to me in stock options. We've got to get this compensation committee sorted." This last aside meant he wanted to force through yet another pay increase for himself, which the compensation committee would recommend to the board for approval to be followed by the shareholders' approval at the Annual General Meeting. It was *pure coincidence* that he also sat on the compensation committees of a number of his peers who were similarly under-remunerated.

Brewster had already brought Lorenson up to speed on how he had been introduced to this UK private banker by some red-headed cocktail party floozy he had met on the circuit, and Lorenson presumed, coveted, but apparently so far unsuccessfully. Lorenson's mind was working overtime. He knew that they were already more than half a billion dollars underwater, more than Brewster knew, and would have to restate their next accounts – they could not hide the losses by pushing them into the future any more, as they had done for the last five years. The problem had grown too big. They would need to put another two billion dollars of commitments on the books to redeem their positions, which in turn would kill their debt ratings by reason of over-leverage, and that meant they would have to pay their bond holders higher rates of interest, which they could not afford, not on the levels of debt they had whacked into the corporation over the last five years. Both he and Brewster were about to hit the end of the line, although Brewster clearly was not letting his ego conceive of this particular possibility. The board would go ballistic when they found out.

What Lorenson could see in this scheme was the magnitude of what they could do with these partnerships. Not only would they rescue current losses, but they could double their bets, keep the upside with them, and stick any losses to the corporation, which may or may not survive. In other words, they could monumentally rip off the corporation by making it take crazy risks that would make the Junk Bond King's fiasco look like *kindergarten.* So what! Jumping three steps ahead, he was thinking, and I have a good deal with the lawyers, so they can draft a memo of instruction from Brewster to me, and if they're worried about what they put in the memo, I'll tell them we'll stick it to Constexo's own internal legal counsel if it turns sour. I will simply be following orders: it's Brewster who gets locked up if it comes to it. If he's game, I'm game. Lorenson had made ten million dollars last year, and here he could see a clear half billion, if he could swing it, so he would try his damnedest.

Brewster was carrying on: "So they want us to meet with some consultant who will set up the structure. I guess they want to distance themselves. Bankers! No guts! Why do they need a consultant? I said I'm in, so long as we act now, next month is too late. So the girl pipes up, says she wants one working day with us in private and we can sign the next day. One working day. That was on Friday. Today's Sunday, so figure it out for yourself. That's why Blim's coming."

"Blim! What do we need him for?" Lorenson countered.

"Do you know about partnership structures? Creative accounting? Derivatives? What your butt looks like? We need Blim." Blim, Brewster's Mr Fixer, the chairman of the Brewster career advisory board. More importantly, the man who undertook all the less savoury behind-the-scenes tasks to keep a flamboyant chief executive like Brewster in the job and out of the state penitentiary. No one knew why he was called Blim, and no one had probably asked him, since any sane creature with a modicum of intelligence steered well clear of anywhere in range of the Blim presence, that is to say unless it was pay day for them.

What the world did not yet know was that Blim was about to enter politics. Among eminent citizens there were not a few who would find it in their best interests to assist Blim, should he ask, which he would. Generally Blim went where he wanted, when he wanted, and did not stand on ceremony. That applied today as well. There was no knock on the door, no announcement by some phoney butler. The door was flung open and there stood Blim, framed in the doorway, even as Lorenson was employing phrases well outside the scope of either the Pope's or the Catholic Church's vocabulary with specific reference to Blim. Blim had learnt to hold his pose in the doorway for two seconds, as standard procedure, to make sure everyone could take note of his presence and fix him in their mind. This was usually accompanied by a booming utterance, in this case, "What's that little troll doing here?"

"I've made him my chief financial officer, Blim, so that he can do stuff for me, like the accounts, right." Brewster replied, in jovial mood.

"Why do you want some spineless little creep, playing with himself in the accounts department?" said Blim.

"That's exactly why I want him there. Who do you want sniffing around?"

Lorenson took great satisfaction out of these exchanges. These thundering buffoons could roar away merrily at his expense, while he cleaned up and banked his stash. And all the while, they would be issuing the memos, evidencing their duplicity, which he would keep safe to leak at the appropriate moment if things turned sour.

Brewster brought Blim up to speed on the proposal. It was no accident that Blim was a fixer. Despite his brash exterior, he had an incisive mind and knew the devil lay in the detail, when it came to legal financial structures. That is why Brewster brought him in for confidential deals where he could not use the apparatus of the corporation. In fact, given a choice, Brewster would use Blim for everything, rather than his pedantic lawyers or his finicky accountants, the cumbersome tools of the big corporation.

"Blim, we're going out on the truck. Lorenson, you do whatever it is you want to do. If you're worried the maintenance man will ramrod you up the rear end, lock your bedroom door. Whatever. I want the presentation ready for tomorrow first thing. I'm flying them in to Escanaba, so they should be here by ten."

Going out on the truck meant that Brewster's massive off-road vehicle had been loaded with shotguns, rifles, beer and Bourbon. Whereas most of the locals respected the environment and the wildlife, it was not in Brewster's nature to respect dumb animals, and in his mind this category did not just inhabit the countryside, but included most of his work colleagues and business associates, or maybe they were a sub-category which he could not legally shoot.

Blim was a willing partner, more for the Bourbon than the beer or the shooting, although he did enjoy going after the geese in season. They migrated along a flight path way above the range of the normal shotgun, so you used the more powerful goose gun. He enjoyed watching the geese doing their version of freefall without the parachute after taking a hit. He had done grouse in Scotland once, but found the process a bit too industrial, as the guns were loaded and handed to him, and the birds fell out of the sky. This is golf, not hunting he had thought, luckily not voicing this unorthodox opinion either on the grouse moor or in the golf club.

At this point Lorenson knew he was free to get his material together. Whenever the other two got back, which could be any time from dusk to the early hours of the morning, they would stumble from the truck to the bar and from there to bed, or maybe not if they did not make it that far but slumped at the bar. What Lorenson did not know was that, despite appearances, Blim would be compos mentis, not that he was a good actor, he was never anything other than Blim: he was simply a born cheat.

***

Nathan was in the back of the truck with Zelda. In the front with the driver was Ferdie Moon, the consultant. Riding through the snow on the lakeside road towards the rendezvous, they made an unusual trio: the elegant redhead, the slim dark haired English banker, and the through and through American who looked exactly like a Cuban, with his curly dark hair and thick moustache. If it weren't for the embargo, he would probably be smoking a Havana. As it was he made do with a cheroot.

"OK, guys," she said. "We play this absolutely according to the rules. I'm chairman of the meeting; you speak when you are spoken to. This is because I am the person without a role to play here, so I can hit these guys as hard as need be without jeopardising the deal. The only time you speak out of turn is if they ask me to leave, when you tell them to piss off, and don't use any euphemisms. If they say it more than once, play it by ear, but take it in turns to tell them to piss off. OK?"

If Nathan had learnt one thing in his short *partnership* with

Zelda, it was that she knew how to run a meeting to achieve her goals and no one else's, but this was the first time she had come up with anything like this."

"I know these guys," she said. "They think they're tough and the world owes them. The share price goes up a dollar and they're heroes, it goes down five dollars and some jerk in the paints division has screwed up, OK so they don't make paint, so it's the jerk in pharmaceuticals who doesn't know a patent from a patient. Got it? They're not expecting us yet, so we'll hit them hard before we've even disrobed, by that I mean got our coats off, Ferdie, so stop grinning."

The truck crunched to a halt on the frozen snow in front of Brewster's place. Like well-trained commandos, they exited the truck in a fluid movement and were banging the deer skull knocker on the front door. The temperature was well below freezing. Brewster opened the door himself, and Zelda pushed through past him into the hall. As Brewster started to ask how come the plane was early, Zelda threw her winter coat over a chair, interrupting him.

"Mr Brewster," she informed him, "I advised you that we needed one working day, and that is today. Our working day does not begin at ten and it does not end at five, so I cancelled your plane. Did they not advise you?" She knew they had not, because she had paid them for this minor oversight, and getting one over Brewster was an opportunity few of his employees would care to miss. "Where are we sitting? Gentlemen, let's go through," she said to Nathan and Ferdie. My holy grandmother, Ferdie thought, she's not just chairing the meeting, she's playing host in Brewster's home, before he can even say, "Hi".

In the lounge, Lorenson was at a desk in the corner looking over his notes, and suppressing a smile at this bit of one-up-manship (or even worse, one-up-womanship) over Brewster. Blim was admiring the lake, and Brewster's interrupted breakfast was lying half-eaten on the table. The introductions were made and the tension stayed. Clearly, Zelda had her reasons for this opening inverted-charm offensive, but it was not an opening move out of Nathan's standard business chess manual.

As the meeting progressed, Nathan began to twig what was going on. He had the time to watch between his own contributions to the meeting. Zelda had a very strict agenda which unfolded and developed rapidly, like a foetus in the womb. Brewster was all bluster, which was why she had controlled him at the outset. He could rule his company with an iron fist, but here, even in his own home, she had exploited the fact that he had no authority over them. He was powerless, except to the extent that she gave him the authority to make a decision, which she would not do yet. Lorenson was the man to watch, sly and in charge of the information, but he soon learnt that when he tried to withhold information Zelda seemed to know. Lorenson began to think she knew more than Brewster, and this worried him. As to Blim, he would never lose his commanding position anywhere; he was biding his time. But by lunch the agenda had passed the point of safe abortion for Brewster's team, so maybe Blim had been thwarted and would have to fight a rearguard action for them to get the best terms they could.

"I'd like to sum up before lunch," said Zelda, taking her fully established chairman role, and knowing full well that Brewster had not had time to do anything about lunch, giving another little twist to the knife. She summarised the financial position, the general outline of the deal structure, and the benefits which would accrue. "After lunch we will fill you in on the mechanism we will employ, and then we will draft heads of agreement, setting out, in particular, the ownership structure, profit entitlements and fees."

Brewster's bluff, that he had kept the personnel clear of the house for confidentiality reasons, but would now instruct them on lunch preparations, fell flat. Zelda was already at the bar suggesting they have a couple of dry martinis, while she busied herself in the kitchen. Nathan thought the suggestion was probably accepted for the relief of having her out of the room. Brewster gave voice to this as soon as she left for the kitchen, suggesting that the only safe place in the house today was in the john, and Blim countered that he wasn't sure he wanted to pull his pants down even in there, and thank his lucky stars he had relieved himself first thing this morning.

But there is little that a dry martini or two cannot fix, and soon the standard raucous tones were echoing over the ice. Brewster had taken them out onto the terrace, and Ferdie, the consultant, was reeling off a string of lurid jokes, as he competed with Brewster and Blim for airspace. This was not Nathan's style, so he moved off with

Lorenson across the snow towards the lake, the elegant banker with the weedy finance man. Lorenson was clearly a very clever accountant. Nathan had been fully briefed on the proposal, but Lorenson, having had no more than a partial view from the morning session, had anticipated what was to come, and more than that, through his questions revealed insights that had not even occurred to Nathan.

After lunch Zelda re-opened the proceedings.

"Mr Brewster, I sure love these off-sites." The initial antagonism had precluded the American style use of first names during the morning session. "You can get so much done without office interference. But out here in Michigan, isn't this something! I could spend my life out here. Well, I guess I don't have that option yet. Work to do. But I tell you it is a real privilege for us to work with you three gentlemen. Men with testosterone who get down to it, take decisions, get things done. Not like those flunkies we met at, well let's just say, XYZ Oils last week. Did they understand what we were talking about? You bet they didn't. We had to tell them to remember to wipe their backsides when they came back from the john. This one guy, he turns round and goes back in, like he forgot. And then, when we get round to decision time, it's like they're saying they don't want to risk leaving any of their anatomy in my hands. So I say, let them go and do what the do in the john if that's what they want to do."

Nathan's sensibilities were beginning to take offence at Zelda's coarse metaphors, when he saw that Brewster had visibly perked up. It dawned on Nathan that Brewster and Blim were visualising whose hands they would willingly put their anatomy in this afternoon, if they were asked to take any decisions and put their sensitive anatomical parts on the line.

"So, gentlemen," she continued, "let's put our heads together, get it down on paper, reach consensus, and then, of course, we all know, that when it comes to the final decision, once it is all agreed, it is down to you, Mr Brewster, to make the choice, press the button. If we do that, I guarantee we can sign tomorrow, twelve noon. Over to you, Ferdie."

"Gentlemen," Ferdie opened, "we're gonna give you a black box."

"Blim?" Brewster questioned, looking at Blim.

"I guess he means like the oil consultants do when they value our oilfields. They don't want us to know their methods, their software, or we don't need to pay them. Once we know how they do it, we can do it ourselves. So it's like a black box that you don't know what's inside, but they put our data in one end and the value comes out of the other end."

"Exactly," said Ferdie, "and our black box is in Liechtenstein. Let me explain what it does." Ferdie looked directly at Lorenson. "Let's just say that Constexo is hiding losses of half a billion dollars in contracts which mature in the future." Lorenson did not flinch, but a chill settled on Brewster, who opened his mouth but was interrupted by Ferdie, before a sound came out.

"Mr Brewster," Ferdie said in a harsh new tone, "let us not beat around the bush. I don't care how many losses you hide. Just listen to the story of the black box."

"Carry on," Blim said. He knew there was no point in getting into a discussion about the losses. He knew that the best way out for Constexo was to make a major acquisition and use it to fix the figures, but with Constexo's debts an acquisition was no longer a realistic prospect.

Ferdie continued, "Gentlemen, what you do with this black box is that as step one you put in the half billion dollars of losses. You do this by contributing half a billion dollars of capital by way of loans and a little equity to partnerships in the black box. What do you have now, Mr Lorenson?"

"Well, I guess you now have a half billion dollars of assets, being your loans and equity," Lorenson answered, "but you've still got the losses."

"That's why we have step two," Ferdie explained. "We also put into the black box all Constexo's trading contracts associated with the losses, so Constexo no longer has the losses on those contracts. This is how the black box, with steps one and two, gives you assets and takes your losses. Oh, and it also reduces your trading exposure, because you no longer have the contracts. It's a very generous box, don't you think? I won't be exact, but let's say the contracts are worth five billion dollars, and we add a margin of cash to secure the contracts. You get net, say, four billion dollars off your balance sheet."

"So you've cleaned up our problem," Lorenson said, "but where do the black box's trading lines come from to take the contracts from Constexo, and what happens when the losses hit?"

"Step three, Mr Lorenson," Ferdie responded. "As to lines, you guarantee some, some we put in, some are secured on cash margins, and some trades are direct with you. And as to losses, well there won't be any."

"Why won't there be any losses?" Brewster cut in, as if forgetting he just wanted to deny hiding any to start with.

"You put in another half billion dollars, or more if you wish," Ferdie replied, "and we leverage on that to trade out of your position. Losses are only ever temporary in this business, as long as you have the capacity to double up your stakes and catch the market turn. In this case, you can start trading in Constexo again, because we've freed up your lines. The only critical point is that Constexo must never own a sufficient stake in any partnership in the black box to require consolidation of any partnership in its accounts."

Lorenson immediately saw the next issue: "And the profits?"

"I said the box was generous," Ferdie answered. "It splits profits between Constexo and us, and, of course, you gentlemen personally if you wish. I see no reason why you should not. The black box includes all the necessary cut-outs to legitimise this, at least according to my legal department." What Ferdie omitted to say was that his legal department consisted of him and no one else.

"And that's what, with your permission, we will move onto now," Zelda proposed. "Let's agree an equitable arrangement to suit all parties and draft heads of agreement."

As the afternoon developed, it became ever more difficult to imagine the Zelda who had entered Brewster's hall in the morning. She was all charm. Ferdie had retrieved his computer from the truck and was tapping away to incorporate ideas and information into a document that was developing before their eyes. He mentioned to Nathan in a coffee break that he had taken a quick look around outside when he got the computer. He said that there was this huge truck strewn with spent shotgun cartridges, empty beer cans and Bourbon bottles, and stacks of live ammo, and he was damned glad he had not seen that before setting their very own she-wolf onto Brewster this morning.

By five they were ready, but Zelda did not close the meeting until six, possibly in deference to her need for a full working day. The departure reflected a full days bonding: lightening, thunder, sunshine, in that order, and all against the backdrop of the Michigan snowscape and the frozen lake.

***

Some marathon runners cross the finishing line looking like prime candidates for the oxygen tent; others appear to have just changed and are having a quick warm up before heading for the start line. Back at the house they had rented, just forty-five minutes from Brewster's place, Zelda looked as if she were having a casual chat at a cocktail party. But for the first time, Nathan saw something vulnerable: she was looking for recognition, for admiration, the Diva expecting the right volume and duration of applause at the end of the opera.

"I think we fixed them up OK," she said. "We hit them below the belt, and while they're still doubled up, we take them past the point of no return. Then we lull them into a sense of regained control and power, but set the goal posts where we want them while they're congratulating themselves, and even Blim gets stuck in midfield when he should be a striker, failing to score. Finally, they're snapping away to swallow the carrot on the string, while we drive a truckload of carrots out of the warehouse. As they say in this country – we just made a bundle of dollars."

"The guy we've got to watch is Lorenson," she continued. "Blim is out of it once they sign the contracts, and Brewster is clueless when it comes to trading and derivatives. That's why he'll probably appear on the cover of the news magazines next year as Man of the Year, the driving force behind energy trading, advisor to the Senate, advisor to Congress, advisor to the President, maybe even derivatives advisor to the First Lady and the Pentagon."

"Do I detect a degree of cynicism towards the American establishment?" asked Nathan.

"Come on," said Ferdie, "they're all good guys doing their thing.

Maybe we just made a bundle, but I take my hat off to them for the corporation they've built."

"Take it off, but keep it in the cupboard in case you need it for the funeral," Zelda responded.

Nathan might have understood Zelda's mood if he had realised the magnitude of what they had just done. What Zelda knew was that they had vindicated Vermouth's grand plan on a scale beyond what Vermouth had even imagined. The only other person who would have appreciated it at this stage was Lorenson, but even he was just looking at his bit of the picture, and wrongly believed that he would outfox the others. Lorenson saw an opportunity to take down Constexo Energy and get rich in the process. Zelda was looking at the first step towards appropriating major chunks of the establishment for free. This was a corporation among the top ranks in the US, and it was her first target. There would be clones.

Nathan was still pre-occupied with aspects of the day. He was taken aback by Zelda's conduct. Until today she had been enchanting and he had taken her at face value, more than that he was drawn to her. What was this new side? He felt an anxiety build which he could not address with her, but he knew she detected his tension. What he could address was how she had seemed to know almost as much as Lorenson about the accounts and more than Brewster.

"Zelda, "he said, "you were fantastic the way you handled Lorenson. Where did you learn your financial analysis? I mean, the figures seemed to trip off your tongue."

"Nathan, you are very observant," she said. "What say you, Ferdie? It's not my analytic skills that helped today. It's my access to their central computer files, as Ferdie knows."

"You'd better close your private banking ears for the moment, Nathan, but you should know, since we are partners. We have to use what is available to us, and I have my ethical standards no less than you, and I am certainly applying higher ethical standards than the top accounting firm which has been signing off on Constexo's accounts for the last two years. If I exposed them, I would be doing a public service. They are hiding huge losses."

"So are you going to expose them? If that's the plan, why are we doing this?" Nathan questioned.

"No, I'm not planning to expose anyone. I'm not an auditor responsible to the board and the shareholders. I'm not a regulatory authority either. Right now I'm simply a private foreign citizen, here on a temporary visa, which expires in ten days. Nathan, let me make this clear for our future co-operation, both personal and business. I intend to act within both the letter and the spirit of the law. I did not hack into their system: the information simply became available to me, when I was outside the jurisdiction of the US."

"I do not plan to do business in the US, nor do I plan to do business with a US corporation, nor do I plan to trade Constexo's shares or pass information to anyone who will. What I am doing here in the US right now is simply airing with a US citizen (who happens to be a chairman) a proposition which relates solely to overseas entities and in no way relates to the US. He may choose to avail of this proposition if it is legal for him so to do (which it is). I have not suggested that his corporation should do business with these entities. If he believes otherwise (and he does), that is his assumption, not mine. If he chooses to channel business from his corporation into this structure (and he will), then that is his choice, which he may take if it is legal (which it is). If you want to run this past your compliance department (which I suggest you don't), they will agree with me, but they will wonder whatever it was inspired you to ask to start with."

"Nathan, I'm glad we are having this conversation so early in out partnership, and that Ferdie is here too, because I want to assure you that so long as we are together, may it be long, I will never become involved with anything, where I, you or any of our team is in breach of the laws of the land in which we are operating, and let me just say some lands have some crazy laws. Did you know that it is still high treason on pain of death in England to have sex out of wedlock with a member of the Royal Family?"

It was time for Zelda to take a deep breath after that speech, but it was Nathan who took the deep breath. He could not fault her logic, which could, he thought, have been incorporated into any private banking manual as standard operating procedure, neither did he want to; not after the bit at the beginning linking "future co-operation" and "personal", him and her.

"Please, Zelda," he said, "don't misunderstand me. I was just confused about the direction your argument was going in. I think you've answered the compliance point more succinctly than they would have done back at the bank, and no I don't have any designs on members of any royal family either before or after wedlock."

The other person who was confused was Ferdie. Why is he calling her Zelda, he wondered? Is he mixing his women up, or is this a reference to some kind of cartoon comic hero like Superman?"

CHAPTER SEVEN - BANGALORE

Bangalore, 26 January 2001

Farah had spent a day with her aunt in Chennai, the south Indian coastal city formerly known as Madras. Her aunt still kept her house there and would visit for several weeks of the year. She and her aunt were the only family members left from the time the family had left Iran during the 1979 revolution. Farah loved the splendour of Chennai with its old buildings and beach front, giving on to a deep blue sea. She could even accept the oilrigs which today stood out above the horizon.

Now she was flying up to Bangalore, a drivable distance or a very short flight, but the contrast was extraordinary. You moved up from the sweltering coastline to the breezy highlands, clear blue skies and pleasant temperatures, despite being just a few degrees off the equator. She was the sole owner of the family business, set up by her much older brother almost two decades earlier. Bangalore is the centre of the Indian aircraft industry and that is what had attracted him, but his love of flying and aerobatics had cost him his life. Farah had interrupted her studies in Moscow to return and take over the business. With her she had brought the somewhat older Peter Arbakhov, twenty-five at the time. If he was interested in her, this had long since been eclipsed by his love of information technology. He was now managing director of the company, which provided software to major corporations in the West.

Many in the industrial world are unaware of the skills and resources available in poorer nations, and they often only learn this at the cost of their jobs when it is too late. If this was proved by the Russians to the Americans half a century ago with a sputnik, it is being rammed home today by the Indians in software. Hitler would have been prepared to sacrifice Eva Braun for their nuclear capability, and if he could have had their software it would have advanced his megalomania by years. In fact, with a smart suntan he could have passed for an Indian, given that many sport moustaches.

The point is that software came to Bangalore not because of the level playing field provided by the information age and the Internet, but because of a history of technologically advanced industry, and the supporting cast that had grown up around it over the years, to achieve critical mass. Farah's firm was among the first to seize and develop the opportunity. Today there was hardly a major corporation in the West which did not employ the skills of her firm or its peers.

Before Peter's arrival, general management of the firm was in the hands of two middle-aged female albino twins, Linda and Betsy, who had worked for Farah's brother. As albinos they had no pigment in their skin and their hair was completely white, their eyes red. They still handled general management, which in their case meant micro-management. For a mother to bear an albino, white as snow, had often been held to be a curse in India, which did not bode well for twins. Conversely, in northern parts of the Indian sub-continent, fair skin and economic power can go hand in hand. Whether this derived from the British Empire, the Moguls before them, who came from the northwest and established their Empire with bullock carts driven against the enemy, or even earlier invaders driving the darker Dravidians southwards was moot to the twins. They had never felt comfortable in themselves and treated their employees as if they were vestal virgins or eunuchs in a harem: it was a very closed community.

Farah always did her rounds of the employees on her infrequent visits in her role as feudal overlord, which took ever longer as the business grew. Today she was thinking that, with the plans she had, there would have to be a one step move to modern professional management. Today everyone knew her, tomorrow no one would. The tour over, she could hear Peter and the twins, assembled in the boardroom, as she approached.

"My vote is Princess Diana," said Linda.

"No, no, Sonia," countered Betsy.

"I would vote for Catherine the Great," said Peter, but then I have never lived in a democracy which would give me a vote, this one included."

Farah entered the room dressed in a stylish sari, lustrous red hair over her shoulders. "I'm glad none of you compared me to Mother Teresa. I'm not Albanian and I couldn't stand the wrinkles."

They stood and greeted her, Peter as always giving her a hug with tears flowing down his cheeks. Farah made a mental note that she would have to send him for some counselling, if she were going to have him sit on a professional board. They sat and chatted.

The meetings were never about current business. Everyone was fully apprised anyway. In this tight structure managers were promoted if they worked well and had potential. There was nothing to gain by profiling themselves in meetings, claiming false credit and misdirecting blame, and as a consequence the culture was to get on with the job. Any business discussion among the four of them at the top was about strategy, and that was Farah's aim today.

"I want to set out some ideas for a new direction she said. We have always been aware that software development has given us access to vast knowledge and information about our clients. We've thought about writing lines into our clients' software illegally to achieve objectives for ourselves, but we never really satisfied ourselves with the balance of risk and reward."

"We have done some first class sleuthing," Linda added.

"Yes, you have, and I shall come back to that. I still have to thank you for the very valuable information on Constexo, which you provided me in December. What I want to focus on first is how we can use the knowledge we acquire."

"Along the lines I have been researching?" Asked Peter.

"Exactly on those lines," said Farah. "But we need to select the industry. Peter, you remember when back in the early nineties everyone here was clambering over one another to get mobile telephone licences. I said I didn't see how you would achieve credit collection in India. I thought people would use our phones and then simply throw them away when the bill came, and there's no way we could chase them in courts *here*. Well, I have researched the many failures around the world and more recently the many successes. We may or may not have survived, if we had gone into mobile phones then, assuming we had managed to win a licence."

"But now the situation has changed. It's turned topsy-turvy. The economic principle of barriers to entry in a mature market says that the big guys have the infrastructure, the money and the market position: the small guys don't, can't raise the money, can't build the infrastructure, can't get a foot in the market and therefore can't succeed. So what's happened now? The big guys have bid astronomical prices for third generation phone licences, saddling themselves with huge debts. Instead of having the money, they've got the debt. It's no win for them, as we've seen time and again. On one hand, the market leaders have to get the licence to continue to be a market leader, on the other hand they jeopardise their future with the price they have to pay for the licence. Eventually it all collapses and a winner comes through, but no one knows who that winner will be. Until then its pandemonium. It's like the arms race."

"I get your point," said Peter, "so what do we do?"

"I'll tell you what we do and how we do it. Software is the key. Third generation phones are coming. We bring out a package which leapfrogs the third generation phones, incorporating voice, mail, navigation, household management, time management, financial management and execution, media, entertainment etc. In fact, everything that everyone else has promised to deliver and failed."

"Farah, you don't even have a mobile phone," said Betsy.

"I don't need one: I meet people."

"And why will this work for us?" Betsy followed on.

"Betsy, you and Linda will manage the existing business, and I want you to do a bit more snooping. I have a list of US corporations for you. Peter will establish a new unit, which will focus on getting contracts in telecommunications. It will then set up a process for parsing the information we acquire."

"We are not inventors, we will simply plagiarise, copy, bastardise, or as they like to say today, adopt best practice. We have a five year window."

"I like the challenge," Peter said, "but it's going to take a few crores of rupees."

"No rupees. We can't risk being in any particular jurisdiction. I have established a Swiss company that will subcontract the work to our company in India. You have full signature authority over the company and its bank accounts, Peter."

Peter opened the package she passed across. "This is capitalised at fifty million Swiss francs. Where did these megabucks come from?" Peter was flabbergasted.

"Peter, do you think I've just been swanning around these last five years, while you three kept your noses to the grindstone? If my plans come through, you'll have a bucket load of dollars by the end of the year. If I do my bit, I hope you can do yours. And, Oh, we'll need a name. We're up against Goliath, several Goliaths, so you might want to call it "David". However, my preference is that the company and all its products be named "Zelda" for branding purposes."

And with that the official part of the meeting was over. If Peter felt he was being asked to be the Bill Gates of the personal communications world, he did not show it.

The four of them left the office building together. They went to have tea on the lawn of Farah's house, shaded by palms. It was quite a sight: even Peter's blonde Russian looks were a contrast to the albinos, and then there was Farah with her flowing red hair. Farah occupied the main section of the house in the few days of the year she spent here. She had many servants: a mali looked after the garden, where they sat; tea was brought out by a bearer; it had been prepared by the cook; an outside sweeper cleaned the terrace behind a wall covered with bougainvillea; through the window you could see the inside sweeper cleaning the hall; the day chowkidar guarded the gate, and would be relieved at sunset.

She did not for one moment believe that this level of servant activity persisted during her prolonged absences, but she saw it as a mark of respect for her presence. A less charitable mind may have considered it an attempt by the servants to keep a cushy job. Peter occupied a smaller wing of the house. Even if he had spent more time here, rather than in the office, he would never have noticed whether the house was cleaned or not, and the garden tended. The de facto head of the household was the cook. In fact, Farah kept the cook on as tight a string as the cook kept the others. She had been used to servants since she was a child, and knew exactly how to control this situation. It had been a wonderful end to the day for all of them, just to be together again, as in the old days. As they left, they each hugged Farah, and she told them, much to their surprise, that she would not only be back soon, but that she hoped to stay in Bangalore again, indefinitely.

CHAPTER EIGHT – THE LANNINGTON

Dubai, 18 February 2001

She breezed into Vermouth's office in her usual style, hair flowing, dressed in an understated grey shalwar kameez. He was on the phone, so she sat on the beige sofa facing him. Nathan had wanted to report in as soon as the contracts were signed with Brewster. She had dissuaded him: they were not to be precocious, no one was expecting results that fast, anything could go wrong, they would wait for the funds to flow.

That was a month ago. She had checked in with Nathan periodically to keep him calm, and to make sure "Bill Robinson" had not called him. Last week the partnership contracts had hit $5 billion, so a report was due. Vermouth had been eyeing her as he spoke on the phone. She looked confident as ever. Why had she come unannounced? he wondered. Now he finished his call and hung up.

"Zenap, hello. This is a surprise. The type of surprise I like, of course."

"You're wondering why I'm here, Julian. I can see that. Well, I thought that you would like to report in to Suleiman, that your grand plan has upped anchor and is well underway."

"It has, Zenap? Fill me in."

"Brewster, he's cloud cuckoo, the financial officer's a very smart crook, and they brought in a fixer whom we well and truly fixed. Nathan and Ferdie played their parts to a tee. Net, net: Friday introduction, Monday negotiation, Tuesday signing. But I thought you'd only want Suleiman to know once the funds flow. Take a guess."

"Well, this is new, they'll want to feel their way. Two fifty million."

"They *are* desperate, Julian."

"OK, half a billion, no, seven fifty."

"Julian, I know you always overestimate my talents, but I did have Nathan and Ferdie with me this time. I'll give you a clue. Round numbers."

"So it's not that much. OK. Four hundred."

"Julian, I can't take the suspense of waiting to see your face…five billion, as in half way up the scale of single digit billions."

"Christ!"

"You're very expressive, Julian."

"You know what this means?"

"I do. This one could go up tenfold, and we'll clone it every bit as well as Dolly the sheep. We'll have a whole flock of them. Where is Suleiman, Julian?"

"I thought you always knew."

"Me? You must be joking. He only ever calls me. I don't even have his number." She responded.

"Zenap, I think it's lunchtime. By the time we get back we'll have an appointment set up to see Suleiman, my guess is the day after tomorrow. You and me."

"And Nathan," she added, which actually suited Vermouth rather well.

The truth is that you never really know where it's going to come from Vermouth thought. He still did not trust Zenap an inch, but she had validated his grand plan, and on what a scale. He had thought *he* was smart, but what about her! It's like the pioneer nuclear physicist Nils Bohr saying during the second world war from his home in Copenhagen: *Zenap, my pal Heisenberg just dropped by from Nazi Germany, where he's heading up this bomb programme. He came up with this funny idea, "the uncertainty principle".* Two days later she comes back with this device and says: *Oh, Nils, that principle thing you came up with the other day. Take a look at this device here. I don't know what you want to call it. I was thinking of something like "atomic bomb". I reckon it has potential to effect a few changes around the world.* Incredible he thought. This really was the scale of magnitude in economic terms.

Vermouth's thoughts turned to his growing concerns about the powder trade: too many leaks; too heavily policed. He felt they could afford to get out of it. But for Suleiman it seemed to be a sacred cow, traditional family business. His reaction had been straightforward as ever: the only trade he knew of which was less risky and offered higher returns was organised crime, and they were not nor would become criminals, they were traders. Suleiman truly believed that attempts to restrict the narcotics trade by western governments, which just a couple of generations before had cashed in selling opium to China, were a temporary blip in the history of mankind, to be ridiculed by future generations, and were, no doubt, motivated by vested economic interest and not social concern. Vermouth had never found the appropriate moment to obtain Suleiman's view on trading nerve gas or anthrax, but he could guess what it would be.

With Zenap's Constexo coup, this was the time to broach the issue again. They were on the verge of shifting economic value on a scale not seen since the oil shock, or so it seemed in Vermouth' mind. Why should they do anything that could jeopardise this opportunity? And the powder trade did. Vermouth's own point of view was simple: he had tolerated the business while it was expedient; now he would like to stay out of jail.

They would meet Suleiman on Tuesday in London.

***

London, 20 February 2001

January had been relatively slow for me, which is what we expect most years. It always seems to take a while for momentum to build in the new budget year. True there had been a fair amount of activity on the energy mandate, but that was mostly account openings, funds transfers, all things for the operations people rather than for me. Settled into my routine, I did not really have any qualms any more about what Ferdie had told me in the briefing at the end of last year in Sri Lanka.

The fees were rolling in and I, Frank Chardonnay, was riding high, to the continued chagrin of my Illustrious Leader. I was even getting cavalier about skipping the Monday meetings, which had never done anyone any good anyway. I was in constant contact with Danny, of course, on the mechanics of the whole thing, but not much else was going on as far as I could see. In the meantime I had upgraded my mountain bike to include hydraulic disc brakes, as well as full suspension, and had got into the habit of going out before breakfast most weekdays.

Yesterday I had expected things to hot up at last. There was a major meeting that took place at the Lannington Hotel overlooking Hyde Park. I have to say this hotel ranks among the classiest of places in London. I entered the foyer and was ushered by a bellboy through to my designated meeting room. As I was led down a flight of stairs at the back of the foyer, I spotted Suleiman drinking coffee, sitting in a raised area towards the rear. They showed me into a large room in the basement, where there was a crowd of people I had never seen before. They were invited in and out of the adjoining room in a bustle of activity.

Ferdie came through a few times. He greeted me, Frank, cordially the first time, but after that he seemed to be rushed off his feet. It was an amazing room with a glass ceiling, so that you had natural light, even though you were in the basement, and you could watch the clouds sweeping across the sky. This may not sound like a banker-like activity, watching clouds, but quite frankly, they kept me waiting for two hours until well into lunchtime, and then when they did call me in, I had just ten minutes to brief them on the subject of my activities over the last two months. Half an hour later Ferdie came out and told me I would not be needed any more. Somehow it was as if I had turned up at the wrong meeting; as if something else were going on.

In the Lannington's Trafalgar Room, Vermouth joined the lawyers and accountants who had put together the Constexo partnerships. He beckoned Ferdie over.

"Ferdie, I just saw Frank Chardonnay on my way through. Get that creep out of here. We don't want him meddling in anything. I don't trust him, or anyone who's dumb enough to stay more than ten years with his outfit. I know we have to use that screwball but let's minimise it, right?"

"Sure, boss." Ferdie disappeared and was back in a couple of minutes.

Vermouth was not a participant in this meeting. He was just making a quick supervisory gesture to keep all these highly paid professionals in line before he and Ferdie joined Suleiman.

When they went in to Suleiman, he was already seated with Vanesh and Zenap.

"You wanted to tell them, Julian, so shoot." Suleiman commanded.

"My position is simple. We've got to get out of the traditional business. Our new enterprise has such incredible potential that we can't, mustn't, jeopardise it. Ferdie is the man who knows the structure. I thought his presentation to you yesterday was fantastic. Thank you, Ferdie. You got it down to a tee. We've come so far since the Singapore meeting last December. It's decision time and it's self-evident. This London meeting has proved it. We should exit *powder* and shift down a gear on *pretties.* "

"Jamal needs charity money now, not next year. This is our biggest year yet." Vanesh cut in, as usual, totally to the point. "Our friends are becoming very ambitious."

"Then give our friends the sixty million balance that we have sitting there." Vermouth proposed.

"I can't. I can't get the funds transferred out," Vanesh retorted. "They're stuck, pending, shall we say, cleaning."

This comment interested Zenap. Last month she had made an arrangement with a bent banker in the Cayman Islands that would allow them to launder one major sum of money in one big bite. Surely this could be it. Vanesh did not know she had arranged things with the banker, because she had routed it through Suleiman to Vanesh. So why was Vanesh not using the opportunity? What was he waiting for? This could be very interesting. There is something here, she thought. I must keep an eye on our good solid chief financial officer, Vanesh, and she decided a little discreet snooping was in order.

The discussion continued, and it became clear that Vermouth was developing a real concern for his personal well-being, and that was what was motivating his desire to get out of the narcotics business. Suleiman was disappointed that personal concerns were being put ahead of business issues, but he did not show it. Vermouth was not getting support from the others, so the outcome was clear. Normally Suleiman would have guillotined a discussion like this, but he determined instead to let Vermouth, for whom he had always had a soft spot, get it off his chest. After some time they moved on to the energy deals.

"I see these as a kind of bridge for us," Vermouth said, retaining the theme that they should move on, breaking free of their more traditional business activities. "It takes us exactly to where we need to be in the financial markets. Let's say, acting as financial engineers rather than as traders. We did a great thing bringing in my old bank. Frank Chardonnay is smart but totally malleable. He does whatever we tell him, never asks questions, and his bank doesn't have a clue either, so we have been able to set up mechanisms to move our money, which we could never have managed otherwise. During the course of this year, the "charities" are going to be huge beneficiaries. I think this is what you were driving at in Singapore back in December, Vanesh."

"Do we want to bring Chardonnay in to give us a report," asked Suleiman.

"I sent him off", Ferdie said. "Basically, he carries out instructions. Since I put the fear of God into him at the Colombo meeting, he'd do anything I ask, right down to pulling a Champagne bottle out of my rectum, if it got stuck up there the wrong way round."

"Can we meet for a drink afterwards, Ferdie," Zenap asked, to a round of laughter.

The meeting ended on a very upbeat note. From Suleiman's point of view, they had achieved all they needed with the energy projects. This enabled them to channel revenues flowing from the "powders" and the "pretties", drug smuggling and jewellery smuggling and trading. As to Vermouth's grand project, Suleiman supported it but had a residual concern that it could backfire, that they may be getting in way above their heads. He closed the meeting. He did not foresee any need to meet before the next quarterly Board meeting. If there were a need to meet, then they should do it informally in the first week of April. He had taken a chalet in the French Alps for skiing.

CHAPTER NINE – ECONOMY CLASS

London, 22 March 2001

Nathan was sitting next to Zelda in Economy on the daytime flight back from New York JFK to London Heathrow. This was their second trip to New York, following the weird Brewster episode. It had been very successful generally. He had generated good business for the bank from Zelda's leads, and the Brewster thing itself was now developing well. He was getting close to Bill Robinson. Bill had dropped in to see him on the two occasions he had been in London, and had said he would become regular in his requests for reports now that the Brewster deal had got off the ground.

Apparently Nathan would have met Suleiman, if he, Nathan, had been able to attend the meeting at the Lannington. In retrospect, he was disappointed: he should have broken off his ski holiday. He looked at Zelda sleeping in the seat next to him. They had been booked a couple of rows further back, but these bulkhead seats had been empty and they had switched after take-off. They were now stretched out with the row to themselves, every bit as comfortable as in Business Class. His thoughts turned to the female executive who had made the news last year for cavorting in-flight in an unseemly manner with her business companion. He could see the appeal as Zelda opened her eyes and gazed up at him. He realised then that this had been the first time he had seen her with her eyes closed.

Embarrassed, Nathan leant back and closed his eyes. He imagined himself telling his mother he wanted to introduce his new girlfriend. Mama would suggest they all go to the opera together: his mother's way of letting the girl know *who the family was.* He had a vision of them heading for the bar in the interval, his father, powerful, white haired, with Zelda glittering on his arm, and behind them, he and his mother, both slim and dark; his mother turning to him and whispering, "I think you have found your Mata Hari, Nathan." In the bar the attention would be irresistibly drawn to their little circle, to the contrast between his slim, elegant mother and the Hollywood vision of the girl in green with flowing red hair, marble features and blue-grey eyes. Across the room he would see eyes drawn, averted, and then furtively flicking back. The vision faded as he felt movement next to him.

Zelda leant down to pick up her document case and sat up.

"The calls went well, Nathan, I appreciate your manner with the clients. They have confidence in you." She opened her case and pulled out a sheaf of papers in a pink transparent plastic envelope. "I got these from Ferdie. They are for your bank. They're all signed, and you should have your people confirm the signatures. They authorise you to disclose full details of all the transactions on the Brewster accounts to Bill Robinson, for physical collection by him when he's in London. Apparently they don't want the paperwork floating around the Gulf, but he needs to know. He's principal advisor. There's a template for the schedule of numbers you should supply him."

Nathan took the envelope. "I got the impression, when you called Ferdie on the phone, that you weren't too happy with the meetings."

"That's not true, Nathan. It's just that we haven't landed Brewster Mark II yet. Ferdie and I set ourselves very high targets."

"I could never have expected a portfolio to develop as fast as mine has since I joined you. My colleagues think the same. That's a high target."

"We make good partners, Nathan. You complement me. Add in Ferdie and we are a full team. I enjoy working with you, Nathan." He looked into those blue-grey eyes, and felt he could see that the depth of her sincerity went way beyond those words, and it seemed that those eyes knew his thoughts and liked them.

"Excuse me, Sir, we are entering turbulence. Would you mind

buckling your seat belt?" the hostess interrupted. The moment was lost.

Zelda took leave of him as soon as they had disembarked and set foot inside Terminal Four. He had no idea of whether she was going to Bangkok, Brighton or the Post House Hotel but that was the way she operated. Secretly, he would have preferred to go with her. He took the Underground to Sloane Square and decided to walk home down the King's Road. Twenty minutes later he stepped through the door of his Beaufort Street flat, just one message on the answer phone. He pressed the button: "I'm at the pub." The Reverend's familiar voice intoned, in a message left just ten minutes earlier. He sank into a chair, both mind and body suddenly afflicted by Gulf War syndrome, shellshock or whatever. The Reverend.

During these last few weeks everything seemed to have come back to normal. Zelda may have been connected to these people, but he could not believe she was involved in any nefarious activity herself. It was also hard to see her as somebody's pawn. He was doing good business; in truth, he had only heard good things about Suleiman and was beginning to doubt the veracity of the incriminating evidence he had seen last year. What did the Reverend want? And the Reverend was there right now, when he had literally just got in from New York. It was almost as if he were being watched. It was late. He had better go round the corner and meet the Reverend. He rose to leave.

"Nathan my boy, how good of you to come. Here, have a pint. The usual?"

"Thank you, Peter. I've just flown in from New York. How did you know?"

"I didn't. No harm. If you hadn't come, I would have come back another day. Any news for me?" The Reverend beamed at him, slurping beer.

"Not really. Jemimah, who is really Zelda, has developed some excellent leads to private banking clients, in addition to Brewster whom you know about already. Bill Robinson is first class. Nothing I have stumbled on leads me to believe they are anything other than the bona fide business people they claim to be."

"I'm glad to hear that, Nathan." He laughed. "Of course, I would generally prefer to hear hard evidence, damning people to hell or sending them to jail, the first being appropriate to my previous occupation in the Church and the second to my current activities. In this case I can live with your response."

The Reverend proceeded to explain that he did not expect to require Nathan's further assistance. It was not clear to Nathan that he had really given any assistance, but he did not object. The Reverend continued to talk in general terms about the continued need for discretion, nonetheless. He interrupted this monologue only to order another couple of pints of bitter. He told Nathan that they would still keep occasional contact, and could possibly request some minor service, but this was unlikely. What he did not tell Nathan was that their suspicions had now moved away from Suleiman and were focusing on Julian Vermouth, a Gulf Banker who worked with Suleiman on a variety of transactions. Nathan would be like a control in pharmaceutical tests, where one group takes the pills and another the placebos. If Nathan came up with anything independently, it could validate another source, prove that the medicine really was working.

For the Reverend's purposes, the less Nathan knew the better, and he should certainly not act as if he were secretly seeking information. This is why the Reverend had told him he was released from service. When it came to the third pint, Nathan requested a gin and tonic instead, and the Reverend was delighted to join him.

"Who's this Bill Robinson chap, Nathan. Any clues as to who he works for?"

"He's a top notch banker, Peter. I can give you his phone number, but somehow, I know it sounds strange, it's always business talk or social talk, but we've never got to any kind of personal exchange. Funny. I have a lot of respect for him, we're really tuned in, but no, I don't know who he works for."

The Reverend was a very meticulous man, but that snippet of information, the phone number, slipped by him. It was only some weeks later that he came upon his note of the number, which he had made at the time, and followed it up. This closed the loop on Bill Robinson, and very helpful it was. They would come back to use Nathan after all.

Entering his flat, Nathan saw the message light flashing on his answer phone, the second message today, no two messages. He was in good spirits, fortified by drinks with the Reverend, and glad that it was all over. He was a free man and back in business with a career before him again. Suleiman was no longer a threat. Nathan had done what he should do, in his opinion if not the bank's, but then they did not know, so they could not tangle him in their bureaucratic web. He pressed the play button on the answer phone

Message one, message left at eleven ten PM today. "Hello, Nathan. You didn't say you had any plans tonight. I'm going shopping for a late dinner. I'll come round later."

Message two, message left at 11.36 PM today. "Nathan, still not back? I'm on my way. See you shortly." She's coming round for dinner! Here! I don't believe it! His spirits, already elevated, soared. The first thing to occur to the domesticated mind might be to tidy up the flat. Nathan adopted a more pragmatic approach and poured himself a gin and tonic while he looked around for a decent bottle of red. Midnight passed and he began to wonder if the messages, by now deleted, were a dream, a symptom of jetlag, when the doorbell rang. She entered, she was in his flat. Unbelievable but true!

"Hello, Nathan. I'm sure you're still on New York time, like me. Since every one else is going to bed, I thought we two could share a cooking experience. Take me to your kitchen, Leader." He took her through and she swung the supermarket bags up onto the work surface. Long gone were the days of the corner late night rip-off shop.

"I have never felt a need for formality with you, Zelda," he said, "but I *am* surprised to see you here. I would have been less surprised, if you had called me from Bangkok."

"You're perceptive, Nathan, I've surprised myself too. Perhaps that says something. We might find out while we cook. Come on."

In fact, she had made a routine call just over an hour ago and heard from the watcher, whom she had forgotten to take off the job, that Nathan was sitting in the Devil's Retreat pub with the vicar. This had surprised her. Was there something she should know? There was one way to find out: talk to Nathan and see if he let something slip. But Nathan seemed in excellent spirits and she could read him. He was not casting those furtive looks, as he had that first time they had met in the wine bar in the City. OK, he wasn't pissed out of his mind yet, but he was well on the way.

"Have you got any red wine, Nathan? It will go well with the main course. I'd like to try it first." He poured her a glass and one for himself.

"See this broccoli," she said. "We're just going to cut off the stalks and fry them with garlic. Try it at a dinner party, and see if any one can guess what it is. Wolfgang Puch would probably get it right, but I have my doubts about the rest of them. You can save the green bits for dinner tomorrow."

"Cheers," Nathan said, pouring Zelda a second glass, and himself, of course. She seemed to be thirsty.

"Can you cut up the onions, garlic and red peppers? I'll deal with the bacon and beef. I want a saucepan." She opened the cupboard below. "Nathan, where did you get this Le Creuset saucepan? This is perfect. They are so versatile. I love this heavy cookware. Once I've heated some olive oil in it, I want you to drop in the stuff you're chopping and mushrooms as well. I'll add the bacon. Then we'll throw in the beef for a minute or so before we add the red wine. This dish takes three hours, by the way."

"I have to be at work by nine."

"I'm joking, Nathan. It's true that it takes three hours, but with this quality of beef it will be ready in forty-five minutes. I thought we could sit down over a glass of red wine while we wait." Her glass was empty again. He refilled it, and his also.

Zelda left Beaufort Street at four forty-five ante meridian. Nathan was as likeable as ever and also blotto by the time she left, three bottles of red wine later. He had let nothing slip, which surprised her. It was as if the vicar had given Nathan's ego a vitamin boost. She did not distrust Nathan. This evening's exercise was just something she had to do, a swift reaction to a changing scenario, pre-empting the unexpected. It was part of her methodology, attention to detail, no stone unturned. The walk back to the hotel would take an hour, and as she walked she realised that she had really enjoyed being with Nathan in his flat.

CHAPTER TEN - AFGHANISTAN

Quetta, 28 March 2001

The plane had started its approach to Quetta in the west of Pakistan, close to the Iranian border. Looking out of the window, Jamal Ali could see the town of Quetta below and the airfield. Apart from that, he saw the most incredible view of bleak dark rocks, unbelievable that this terrain could support life. It might be different after the monsoon rains, he thought, but he knew that the heavy, grey monsoon clouds which floated across for months in the summer would seldom shed their load here. This was not the desert as he knew it from his youth in Saudi Arabia. He could never live here.

He ran through why he was coming to this place and what he must do, what was to be discussed and agreed. It is my conscience which is prompting me, he thought. I must take the true way and this can no longer be in the company of Suleiman, my one true friend.

From Quetta he was taken north by helicopter over rugged, impassable terrain into Afghanistan. They landed in an open area bounded by barracks which looked as if they had taken a few hits from cruise missiles. He was told the story later that day, when he was introduced to the camp's mascot. The mascot was a skeleton wired together and suspended by a rope around its neck. Some months before, a commando team had attacked the camp, planting explosives and destroying many buildings. One of the commandos had been shot dead, probably by the friendly fire of another commando, Jamal thought, when the camp finally awoke and reacted. Was that not the chief cause of death of the attackers in the war against Iraq? His hosts insisted the dead man was an American, but apart from his fair skin, which he had now shed for his new role as camp mascot along with his other soft body parts, he had carried no identification. His broad toothy smile seemed to signify that he had known death was better than capture.

Jamal was led into a building, where a number of bearded men dressed in local garb were seated on ammunition cases and on the floor. They were consuming a meal of rice boiled with goat's meat. The rice was in a large aluminium saucepan next to a pile of chapattis. The men smoked, and Jamal hoped the ammunition cases did not contain explosives. Three of the men rose to meet Jamal. The others continued to eat, forming balls of rice with fingers and the thumb of the right hand, in a practised manner, disinterested.

"Salaam Aleikum," Jamal said in greeting. He would use Urdu until another language was proposed in situations like this. Urdu, and its sister Hindi, had grown up as the language of the soldiers and camp followers centuries before. With all the different tribal groups of the Indian sub-continent, and their multiplicity of languages Urdu had become the lingua franca. You spoke your own language to your community and Urdu to others. Their leader switched immediately to Arabic. Jamal knew of this man, but had never met him, although a number of his companies were recipients of Jamal's "charitable" donations. They had much in common. They had both grown up in Saudi Arabia and moved in affluent circles there in their youth. It was surprising they had not met.

There were no formalities. Each knew why the other was here. Time was not important as they conversed. They broke in the middle of the afternoon while Jamal was shown around the camp. Then the discussion resumed with just the two principals, and the afternoon turned to dusk as they left the barracks and climbed up into the surrounding hills, still just the two of them. Jamal began to voice his misgivings with regard to his own situation on the Board. They were following a narrow track created by a goatherd and his charges, but no goats were in sight. Sometimes they walked in single file with Jamal behind and then the track would broaden again.

"My group, inshallah, is generating more funds than ever this year," Jamal said. "I have distributed five times as much money this year as last year. This is because we have become much more efficient at moving funds. We have been able to establish our people within international banks and also to use their people for our purposes. The international bankers are driven by money and this makes them easy meat for us. They are naïve and stupid, but very clever at what they do. This combination works well for us. Their police and regulators are left far behind, far far behind."

"I have appreciated the funds you have made available in Germany," the leader said.

"Suleiman has employed very efficient people, but now he has a secret scheme. It is on a scale which is not to my liking, which I think may threaten us, and you." Jamal continued.

"What is this grand scheme?" the leader asked.

"It is not for true believers to learn of the details of these financial schemes, but Suleiman may bring down one of the largest US corporations and take their money." For the moment this was as much as Jamal wanted to say, before he had a reaction.

"We are not thieves of the night, Jamal; we are holy warriors. We do not need to steal their money," was the leader's disdainful reply. "It is the will of Allah that we fight against those forces which threaten Islam, that we destroy their leaders. We will destroy their symbols of power. We have no need of their money."

Jamal was in agreement with this, and he elaborated.

"I think that Suleiman is wrong. There is an unbeliever who has proposed this scheme to him. Suleiman's mind is clouded. We should trade goods. That is our world. We should establish modarabas to buy and sell goods, even hashish, as has been done here for centuries. We should buy weapons and we should use plutonium as we have previously used the sword. We should respect the pillars of the one true religion and give to the poor, zakat. We should not sully ourselves with usury, with the dirty money, with schemes of the Crusaders."

"You are right, Jamal." The leader was almost wistful. "It is the true believer who will win the battle for Islam, the true believer. The practices of the West, you call them Crusaders, are ungodly. We will take the fight to them. Those to whom it is decreed will die at our hand and our martyrs will earn the rewards of paradise." They launched into a fervent discussion about the spread of Islam and the action to be taken, of Jihad, holy war, of their own Jihad.

Jamal knew that this was where his own allegiances must lie. In his mind, the two of them were ranked among the few who understood what must be done to further their cause. It was a private battle: even Islamic states would not openly give them the support their cause deserved. The two of them were fervent in their belief and certain of what they must do. Others, contemplating the actions of these men, would later claim that men like these had hijacked the cause with their extreme beliefs and their extreme measures.

Finally, they came back to Jamal's personal circumstances. He wanted Jamal to join him, and Jamal agreed. Jamal should distance himself now from Suleiman and his group. Then they discussed the specific steps Jamal should take. What it came down to was that, as soon as Jamal had set up his exit strategy from the Board, he should assume control of the businesses and plunder Suleiman's finances. They thought it would be right to eliminate Suleiman himself. That would be taken care of, if necessary, once Jamal had completed their plan. They talked through the steps they should take, setting an October deadline. In their eyes Constexo Energy was Suleiman's downfall. He had stepped outside the fold with a scheme that embraced the evils of the unbelievers. They were convinced that Suleiman had intentions that he had not revealed to Jamal. Jamal must break away: this was prescribed for Jamal's own Jihad.

Jamal slept at the camp that night. He left the next day by the same route as he had arrived. As the helicopter lifted off, he looked down at the camp below, disappearing behind rocky hills, grateful that his mission had been decided, glad that he did not have to carry it out from here.

From Quetta Jamal flew to Karachi. If he was going to take over the Suleiman Empire, he had to secure the underlying businesses. He was confident about retaining the "powder" trade. He was a frequent visitor to Peshawar and its hinterland. It was from here that their operations were managed. He knew the people well and he knew that he would have support from the friends he had just left. There was no problem taking control of this business. Where he felt less confident was in the gem trade. Landing in Karachi, he was picked up by his host's driver and taken to a house in KDA, traditionally a smart residential area of Karachi but now being challenged by the various phases of the Defence development adjacent to Clifton.

Gates swung open to allow the car through and it pulled up opposite the main door. A servant led Jamal through the house and out into a walled garden behind. Magnificent Bougainvilleas grew up the walls in the shade of young palm trees. One side of the lawn was covered by a red and blue striped shamiana, an awning intended to hinder the evening dew, rather than provide shelter from rain, which seldom came. The main part of the lawn was set out for croquet and a couple of mallets lay on the grass. A group of westerners were sitting at a table under the shamiana. When they saw Jamal Ali, they rose to leave, taking their empty Murree beer bottles with them. Jamal's host, a tall blonde Englishman walked across to greet him.

"Jamal, it is a pleasure to receive you here in my home, a pleasure and, indeed, an honour." He embraced Jamal.

"Thank you, David, it is most courteous of you to invite me."

"You will take some green tea, I am sure," David said, motioning to the servant to bring some for them both."

From formalities they moved on to discuss the political situation and debated who was likely to succeed the present military regime. David was much in favour of the military. They provide order in this chaos, he told Jamal. They then moved to the reason for Jamal's presence.

"David, Suleiman does not know I am here, and I would prefer it to stay that way. This is a personal initiative of mine. I want to ensure that we do not become too dependent on Suleiman. This business has become too important for that."

"You may rely on my discretion, Jamal. I also feel that you and I have a special relationship. It was you who brought the tanzanite connection."

David was the key figure in the Board's gem trading business, or some would say gem smuggling. He had traditionally placed their emerald and diamond stocks in the European market, as well as semi-precious stones. He travelled frequently to Europe in general and Hatton Garden in particular but he preferred to live in Karachi.

He was doing nothing illegal here and considered it to be a good place to stay out of jail.

Some five years earlier Jamal had travelled to East Africa and spotted the opportunity to pick up tanzanite. Almost 90% of tanzanite was smuggled anyway, so it would be easy for the Board to step in and take a big position in the market. The Board had both the financial resources and the mechanics of transport and distribution in place. Since then commissions on tanzanite had become David's biggest source of revenue, and he felt that he owed this in some measure to Jamal. Apart from that, the two of them had become firm friends, even if they met infrequently.

"I am going to be blatantly honest, Jamal," David said, fixing Jamal with his clear blue eyes. "If you want the tanzanite business and the rest, I really don't mind. It doesn't concern me. I do my job and make my commissions. Who receives the proceeds of what I sell simply does not matter to me, as long as the source of the tanzanite is not compromised. As to the emeralds, I think you will find it more difficult. I have no control over what they do in Sri Lanka." David waved to the servant to bring some more tea.

"David, you have great understanding. You are wise beyond your years." Jamal smiled at him.

"Plan it carefully, Jamal. Suleiman is a powerful man in all senses of the word," David cautioned.

"I will," Jamal replied. "I will be honest with you, too. I believe we must separate this business from Suleiman's other activities. When it comes to the point Suleiman will be obliged to agree. He will have no choice. I too have powerful friends. But David the arrangements with you stand. I could not have a better or more trusted intermediary. You have to be aware of what is going on. I plan to set up a smooth transition with completion scheduled for October. What I have to develop is the practical steps which will allow this to happen, and that I am well qualified to do."

"I wish you well, Jamal. I have seen nothing but utter professionalism in all our dealings to date and I have no doubt that you will achieve your objectives."

After Jamal had left, David's friend returned from the side garden, where they had continued their conversation over a few more Murree beers. They had retired there as a matter of courtesy towards David's strict Muslim guest.

"Who was that guy?" a red haired oilman asked.

"Oh, I knew him years ago back in Saudi," David replied. "He drops in when he's passing through, a kind of family friend you could say. The Saudis are into jewellery, so I guess that's why he likes to meet me."

David was a well-respected buyer for the London jewellery trade.

Jamal flew up to Lahore that evening, where he was to attend a meeting of Islamic scholars. As the 747 took off from Karachi, he reflected on the events of the last two days. His immediate future had been mapped out in Afghanistan. The meeting with David had been the first step towards implementation and it could not have gone better. His personal intervention in the businesses was not sufficient, however. He would need to assemble a team to establish a command and control system for the diverse businesses of the Board. He did not know how Suleiman managed the business; that was never disclosed, but he, Jamal, would set it all up on a professional basis, without Suleiman's knowledge and against his wishes. The very last step, scheduled for October, would be to take over the central finances. This would be the most difficult task. They would need to brainstorm a solution.

As the plane began its descent to Lahore, Jamal was disturbed by one aspect of the meeting in Afghanistan. He had always respected these people who were leading the faith. He had never questioned the rightness of their interpretation of the Koran; rather he had looked to them to help him in his understanding. But one detail kept surfacing in his mind to disturb him: the mascot, the skeleton. How can it be right to desecrate the remains of your enemy in this way, an enemy who was a simple soldier? This was not in tune with his understanding of the true way. He felt a sense of menace. Was there something beyond this that he did not yet understand?

CHAPTER ELEVEN - MERIBEL

Méribel, French Alps, 2 April 2001

Danny called me up out of the blue in the first week of April with the words: "Frank, you have to be at an urgent meeting. We have a major problem on the energy deals." I was supposed to fly out the next day and return on Wednesday evening, but since the meeting was in Méribel in the French Alps, I decided to add on an extra day and do some skiing. That was how I came to meet Nathan, that one and only time. In a way, I wish we never had met. It would have been easier for me that way.

I was collected on landing in Geneva as promised, and then whisked across to a waiting helicopter. This meeting is urgent, I thought, and I am glad they have at last appreciated my *very important person* status. This is what big bankers do, and I was the only passenger on the helicopter. Good for them, those exalted few in the top echelons of banking; they might like helicopter rides - I don't. First, there is the clatter of the blades above you and then the vibration of, well, everything including you. It is even worse in the mountains. When you are looking down on the white peaks of the Alps just below you, you realise that you *do* want those rotors to keep spinning.

When you crash-land in water, you are supposed to wait for the helicopter to submerge, so that the water stops the blades turning, and only then do you exit the craft and swim up to the surface, avoiding decapitation by the blades. What do you do when you come down on a snowy mountain slope and proceed to take an impromptu toboggan ride down to the valley at a hundred and sixty miles an hour? Indiana Jones would have known. I had visions of me grabbing the controls from the pilot as the helicopter plummets from the sky, apparently doomed, but no, it hits the mountainside and does a rendition of white water rafting without the water.

On arrival at the Altiport in Méribel I was met by an American driving a white minibus. His name was Jude, or at least that is how he introduced himself to me, and I introduced myself as Frank Chardonnay. He struck me as being in his mid forties. He was about five ten, and was as forward in his manner as his belly lay forward of his trouser belt. This was his first season in the Alps, he told me. He was managing the chalet, which included ferrying people around and doing the cooking. His previous life was as a cook on yachts chartered in the Caribbean. He put the emphasis on the second syllable in the American manner. A girl came in to do the cleaning, and baby-sitting he told me winking, but not much else.

"The chalet sleeps twenty," he said. "No offence meant, but you're joining a weird bunch. They spend their time sitting in the chalet in meetings and out at hotels meeting people instead of getting out on the slopes. In a manner of speaking, not what you do on ski vacation. Still, you and me can go out this afternoon."

The chalet was in a new development of chalets on the Altiport side of Méribel. It was at most a year old and in stunning condition. The main dining and living area had a huge wooden dining table, an open hearth and sumptuous sofas. It gave on to a wrap-around balcony with views over Méribel and across the valley, stunning. On the two levels above were bedrooms, and down below was a games room, TV room and a terrace outside with a hot tub and open air Jacuzzi. Five stars would be an understatement, I thought. Jude told me that the top storey bedrooms were functioning as meeting rooms this week. He showed me to my room on the second floor, and he suggested I change for skiing and meet him down below. I did as instructed in about one minute thirty seconds – the ski slopes were beckoning – and found him in the kitchen ready to go. He had made a couple of baguette sandwiches with *jambon du pays,* which we munched as we went down to the minibus. Jude suggested I try on the boots he had hired for me and they were fine.

It was a beautiful day with clear blue skies and glittering white peaks. I love skiing. Jude took us on a route that took us across to Courchevel. Méribel is the middle of three valleys linked by ski lifts; hence, the name Les Trois Vallées, the three valleys. Jude considered Saint Martin de Belleville to be the fourth valley, linked to the other three valleys after the name was coined, which only permitted three. We had a perfect afternoon's skiing. Jude's belly belied his elegant style and speed. We must have covered at least a hundred kilometres before we took our last run back down through the woods. This was a relatively new, and very difficult, piste named after some recently dead French Olympic skier, Jean something or other. We cruised through a couple of icy mogul fields, hit a high speed schuss and landed in the village below, as they say in German, *in null komma nichts*, breathless, aching, and yes, very thirsty. We had skied non-stop, excluding lift rides, for three and a half hours.

Back at the chalet I went up to my room, changed, showered and came downstairs. I still had no idea of the agenda, which did not appear to have the urgency suggested by the helicopter ride. The fire was blazing and a few nibbles were set out on the coffee table. I found Jude in the kitchen. He opened the window, grabbed a Kronenbourg, which was cooling outside on the sill with a number of its friends, and thrust it into my hand, a process that he repeated as often as necessary, as he cooked and chatted about the Caribbean. It was getting on for seven, when a voice boomed out from the lounge.

"Frank, what you doin' in the kitchen? Makin' toast? Get your butt out here!"

It was Ferdie, who was mixing himself a Bloody Mary at the cocktail cabinet. I had not heard him come down. Some minutes later we were joined by Danny.

Dinner was just the four of us, Jude, Danny, Ferdie and me. The starter was sumptuous, a seafood cocktail in a balsamic vinegar dressing. After Jude had done his *welcome to Méribel routine*, I told Ferdie how I had been helicoptered in.

"You think that's something, Frank? Well I picked up my plane in Teheran. It turns out I was added into some kind of official delegation, not Iranian by the way, on a special official plane. It was full of senior politicians, businessmen and at the very back journalists. Everyone wants to talk to the head honcho, right, but he comes and sits next to me, like he wants to talk about his student days in California, and not some political bullshit with these other guys, or concessions and payoffs with the business guys."

"So we land in Zurich, but we don't dock at one of those bridges that go straight into the terminal. Instead we do the old fashioned thing of walking down steps to the tarmac. As we come down the steps, this line of about thirty stretched limos sweeps over to us. In hierarchical order the politicos get into the limos. My turn is ahead of the businessmen, and it didn't look like the journalist would get a look in on the limo scene. There weren't enough limos. So, the driver asks me if there is anyone with me, as he opens the rear door, but I'm on my own, so he asks me where I want to go. Then we simply drive off the runway and out into the Zurich traffic."

"You came up here through the snow in a stretched limo? That's incredible." Danny exclaimed.

"I did, but there was no snow on the road. It gets better. So just before Moutiers, they've got these traffic lights. When the traffic gets too heavy on main arrival days they switch them to red. This is to control the flow of traffic up into the mountains. So there we are stuck on this highway, which has been turned into a temporary parking lot. I light up a Havana and wind down a window."

"After a while the would-be skiers, stuck in a temporary parking lot, start getting out and hanging out in the road, like they're watching break dancers down at pier number eight. So I put on my mirror sunglasses, clench the Havana in my teeth, lean out of the window of the stretched limo, and holler, *if anybody's thirsty, I'll check out the bar for chilled Champagne.*"

"And they came running," I said.

"You just bet three thousand percent wrong. They're thinking, like, who *is* this frigging freak in the limo. But the driver gets out. Turns out he's some Greek kid doing a student job. And you won't believe this. He pulls open the other door, reaches in the bar and pulls out a bottle of Champagne. This could take half an hour, he tells me, before we move, and he'll join me if no one else will. So I get out, and we go round to the trunk. By this time I'm suspicious of what might be in there, what with the stretched limo and all, but it's only my bag and two director chairs. The Greek kid unfolds the chairs, and there we sit, sipping Champagne, right there on the highway, in the fast lane."

"Grand juries behold this, Ferdie," Jude says, "you just pulled one over on Frank with his bullshit about chopper rides."

"Yup, you see, Jude, our host likes us to blend in. You don't hire a chalet like this and then pull up in a tour bus. He just wanted us to be inconspicuous, I guess." As dinner progressed, the level of conversation deteriorated to about two grades below bullshit. It was as we headed upstairs for bed that Ferdie told Danny and me that we would be on together, at eight sharp, down below in the TV room.

Jude prepared a cooked breakfast, which I consumed on my own. At eight I entered the TV room to be greeted by Vermouth. Danny arrived a couple of minutes later. The nub of the problem, Vermouth explained, was that we had to move some funds fast. That was why they wanted Danny and me here together, so that we could work out a plan. It was all connected with a power project in which Vermouth's people had a behind-the-scenes interest.

For a few years in the early nineties private power was the flavour of the month in international financial circles. Emerging market governments wanted to attract foreign companies to build power stations, so that they did not have to use their own money. Concessions were agreed which would make the foreigners very rich, as long as they could trust the governments to honour them. The foreigners would build the power stations and local (often state-owned) utilities would buy the power. In some cases the foreign currency loans taken up by the foreigners were even guaranteed, so they were well and truly home and dry, as long as they could build a plant which worked, and this they knew they could do.

The subsequent problem arose from two underlying polar bears: first, not each faction in the government, be it central or local, would agree; and secondly, governments change. You could be iced out, just like that.

"Right now it looks as if the whole thing has unravelled," Vermouth was saying. " We have to find a way of baling out at least cost to ourselves. The others can fight a rearguard action, and if they win good luck to them. We're getting out." My job was to shift funds out of reach of disgruntled partners etc. We talked it through for about an hour and came up with an ultra-nifty solution.

Vermouth thanked me for coming, saying he was very pleased with the result of our deliberations.

Danny stayed on with Vermouth, and I stepped out into the hall. There was this English looking banker type standing there, slim, dark haired, leaning against the pine banister of the staircase, who introduced himself as Nathan something or other.

I said, "Well, Nathan, I've finished here for today. Frank Chardonnay." I reached out to shake his hand, a firm, assuring grip. "It's nine and I'm off skiing, as soon as Jude the cook boy can bring me down to the lifts."

It so transpired that Nathan planned to do exactly the same. He, too, had tacked on an extra day. As we were talking there was a light step on the stair. A pair of slim legged jeans came down, and then the familiar figure and red hair and slender shape of Zara were revealed progressively upwards as she descended. She set about introducing us, and was startled that we would be skiing together. She insisted that she join us as soon as she could. Her manner was almost as if Nathan and I were not supposed to be alone together, and she wanted to chaperone us. Nathan suggested we ski over to Val Thorens and that she should join us there for lunch – we could ski back together. He tossed her his car keys. You drive over. I'm sure Jude will appreciate the drive back, he told her. As we went out to the minibus, I understood what he meant. A deep blue, UK registered, Audi TT stood in front of the garage.

"You drove down?"

"I did. Left work at lunchtime, drove off the shuttle in Calais at three and by nine thirty I was here. My record time, actually."

Nathan had a very pleasant manner. The weather was excellent, and we had had a fantastic morning's skiing by the time we reached the restaurant rendezvous above Val Thorens.

"You're a superb skier," I told Nathan.

"I've been doing it every year since my first school trip when I was twelve. I thought about doing a ski instructor course in my gap year before university but the standard of skiing was too low for me at the instructor school. You get by with your stamina, Frank, but I could help you clean up your style."

"Lucky you, skiing. In my time gap year I ended up on an oil tanker, a crew of forty one, eighteen different nationalities, a tinderbox set for stabbings and who knows what else. I jumped ship in Las Palmas."

We did not ski down to Val Thorens itself, but stayed above on the mountain looking down at this moonscape high above the tree line. These wide-open slopes are for posers, film stars and members of the Royal Family. Me, I prefer zipping in and out of the trees, cutting through narrow gorges strewn with boulders, and taking every risk you can think of, except, of course, avalanches, which are bad news.

"Deux grandes bières," I said to the waitress, when she finally managed not to avoid seeing us.

"You what?" French has long since ceased to be the lingua franca of the staff in Alpine ski resorts, so I amended this request to two half litres of beer.

After a second beer Nathan suggested we move on to vin chaud. It was then that we saw Zara sweeping down the slope towards us in perfect curves. Far behind, losing ground fast, was Ferdie, who seemed to manage to slide, but not much else.

Descending from the restaurant, we came upon what appeared to be a cross between a ski jump and a motorway speed trap. You launched yourself off the top and went hell-for-leather. As you flashed past the sign at the bottom it indicated your speed. Zara went first and triggered the display at 83 kmh. Ferdie turned to Nathan.

"She likes you, you son of a gun." I had also noticed how she was looking at him in the restaurant.

"I can only dream. Way out of my range," Nathan said, launching himself into the speed test, to hide his confusion, and hitting 71 kmh. My extra fifteen kilos gave me 73 kmh and then came Ferdie. In a manner totally inconsistent with the intended design of the speed test, Ferdie somehow managed to swerve left, head up a wall of snow and take off. He performed an impromptu acrobatic display worthy of the Moscow State Circus, and, *manque de filet de sauvetage,* commonly known as safety net, fell flat on his back. In true Bond style, shaken but not stirred, he recovered his skis and sticks and skied down to join us.

Zara addressed the troupe, reassembled below.

"After that display, I am enrolling you all in the Girl Guides. I am your patrol leader for this afternoon. Frank, 73 Kmh, Lord help you," she taunted. "Now, let's get down to business after all this pathetic pissing around on the slopes, and as for you, Ferdie, your ski suit is two sizes too small. You look like a matador, not a skier. I might have said you showed excessive testosterone with your acrobatic display just now, except this ridiculous suit had already made that self-evident. You remember the helicopter gunship scene in that Vietnam film?"

Ferdie jumped in, presumably to redeem himself, "You mean when the gunships are gliding over the green canopy of the Vietnamese jungle. Then they drop napalm all over the Viet villages and paddy fields, which explode into flame. They blast away at the villagers, massacring every thing that moves and eventually touch down, pile out of the chopper and finish them all off, men, women and children."

"I don't think the film had quite that degree of verisimilitude, Ferdie, but you've got the gist." While he had been talking, she had removed her backpack, slipped Wagner's *Ride of the Valkyries* into the CD player and attached powerful external speakers to the side pockets of her backpack.

"I don't do this under avalanche conditions," she said, clicking it on, and turning it up to full volume. "May the good Lord help the other skiers! Let's roll!"

They launched themselves into a black mogul field in a tight group twisting, turning and leaping in unison, as Wagner blared his version of the apocalypse across the mountain with modern electronic assistance. Wagner, the composer who took the *fat lady* off the stage and introduced theatrical action to the opera. What would he have thought of this powerful rendering of his opera as it shattered the frozen Alpine air?

Ferdie strove to catch them up at the bottom of the piste, while keeping himself from becoming a candidate for the clinic's emergency ward. Further down the slopes, for scene two, Zara decided to switch the CD, saying, "This time, girls, we do a sing along, like we're by the campfire", and they took off screaming out the words of a very un-girl-guide-like classical rock song. Again, we stopped at the bottom of the slope to wait for Ferdie. Nathan seemed to have christened Zara with some kind of joke name for the afternoon, “Zelda”. I tried to think whether there was some TV character he was referring to. Then we came to a sweeping track which veered in a right-hand curve across the side of the valley. We could see Méribel, vertiginously far below, as we sped past groups of astonished skiers sounding as if we were Queen in concert in Hyde Park.

It was only years later that I thought back to this scene. If Zara's purpose had been to prevent Nathan and me from talking shop, she could not have done it better.

CHAPTER TWELVE - STEELVILLE

Steelville, Russia, 10 May 2001

Brewster and Blim had determined that there were great business opportunities to be had in Russia and the other states of the former Soviet Union. They decided to go for a week in May to check out the lie of the land. These were personal investments: they could not see their corporate flunkies having either the nous or gumption to do any business outside the strategy manual. From what they had heard, this opportunity lay at least two circumnavigations of the equator outside the scope of the manual.

Brewster had got the business model from a US senator who claimed to be making a fortune over there. His instructions were very straightforward. You take over a factory. They have no idea of what anything costs, but they know that they sell their product for next to nothing over there. You tell them you will sell it for twice the price overseas, and they are over the moon. Then you have them make stuff. You sell it abroad and take the sales proceeds into your offshore bank account instead of paying the factory. They are used to not being paid in Russia, he had said, and they do not pay their bills either. Half the time it's the state utilities that they fail to pay anyway, so everyone is happy.

In the US, if you sell something for a hundred dollars, it probably costs you eighty dollars, so you make twenty dollars. Over there you sell something for a hundred dollars, and you pocket every last cent of that one hundred dollars in an offshore bank account.

Brewster was all for adopting this business model, and almost wondered why he had never tried it in the States.

Blim agreed to join the trip, because Brewster paid him to come. To Brewster's surprise Blim also wanted Lorenson along. Since the January meeting on the partnership deals, Blim had begun to appreciate Lorenson's insights. He now realised that if he had spent ten minutes with Lorenson instead of rampaging through the snowscape in the truck the day before, blasting away with shotguns at phantoms of Brewster's business associates, he would never have let Brewster agree the deal the way it had been done. He wanted some time with Lorenson to see how they could fix this situation and recover the advantage, and the Russia trip looked like a good opportunity. He wanted to checkmate the hamsters who had set them up, including him, in Michigan.

They had blustered around in Moscow for a couple of days and were now in Brewster's Gulfstream jet, heading south for Steelville about an hour to the south. Brewster was knocking back vodkas like a true Russian president, because he was totally pissed off at the way it had gone in Moscow. Both meetings had gone the same way. They had been ushered into a room with a table approximately five miles long. The Russians had filed in to take the places opposite them in order of *height*, for which read *rank*. Between Russian utterances, the interpreters had spoken in broken English all this claptrap about introducing the companies and Lord knows what else, and it seemed that Brewster had responded through his interpreters in kind whether he wanted to or not. They had got nowhere, not a contract in sight. This kind of stuff was for his lawyers and accountants back at head office, not for him. So Brewster drank vodka and slumbered.

Blim was very focused on the partnership problem. The partnerships had made a lot of money but their share was too small. Lorenson was very clear about the fact that this did not matter (it was relative) what really counted was the actual amount of money they could make for themselves.

"Look, Blim, we just increase the stakes."

"But there must be a limit to that."

"There is, Blim, but I think there's a way round it. At the moment we three are in there as owners, together with those other guys, who you agree outsmarted us. They knew what they were doing, while we were the new kids on the block. So let's look at it differently. Let's get all your smarty-pants senators in. We'll tell them it's like they're investing in a hedge fund. They'll come in behind us, so the other guys won't even know."

"OK," said Blim, "so then we can treble the amount we do. No regulator will dare complain, because "smarty-pants", as you call them, will rap them on the knuckles if they do."

"In practice, more complicated, but yes," Lorenson replied. Blim was thirsty. Breakfast in Moscow had been at five thirty, and it was now almost eight, so he asked the hostess to bring a couple of beers.

Lorenson continued, "We went in at five billion dollars. I say we go up to fifteen billion now, and if you tell Brewster that we should, he will, because he doesn't have the faintest glutinous clue of what we are talking about. Secondly, we'll scare that little redheaded floozy pantyless. She knows exactly where Constexo stands and that it cannot support this, even with the partnerships. My prognosis: they will sell out to us, and then we will be back where we should have been to start with."

"Lorenson, you are the meanest little sewer rat. It's a deal. And when that screwed up red haired bitch comes to you begging for mercy, dollars or whatever, send her to me and I will oblige."

Lorenson was pissed at himself for talking too much: now two people knew what he was doing.

In Steelville things went better for Brewster. First of all they met a Russian banker. He told Brewster he was willing to bank him, which was a great start. Then Lorenson started asking all these dumb questions about the bank, and these dumb questions looked like they could kill the deal that he, Brewster, had just cut. The Russian patiently explained to Lorenson that the reason he had just seven clients was because he liked to deal with people he could trust; yes, they were also owners of the bank, and that was why he could trust them; and yes, they were all in the same industry and this was a strength of the bank because that is where the bank's expertise lay. Exasperated, Brewster had turned to Lorenson and told him to get his butt out of the room so that they could start talking business.

On the tour of the steel works, Brewster was all praise for the local management, omitting to mention that he had never seen a steel works in his life before, even when they asked him directly, probably fazed by his exuberance for their production methods. His hosts duly informed him that steel works were introduced to Russia by Peter the Great, who had travelled incognito in Europe to learn how to build a navy and saw that steel was an essential requirement. Brewster wanted to ask why Peter the Great did not just buy steel from the other guys to make his boats, but at this point they arrived at a manufacturing facility adjacent to the steel production. His hosts explained that the steel works covered over a hundred square kilometres of land, and anyone who wanted to invest in a plant which used steel as a raw material would have huge benefits by locating it right here where the steel was produced, saving raw material transport costs.

While Brewster's internal cash register switched into overdrive, Blim was more circumspect. What struck him was the fact that the armed forces used steel for guns, tanks, bombs, you name it. The facilities in this Russian steel plant included sophisticated computerised and digitally controlled western production equipment from every industrialised nation you could think of before you could say "Jack Robinson" ten times. So what about the cold war? Who was kidding whom during the cold war, and who was kidding whom now? If nothing else, Blim was a patriot who did not believe that commie reds changed their stripes any more than a leopard its spots, a lion turned vegetarian or an elephant carnivore. He had a good heart, despite his bluff exterior and habitual cheating, lying, tricking, bribing and generally corrupting to further his ends. As for Lorenson, he just wanted to get out of there and stick fifteen billion dollars on the books of the partnerships.

The next stop was Ukraine to look at some of the facilities which used to build nuclear submarines and were now looking for alternative business, unless they could find a buyer for nuclear submarines, or even just the missiles would do. However, Brewster's schedule was curtailed just before they were due to lift off from Steelville, and they headed back to New York. Blim shared Lorenson's view that the sooner they got Brewster out of there the better. High above the Atlantic, Lorenson began to wonder whether Blim had engineered the change of schedule.

Riyadh, 11 May 2001

As Brewster's Gulfstream crossed the Atlantic, Jamal was drawing spidergrams, thought maps, of the plan he had agreed in Afghanistan. It always came back to one theme, right there in the centre of the web: he needed someone in addition to himself, inside the organisation of the Board. The ideal candidate was Vanesh in his capacity as chief financial officer, but he could not see himself persuading Vanesh with the arguments he had employed in Afghanistan. Vanesh was not even of the faith, although he realised that this did not necessarily matter. Jamal was methodical. He had eliminated Suleiman, as a matter of definition. Vermouth, the architect of the blasphemy, as he now thought of it, was also eliminated for the same reason. In his mind, Vermouth had espoused, if not the devil itself, then the dark side of life. He had then run through each of the formal members of the Board and drawn a blank. Who else? For the third time that evening, bent over his desk, the Koran by his side, he went through the list.

An image of Suleiman's red haired girl came into his mind. She had Suleiman's trust, he thought. Could he use her? Would she agree to work with him? He had often talked to her after Board meetings. The others did not socialise, and he had always missed that aspect at the meetings, but this was Suleiman's way, his leadership. In contrast Jamal's life was spent with people, discussing, debating and then acting, so unlike Suleiman, he thought. Suleiman, a rational man of action, erudite, powerful. The more he thought of it, the more he realised that she was like him. She had told him that she did not have a cell phone; she had asked him why she needed one, as she preferred to meet people face to face, to live her life. She was also very devout and had often talked to him about prayer, about the strength of Islam, how a true believer would watch for that band of light on the horizon at the point when the sun crosses, or seek to glimpse the moon as it signalled the start of Ramadan, the time for fasting. He would approach her. How should he approach her? He would use her as a foil against Vanesh.

Jamal planned meticulously for everything he did. Usurping the finances of the Board would be a complex task, requiring a professional team. In parallel to assembling his team he had made discreet approaches to Zenap. It was as if she understood what he wanted. She told him that she did not like Vermouth's grand scheme even before he asked her; that he, as a member of the Board, must do something as she was sure that he, Jamal, must share her viewpoint. When he suggested she might help, she said that she did not know how but she would do what he instructed. It was so simple. He had Suleiman's trusted aide in his pocket. Reflecting on this, he thought that he now understood why Suleiman wanted her as his aide.

***

An Island off the East Coast of Malaysia, 15 June 2001

Jamal had assembled a team of thirty professionals to execute the plan. He was a man of modern times. In the same way as a US investment banker would employ a cast of thousands to advise on an acquisition which a traditional merchant banker would have completed with a team of three, so too did Jamal require a team of thirty to achieve one fifth of what Zenap was routinely carrying out for Suleiman and others. Most of the thirty would spend their time rectifying one another's screw-ups, tracking down leaks, fixing the consequences of leaks and liaising with one another. Fortunately, this task did not require a public relations team.

Jamal had made a number of private investments in Malaysia. He felt very comfortable in this environment where the inner circle would seldom be taken by surprise by market forces. The exception to this had been in the Asian market crash of 1997, as a result of which Malaysia had deemed it pragmatic and expedient to exclude market forces, quite simply freezing everyone in until such time as the foreigners should see sense, bethink themselves. With this in mind, Jamal had chosen to hold his strategy and planning meeting on an island just off the east coast of Malaysia. Participants could either fly in to Tioman and take a ferry or land at Singapore, cross to Johor Bahru, drive up the coast to Mersing and take a ferry. On the island was a resort consisting of a number of air-conditioned huts, which Jamal had been able to rent for the occasion.

Zenap had chosen to take the Singapore route to the meeting. There are fast modern vessels that make the crossing from Mersing.

Zenap had preferred to take a fishing boat. She was now approaching the island, standing at the bow of the vessel and surveying the island through binoculars. It rose up from the emerald green sea as a green clump of trees. She could see a smaller island to her right and in the distance, through the haze, she thought she could make out Tioman, which she had previously seen only in a James Bond film. Her natural caution had led her to take a fix on the geography just in case.

She always liked to be prepared. Straight ahead she could see a rickety jetty and behind that a clearing with a number of pyramid structures, which were obviously the huts where they would stay. The only other landing point on this side of the island was up to the left, where an older holiday development snuggled against the hill behind. It looked deserted, and she thought it might well have fallen into dilapidation. This could be a place to hide if need be. The fishermen told her that most of the coastline of the island was inaccessible by reason of rocks and cliffs; however, there was a deserted bay directly across on the other side of the island. They often landed there. They never went on to the island itself, but they had heard from tourists that there was a path over the island, so steep that a rope had been installed for you to pull yourself up over the central ridge of the island. She asked them to go to this bay after they had dropped her, on the pretext of fishing. There they should deposit a suitcase, which she had closed with a combination lock. It contained an inflatable dinghy, hopelessly inadequate, but the best option she could devise, as an emergency fallback if things went badly wrong. Swimming would not be an option.

It was with amusement that Zenap watched the unfolding of Jamal's meeting plans, so different from Suleiman's efficiency. Jamal was a methodical bureaucrat doomed to failure, she silently told herself. The whole place was hopelessly inadequate for a clandestine meeting. They had drawn attention to themselves by monopolising the local travel infrastructure just to get everyone here. Some ferries pretended to have changed their schedules, so that the participants had to pay for privately booked journeys across. To extort higher prices driven by frustration the boatmen kept participants waiting for up to four hours. By the time the meeting was due to start less than half the participants had arrived. Two of the huts were occupied by bemused tourists whose bookings Jamal's people had neglected to cancel. Meetings were held at the restaurant, and the saving grace was the excellent chef, who produced wonderful fish dishes and spicy Thai Thom Yum soup.

On day two Zenap decided her fallback dinghy on the far beach was redundant, so she took three of the nicer participants on an expedition across the island to use the dinghy for recreational purposes. She told Jamal that this trek would be a bonding session, and he was fully in favour of employing modern management techniques, so he acceded at once. The members of Jamal's group were professionals, a combination of accountants, consultants and lawyers; presumably Jamal had used various subterfuges to engage them. They were all of Arabic, Turkish or Pakistani extraction, but worked in various locations, including, London, Saudi Arabia and the Gulf.

Zenap developed an immediate affinity to an Egyptian lawyer, Nabil, and had also invited a Syrian, Khaled, and a Turkish accountant, Sufi. Behind the huts was a coconut grove strewn with fallen coconuts and piles of empty husks, and almost immediately the path began to rise. It was crawling with soldier ants most of the way up. By the time they reached the ridge of the island, even the fittest of them were panting from the heat and humidity, particularly Nabil who carried a few surplus pounds. As they descended to the sea on the other side of the island, an amazing sight greeted them, a perfect sandy bay ringed by rocks and boulders, shaded by palms. Pieces of coral glistened in the sun on the beach and the sea, a shimmering blue in contrast to the emerald green she had seen on arrival, stretched away to the horizon. The scene was spoiled only by a suitcase discarded on the sand, fastened by a combination lock, which immediately drew Nabil's attention. What was this suitcase doing on a deserted beach? He questioned.

They sat drinking cool water, which they had brought with them. Zenap suggested a competition: who could crack the combination to open the suitcase? They took it in turns unsuccessfully, until Zenap finally won. Inside they found an inflatable dinghy, a pump and two paddles. It was suitable for a load of three and they were four, but Zenap suggested they give it a try anyway to get around the island by sea rather than braving the rigours of the hot return climb over the crest of the island through the humid forested slopes. Nabil, still red in the face, despite rest and a cold drink, agreed whole-heartedly.

The mariners launched their new toy and set off following the coast in a northerly direction. As they rounded the point of the island, the real bonding session began. They were caught by a current, more powerful than strong paddling, with just two paddles for a load of four, could resist. Fortunately, a gust of wind caught the inflatable and its shallow draft saved the day as the wind swept them closer to the point, but not close enough. They abandoned their craft and swam the last fifty yards. They clambered over rocks to the shore and made their way past the abandoned settlement that Zenap had espied through her binoculars on arrival, back to the safety of their encampment and the cool drinks of its restaurant. Zenap was exhausted, physically by the effort, and mentally by the risk they should never have taken.

The conference ended with an open-air dinner at the restaurant. Barbecues were set up above the beach, and kebabs were grilled, meat and fish. It had been a memorable two days for the participants, very exotic. Jamal, meanwhile, was confident that roles had been duly assigned, and he had set out on a chart a timeline showing who was responsible for what and when up to the October deadline.

Zenap thought everyone knew their responsibilities, but no one knew who would carry them out. In fact, it was clear that no one had any idea of what to do practically. They were like an army with officers and no men, chiefs and no Indians. As the meeting drew to an end, she went up to Jamal and spoke with him. She thanked him for having the confidence in her to invite her.

"You have allowed me to recover my faith," she said. "You must tell me what you want me to do to support you. Even Suleiman, if he knew, must admire your skill in forming a team so perfect for the task they must perform." And Jamal felt vindicated on his choice of Board insider. His plan would succeed.

Fiasco though this may have seemed to Zenap, what she did not know was that Jamal had been successfully infiltrating his people into the various businesses and was well poised to take control, as soon as the opportunity arose. This Malaysian exercise was focused solely on the plan to plunder the central finances of the Board, which in Jamal's mind was desirable but secondary to his main purpose. He had now thought through his game plan and was determined to follow a twin path of furthering his control in the field, while pulling back from involvement by him at the centre. He did not wish to alert Suleiman, take personal risks or provoke suspicion.

CHAPTER THIRTEEN - KLAIPEDA

Klaipeda, Lithuania, 21 July 2001

Klaipeda in Lithuania is a port on the east side of the Baltic. Its traditional wealth, from the time of the Baltic's Hanseatic League, is still visible in the architecture of its old buildings. The port itself has benefited dramatically in the post Soviet era, charging the Russians for the access of their freight to the sea. The town has its own airport, where Zenap had landed two hours earlier on a chartered Aeroflot business jet. She had been the only passenger, while the flight crew had consisted of two pilots, a flight engineer and two hostesses. She suspected that this overkill on the flight personnel front had less to do with her arrival than with the departing passengers, who would use the jet tomorrow.

Zenap had flown over the flat woodlands of Lithuania, the last holdout of European heathens facing the Christianisation programme started by the Romans, which took hundreds of years to push this far north. Some locals were said still to conduct their ceremonies in the forests, not like the new Satanists but in an unbroken tradition preceding Christianity. These stories were fun, she told herself. They should go out and look for a few pagans in the forests. She knew that the old religion and culture here had branched from the same tree as her own, centuries before Christianity. The Lithuanian language was used by scholars of linguistics in their research on Sanskrit, the ancient language of India and ancestor of the modern Indo-European languages. The Lithuanians, cut off in the swamps, had retained a language distinct from the European languages which together with the Slav languages now surrounded Lithuania. Incredible how a tiny culture and language can survive thousands of years in an ocean of hostility, she thought.

Zenap had walked along the sand beach as far as a wooden pier stretching far out to sea. Ignoring the prohibited signs and a boozy guard in a tent, she had walked out as far as the maintenance of the pier permitted, before the slats of wood no longer permitted a foothold. Probably for loading missiles in the old days, she had mused, looking down at the steel rail tracks running out to sea over the wooden slats of the pier. Now it was ten minutes to three in the afternoon and she was due to join the meeting at three.

Zenap turned off the sand beach and walked towards the meeting room. It was housed in a modern, brick building, raised up from ground level on pillars, surrounded by trees. It must have been constructed as a holiday spot for the Russia communist elite before the Lithuanians booted them out. In true David and Goliath form they had stood in front of tanks, protested and died, to become the first Baltic state to achieve independence. Estonia and Latvia followed soon after, while Kaliningrad remained as an isolated Russian enclave, a Gibraltar on the Baltic. It was Vermouth's idea to meet in a completely off-the-wall place. He was becoming increasingly paranoid about the drug business. She, Zenap, knew that it did not make a blind bit of difference if they met here, Dubai or even New York, though she knew that New York had been declared off-limits this year, something to do with the "charities", but she had not found out why.

It was Suleiman's form to call her in when a meeting was pretty much concluded, so she was not surprised to find Vanesh, Vermouth and Moon with him. Jamal figured less and less these days and she wondered why, given his plans, of which only she in that room was aware. What I learnt last month in Malaysia must be just a small part of his plan, she thought, in a moment of lucidity. In contrast, she had learnt a lot more about Vanesh. Ferdie Moon brought her up to speed on what had been discussed. What it boiled down to was that Brewster and Lorenson had gone way over the top with the deals they had put into the partnerships, to the extent that they now jeopardised not just their corporation but the partnerships in which the Board had interests as well.

"Give me your take, Zenap." Suleiman said, after she had been given a chance to review the material on the table in front of her, five pages of a report and two pages of figures.

"The way I see it, we were looking to pull out three billion dollars net. Today they're in the negative zone. It's their fault. What we do is pull out the good bits selectively and dump the rubbish on Brewster and Constexo. The whole thing will fold, but we will clear two billion dollars the way I read the numbers."

She looked around at them and continued with her set piece.

"We have powers of attorney which will permit us to close out the positions which suit us and remit the proceeds to our accounts without telling Brewster. He won't find out until it's too late. The US bankruptcy lawyers will make a killing out of Constexo's demise, congressional committees will get the chance to meet forever investigating the scandal, and maybe even justice will be done and Constexo's auditors will be brought down for negligence and wilful misconduct. How does that sound?"

She knew Vermouth would not like this. The Constexo partnership structure was not just the keystone of his grand strategy; it was the only stone so far. She and Nathan had met several US corporations without success. The nub of the problem was, and only she knew this, that the albino sleuths in Bangalore had not been able to come up with the goods. They had not been able to burrow into the confidential financial data of other corporations in the USA who might be in a similar situation to Constexo. She could guess which corporations they might be, but she needed hard evidence to coerce or seduce their managements to follow the Constexo path. Without the information it was down to plain luck, and this they had not had. Vermouth argued his case forcefully but it seemed to be going her way. Vanesh was supporting her every step of the way. This made her confident that she had sniffed out his hidden agenda. She would tackle him tonight.

After dusk she saw Vanesh standing alone among the trees. Her plan was bold, but she knew that if it came to the crunch, Suleiman would believe her over Vanesh, and Vanesh probably knew this too. She joined him in the shadows, the fragrance of the forest hanging in the air. She had been taking pains to get closer to him and now was the moment to go all out, a little bit of endearment and then simple hard-nosed business. Business was his first love; maybe she could come in second, for as long as it took.

"I used to have a brother very similar to you. I called him Zuri. I should call you Zuri."

"Zenap, I am charmed by whatever you call me."

"Zuri, I'm unhappy. Suleiman's cause used to be defence and furtherance of the Arab World. Now the Board supports groups who take direct action to destroy their enemies, who usurp the cause they claim for their own violent ends. We have been giving these fighters money to pursue these ends. Now we are looking at paying out hundreds of millions to them. It's not right to supply funds to them on this scale. It's not my cause, or yours, and I would prefer to keep the money and use it better." In this she was speaking the truth.

"I am surprised to hear high treason from you, Zenap. Are you testing me?" He chuckled.

"It is true," she stated with indignation. " It is what I think. I cannot believe that you think otherwise. We must impound these funds. We could give Suleiman a share but he will not want it. For him it is all for the cause or nothing for the cause. He could not share these funds, allocate them as we would. That is the problem." She leant closer to him. "I explained in the meeting today how we should withdraw the money from the partnerships, but you must tell me how we withdraw it from the Board, from the accounts, for us. It is only right."

He gave her a quick hug with one arm around the shoulder, released her and said, "I think we should retire for the night."

In Zenap's book that meant she had won him over. Now it was just a question of mechanics. She knew how to extract the funds from the Board's accounts in Switzerland as soon as they were transferred to these accounts when the Constexo positions were liquidated, but she would need Vanesh's signatures on the paperwork, and what better way to get those than to let him work out the plan for himself. In fact, she was sure he had worked it out already. Would he let her in on his deal?

Sitting in his room, Vanesh was unable to focus on the novel he had been reading on the flight. His mind kept returning to the girl, which was how he thought of her. Maybe this was the solution, he thought. He had been planning to take the money for exactly the same reasons as she had voiced in their talk this evening. He had moved closer to her over the last couple of months. As witnessed this afternoon, her business judgement had matured. Perhaps they could get together. She was exciting. Could he keep up with her? He found these trips tiring, needed rest for few days afterwards. But from what he knew of her schedule, she just launched from one trip straight into the next. At the end of last year when they had been pulling everything together, she had been in London several times, Singapore, Colombo, Dubai, and the States in less than a month. Maybe this was why she wanted to settle down with him.

What did he want? He thought this was what he wanted. And there was something very Indian about her, the way she reacted to him. He was from southern India, but he had no idea of her background; no one seemed to know much about her, except Suleiman. Suleiman, his one true friend, a man he admired, but off the rails now. Sad. Sad but true, and sentimentality was worthless. He would get on and do it. If she were there and ready to come, he would take her. He had nothing to lose. He was not doing it for the money, in the common sense.

From his window Vermouth had watched Zenap go to Vanesh under the trees. It troubled him that she should be outside with Vanesh. Vanesh and she had never had more than the briefest of business exchanges. Was he missing some link in the chain, some part of the pattern? In the end he decided it was just his growing paranoia, his fear of the drug trade, of the consequences, which swirled daily through his head. The problem was that he had no control over his unknown opponents, the customs men and drug squads out to trap him. He imagined a web being woven, and he the harmless fly flitting towards it unknowingly. But the worst of all was the fear that all would unravel just as he was about to achieve this unimaginable financial coup that they were orchestrating. He thought back to that meeting with Suleiman on the South Downs so many years ago, fitting that this scheme should have drawn first breath in a hurricane.

***

The next morning they all boarded a white minibus to go out to the airport. The Aeroflot machine Zenap had flown in on the day before had been up to Moscow and returned late in the evening. Within five minutes of their arrival it was in the air. The front cabin was fitted out with plush grey leather seats around a table, and the rear cabin had twelve seats in standard aircraft configuration. Suleiman, Vanesh, Vermouth and Jamal took the front cabin. This was to be a strategy meeting to take a decision on the Constexo Energy situation. Zenap and Ferdie were in the rear cabin. It was they who would execute whatever plan were agreed in the front. The only other occupants of the cabin were the flight engineer, two hostesses and twelve cardboard boxes, the booty of the Moscow trip. They did not yet know where they were going; that would depend on Suleiman's decision at the front. He had filed a flight plan, but he could always change it.

Ferdie was sure they would be in the air for at least two hours, so when the hostess suggested a vodka before breakfast, he decided on a beer and took a couple of cans. Zenap stuck with the vodka.

"I have an active enquiring mind," Ferdie said. "I'm gonna take a look in those boxes on the back seats."

"You can't open Suleiman's boxes," Zenap said. She had no idea what they were or what was in them. It was hard to believe Suleiman would risk taking in drugs on a chartered plane on which he was a passenger. Ferdie had no such qualms because he had no idea of Suleiman's business apart from the business schemes he, Ferdie, set up, and elaborate they were these schemes. He saw himself right now as one smart dude.

"You'll be amazed what this little thing can do," Ferdie replied, as he stood up, unfolding the blade of a Swiss Army knife, and moving to the rear of the plane.

"This is a hijack," he said to the hostess, laughing. "What do you have in your boxes? I see twelve very valuable boxes. Stand and deliver." The hostess continued with what she was doing. He zipped the knife along the seam of the box in seat 6B.

"Suleiman wouldn't trust me to do my job if he thought I wouldn't check these out. Zenap, it's caviar in cans, thousands of bucks worth of caviar. This guy's something: he's an incurable trader. This little haul pays for more than the cost of chartering the plane.

We're flying for free. Good that I've got my Swiss Army knife." He came back with a can for himself and one for Zelda and proceeded to open them with the knife's tin opener.

"What about the guys in front, Ferdie?" She called the hostess over, who, of course, had somewhat more sophisticated equipment than Ferdie's Swiss Army knife. While Zenap and Ferdie munched straight from the cans, the hostess prepared a sophisticated display with ice and vodka, and took it forward to the front cabin and to the pilot with whom, unbeknown to them, she had a close relationship.

"One of Suleiman's standard quotes is *God helps those who help themselves*, Ferdie, which is what we are doing with the caviar right now, but it brings me to the point. Up front they are going to decide to do what I said they should do yesterday. It's just that they think they have to discuss it first. So how are we going to do it, Ferdie? It's down to you and me."

"Well, I guess we should stick with the Bible and teach Brewster that if you live by the sword you die by the sword. We have two problems. The first is to get those positions unwound and take the profit before anyone knows what is going on, because there is one certainty, and that is that the market will tank as soon as they *do* know. The second problem is to get the money out and into the Swiss banks before anyone can get to the courts or whatever; possession is nine tenths of the law. The other certainty, sorry did I say just now there was one certainty, is that Brewster et al will be out cold to the count of ten, dead, muerto, mort, tot."

"So we will need to spread the dealing around when we unwind the positions, Ferdie, and then move ultra-fast." Ideas were running through her head.

"Yes, and we've been planning for something like this, so we have enough dealing accounts and dealing lines to handle the volumes we need to transact. But since yesterday's discussion, I've been thinking about how the sheer scale of the thing will affect the markets. If word gets out too early, which it easily can, we're dead in the water and might as well go home, finito. So how can we influence this?"

"The proverbial red herring?"

"Yeah, we'll divide the firms who deal for us into two groups. Group A does the business. Group B is put on standby that we are about to give them an instruction to do the opposite of what Group A has been instructed. That way, half the market is going to be expecting exactly the opposite to happen of what we really intend to do. If Group B see the market move they'll be laughing, and even front running, until they realise we've not confirmed their instructions to deal."

"You handle that Ferdie. I'll fix the money side. The issue is time zones. You give me an exact scenario of your projected deal settlements, and I'll route the funds through multiple channels. Destination Switzerland is my vote."

"Zenap, I've never thought of you as a democrat. Who else is voting?"

"No enfranchisement beyond red haired thirty year olds, Ferdie. And what about the powers of attorney?"

"That's my baby, Zenap. You're not ripping off my bucks." What else would Zenap expect from a professional like Ferdie?

An hour into the flight Vermouth came aft and let them know they would be landing at Gatwick. The decision was to liquidate, as Zenap had guessed. They would have two days for preparations in London and then they would fly to New York to do the dirty on Brewster.

"And Ferdie," Vermouth said, "this exact structure we've used for Constexo will not work a second time. Please think up some ideas, because we've got to replicate the transaction. We've done so well on this one and Zenap has more irons in the fire." With that he was gone.

***

London, 23 July 2001

Some days everything goes right and you have masses of energy. This was one such day, or by now a warm July evening. I had just taken some foreign clients to the theatre to see London's longest ever running play. I had seen it as a child, but I have to say it was great fun and very well performed, not the least stale after fifty odd years. I anticipated the clients would want to go out afterwards, so I had booked myself a room in the club for the night, rather than trekking back home. As it turned out, if they did want to enjoy London nightlife, they had made their plans excluding me, so I found myself at the club bar soon after ten.

Not the place to be on an evening like this, I thought, and headed out. I was walking up Pall Mall towards Trafalgar Square, when I saw a vaguely familiar figure coming towards me, which developed into the unmistakable form of Zara. Just as I was reaching her a free cab came by, which she hailed and bundled me into the cab, one of the new type.

"I'm kidnapping you, Frank," she said.

"Zara, what are you doing here?"

"Looking for you."

"Here?"

"No, I thought I'd have to go into the club and get you out. Are ladies allowed in the bar? Your secretary told me where you would be when I called your office earlier. I left a message on your mobile as well." Which, of course, had been turned off in the theatre.

"I know you've been to the theatre, so you haven't eaten, and I've booked a table at a place on the Aldwych, because I'm staying just around the corner." I noted her "because" which did not lead into a clause stating "why" she wanted to see me, but who could complain about being picked up off the street by this manifestation of the female form?

At this time of night the taxi took about two minutes and thirty seconds to get there, across Trafalgar Square and along the Strand, but it was time enough for Zara to explain that she was just here for two days, apologize that she had not been around recently and express her desire that we meet socially more often. As I said, some days just seem to go very well. We were greeted at the entrance and led downstairs into this very elegant restaurant. The tables are well spaced, so you have privacy from other diners, and this did bode well for the evening, the rest of the evening. I said that it was a bit late for aperitifs and asked for the wine list. I chose a Lebanese red, but the waiter did not agree with my choice, and we ended up with a Burgundy.

The Burgundy tasted to me as if it was from Algeria, all a matter of taste I suppose - it was clearly a first class wine, or at least labelled as such - but I was determined to insist on the Lebanese bottle for round two. Zara was bubbling with stories of where she had been and what she had just done. Today she had just come in from Lithuania, and she got a great kick out of describing the well-built Russian air hostesses who offered you vodka for breakfast and fruit juice for lunch. It made sense to me: the vodka was clearly just a continuation of the previous night's drinking session, while the fruit juice was the punctuation mark before the next session started – maybe I should move to Russia.

By the time the first course arrived, we had already moved on to the Lebanese red, and I was pondering what to choose next, when Zara suddenly turned serious.

"I have an ulterior motive tonight, Frank." She pulled out a stack of papers which looked as if they had been printed off her computer.

"This package carries a health warning," she said. "It can make you seriously rich."

"I have been warned. What is it?"

She passed across various pages, asking me to look at extracts which she then cross-referenced with other extracts. What we were looking at were the published reports of Constexo Energy of the US, a top ranked US company, and its filings to the regulatory authority, the Securities and Exchange Commission.

What she demonstrated was that, if you made certain assumptions, the company was disguising important information; in fact, so important that the company was going to the wall, going bust, belly up as they say in the US. Zara made two points: first, that I had less than a week to deal; and secondly, that my dealing could not he construed as insider trading because it was based on an interpretation of publicly available information, which she had assembled for me.

"Why are you telling me this, Zara?"

"I would expect no less from you, Frank. If you could make me rich, would you withhold the information from me?" That seemed to me like the answer of a reasonable person. The waiter came with the main course and acted a bit supercilious about all the papers spread out on the table, so I asked him in an American accent, using expressions native to Chicago, if he knew who his mother was. He did not take it personally, thinking it was a gripe following on from the Lebanese/Burgundy wine altercation.

I took another look at the papers. Most were SEC filings, some were copied out of annual reports, but it did strike me at the time that a few key items had a different source. Only at a later date, after the collapse of Constexo, did this make me shudder with apprehension. Right now I was enjoying dinner, the company and the prospect of getting rich. We skipped dessert and coffee.

Back upstairs we stepped out onto Aldwych and then turned right along the Strand. The young after-hours crowd was out in force, running around, shouting, vomiting, and doing all the things that make weekday evenings around Charing Cross Station such fun. Having refused the kind offers of approximately eighty five mini-cab drivers, Zara decided we should go into the burger bar just before the station. Lithuania must have built an appetite. A burger on her part and nothing on mine, and we were back out on the street. She had some figures that she thought I needed to see back at her hotel. So back we went, this time in a taxi, to the hotel, literally a few seconds walk from where we had dined.

We went up to her room. At the desk Ferdie was tapping away on a computer. He had two more computers up and running on the desk, connected by mobiles to the Internet, and another on the floor next to him. It was a bit incongruous in this very traditional hotel room. He looked up. "I'll just get this halfwit off the line and I'm with you," he said.

"I've just told Frank to sell Constexo forward and cash out next month," Zara said.

"Right," Ferdie responded. "I've already done it. The multiple's gonna be at least 20. You put in a hundred thousand bucks, you get two million back."

Ferdie proceeded to close down his computers. He brought me a folder of papers, which he quickly ran through.

"We wanted to show you this, Frank. It shows all the funds that have flowed through your bank on the energy deals. This is very impressive, Frank. Personally, I think I owe you one. I say, go for the Constexo deal, Frank. Make a bucketload for yourself and screw the bank. After this bucketload of dollars you won't need the bank anymore. They'll come running after you." I felt he had a very convincing line of argument, particularly as I had this vision of my

Illustrious Leader chasing after me to get my very own bucketload deposited in his bank, so I asked him to develop the argument.

Somehow that led into a game of three-card brag. Zara said she didn't know the rules. I have learnt from experience that these types clean you out. In this case, she lost big time, so having cleaned her out of cash, I suggested we move to strip poker. Ferdie was keen, but without the poker bit. Zara called room service because we had emptied the mini-bar. Obviously remembering Lithuania earlier in the day, she could not decide between vodka and Champagne, so she ordered both, and we forgot about cards. By three o'clock we had run dry, so Zara put Ferdie in charge of organising refreshments, while she called up some guys in Hong Kong and then in Singapore about some funds she had to transfer in a couple of days, and by now they were open for business in their time zone. Her calls took about forty-five minutes. Ferdie had underestimated the cognac we required, so by the time Zara got off the line, we had moved on to Tequila.

The Tequila prompted Ferdie to launch into a learned discourse on South American civilisations. I did not point out to him that Tequila came from Mexico, which is not in South America, but he soon moved on from South America anyway.

"You know what really strikes me," he said, "is that Homo sapiens like me have been around for fifty odd thousand years, but these smart professors talk about early civilisations from five thousand years ago. This is not early. What do these dudes think a smart guy like me, or you, would have been doing twenty thousand years ago?"

"Drinking home brew," I suggested.

"No, Frank, get this. Oceanographers working in the Arabian Sea just off the coast of India have discovered two submerged cities, measuring two miles by five miles. These are full blown conurbations. And guess what: artefacts lifted from the ocean bed have been carbon dated at nine and a half thousand years."

"That's the end of the last ice age," I said.

"You've got it. The sea level rose several hundred feet when the ice melted. Now where would a smart dude build his city? Think of Los Angeles, San Diego, Rio de Janiero, Biarritz."

"OK, OK, I get it. By the sea," I answered.

"Exactly," Ferdie continued. "All the best land around the world was flooded ten thousand years ago, an area taken together bigger than the Americas from Tierra del Fuego at the bottom to the US / Canadian border at the top. So if you were smart that's where you would look: in the sea, and not in the Iraqi desert. Not one random archaeologist to my knowledge has been smart enough to look in the most obvious place. I mean, they even tell us about it in the Bible. You know, the Noah thing, floods."

"Maybe they don't like getting wet. What about Atlantis?" I asked.

"Those guys looking for Atlantis are adventurers. Anyway, we know that was Santorini." Ferdie had either run out of steam, or he felt my argumentation, focusing on the psychology of staying dry rather than fact of the submerged artefacts, belonged at a lower academic level. He drained his glass.

The Tequila seemed to have a high evaporation rate. Ferdie was fed up with room service always bringing up the same old stuff and wanted to move on to a pub. I am not clued up about which pubs are open at four in the morning, so, thinking of Santorini I suggested that we should challenge room service to find us a bottle of Metaxa, failing which we could try a few of the other guests' rooms, and maybe check with reception to see if there were any Greeks on the room list. Ferdie wanted to check out the Greeks right away, but I prevailed upon him that we really should try room service first, and sure enough, they came up with the Metaxa.

It was only when Ferdie was pouring the last two glasses of Metaxa from the bottle, that I realised the time. Zara was already on the line to banks in Switzerland. OK, so they have an hour's time difference and get in early, but still. Part of the idea of staying at the club had been for me to arrive at the office early today. I had an appointment with my Illustrious Leader in which I planned to tell him to double my salary, in the hope that I might have my annual pay increase bumped up from 3% to 5%. I stood up. Zara hung up, came across and gave me a hug.

"It was really nice to spend some time with you, Frank. I'm serious about the share deal. Do it. Ferdie and I will." I thanked her and left the room, trying to work out survival strategies for the day ahead.

As the door closed, Ferdie turned to Zenap. "What's all that crap about selling Constexo shares forward?"

"He'll make a bundle from a forward deal on Constexo, Ferdie. I liked the way you winged it with the multiple of twenty, when you had no idea what we were talking about. Anyway, I showed him some inside information. So if he deals, he will win out big time, and then he has a choice of doing what we want, or being sent down. It's just insurance, Ferdie."

"I'm glad you're on my side, Zenap." She had to think about that one.

CHAPTER FOURTEEN – NEW YORK

New York, 26 July 2001

Brewster's office had called for a meeting. Apart from the initial New York meeting and the Michigan meeting, all dealings with Brewster's side had been conducted at the flunky/gofer level, rising only occasionally to Lorenson, but no higher. So even before they met, Brewster had put himself on the light side of the scales, being the one who needed to talk. Brewster's timing was good because Zenap and Ferdie were in-flight due to land in New York, so they would be available to meet him. Brewster's timing was bad because Zenap agreed with Suleiman that she would meet Brewster on the evening of the day on which they had closed out the whole situation. She felt that this was good, because his focus would now be on the meeting, by which time it would be too late for him to do anything, and if he had seen any warning signs by that time, he would not take action, expecting to deal with these matters at the meeting, and by then it would be too late. A truly excellent negotiating situation, she thought, in sarcastic mode.

Zenap called Brewster personally. After being transferred up through a routine ladder of three secretaries and one chairman's executive assistant, she had him on the line. She bantered with him for forty-five minutes, presumably while his dynamic corporation was adding a few hundred million dollars of shareholder value under his direction, before she suggested the meeting time and location. She named the hotel in Manhattan where she was staying and suggested they meet there. He was very keen to oblige, having misunderstood her intentions, no doubt, after the last forty-five minutes of intimate conversation. Otherwise it would have been Brewster who fixed the location.

The hotel did not have a high star rating, but it was one of New York's historic hotels, and the scene of many famous meetings, a very acceptable venue. In fact, Zenap was not staying there, but had chosen it by design. There was a small chance that Brewster could turn extremely nasty. While she did not expect anything to happen at the hotel itself, she wanted a safe route out. The hotel had front and rear exits, so you could be on the street and away in many directions, but then many directions can be covered.

What was interesting about the hotel was that it had been built in the days of the railways and a direct but very long tunnel had been constructed to the station. This was the way she and Ferdie would leave, whatever happened. Given that within the hotel the norms of social behaviour would be maintained, any Brewster thugs would have to be very fleet of foot to track them down through the tunnels, assuming the thugs worked out that that was where they had disappeared. When it came to personal safety precautions and planning Zenap was a master of overkill, and Ferdie killed himself laughing when he heard the plan. But then if she wanted to walk down underground tunnels late at night in New York, that was OK by him.

The meeting itself was as much of an anticlimax as the Eiffel tower must have been to the Parisians, when it was constructed for the World Fair. Brewster, Blim and Lorenson arrived on the dot of eight. Zenap and Ferdie walked across the Foyer to meet them, and Zenap asked Brewster if she could first have a moment with him alone. He was chuffed to be given this personal treatment by her, and they walked a few yards up the foyer, leaving the others standing in a group. She thanked him for inviting them, his time, his courtesy, and just wanted to say, personally, how grateful she was, before they started the meeting.

They moved back to the others, and Ferdie suggested they move up to the bar. Raised to one side of the foyer, this was a dimly lit traditional New York bar. Blim did the ordering for them all, and trays of nuts arrived with their drinks. After an uncharacteristically short blustering by Brewster, he turned the meeting over to Blim.

Blim knew the best negotiating style would be to go straight to the point. He had seen *them* operate in Michigan.

"Lorenson has some numbers." Lorenson handed round a sheet of paper. "The markets have not moved as we anticipated. We now have fifteen billion dollars at stake and we are underwater financially. We do not believe that it will be possible to recover from this situation unless we get our timing right and take decisive action. Too many people in the decision making chain will not work. Therefore, we propose that we buy you out."

This was the last thing Zenap expected, so she said, "Mr Brewster," looking at Blim, "this is indeed fortunate. My principals authorised me to make an offer to you to sell, subject to my agreeing their floor price, although we did not for a moment expect that selling would be your intention. My authorisation is unusual. My principals believe it is the nature of the business that values can change very quickly and, therefore, that I should have all possibilities covered in my power of attorney to act on their behalf, including sale. As they cannot be here personally, they have asked me to negotiate for them. I had not been expecting to make a sale. However, let us discuss this as it may be in the best interests of my principals."

Ferdie beckoned the waitress across for refills. Brewster muttered under his breath that they should order two each to keep that surly bitch of a waitress out of sight longer. Ferdie whispered something to her. She smiled and was back almost immediately with three drinks for each of them.

"Then I think we should ask Lorenson to work out the price." Blim said. *Work out the price*! Ferdie thought. We just closed out the whole shooting match for two point two billion dollars, and they think they can pull one over on us, *working out the price.* Get real.

Sure enough, Lorenson was switched to generous mode. After a lot of tapping on his machine and questions to Blim about assumptions, he came up with seven hundred and fifty million dollars. Zenap failed to conceal her surprise at the *high* value offered to her principals, so she did not manage to negotiate it up to more than eight hundred and ten million dollars. She regretted that they could not meet tomorrow to sign the contracts, but noon the day after was agreed.

No more drinks were required before the meeting wound up. Brewster was clearly too pleased with the result to press for an extension of the meeting with Zenap in her room, so they took leave of one another. The Brewster Team left by the main entrance. Zenap and Ferdie took the tunnel, as planned. And they ran, laughing like hysterical adolescents. They were so used to serious business meetings that a spoof like this one was the biggest joke they had had in years. Brewster would find out, tomorrow, that he had been sold out: there would be no signing the next day, Brewster would be fighting for his life, and Blim would discover that he had more important business connections than Brewster now was, consigning Brewster to history, maybe the stone age. As to Lorenson, Zenap thought, so near yet so far. Goodbye, Mr Lorenson, no billions for you.

Zenap and Ferdie split up at the station. Zenap intended to fly to London to deal with Nathan and the fallout from the impending Constexo crash, which would affect a number of the accounts Nathan handled. Ferdie walked the few blocks south to his Manhattan apartment. He took the elevator up to the eighteenth floor. He rang the bell to warn his wife Sue that he was coming and stepped into the hall of the apartment. It had very stylish décor in pastel shades. On the green marble floor was a Persian rug, a Tabrez. Finely woven and inlaid with silk, it glittered like a jewel. Sue called from the lounge to the right. He said he would be five minutes and turned left through the door into his study. It was a small room with traditional French chateau style furniture, a desk and a couple of chairs. He clicked on the CD player and the soft tones of a breathy female floated across the room.

Ferdie's task was to send out confirmation of the day's work to the Board. He had prepared an eight-line email in advance, and now he connected to a teenage chat room on the Internet, in order to transmit the email to each member of the Board. Originally the Board had used a book code to disguise its communications and then they had added in prime number codes, but Ferdie had suggested they forget the idea of codes. His method was to send bits of the email scattered into the sort of drivel and sexual innuendo that is common in chat rooms. The real bits of email message would be identified simply by the fact that they would be the only contiguous portions of the author's text in the chat room not containing a spelling mistake.

Ferdie had written a programme that would automatically respond to the chat of bona fide chat room participants, while feeding in bits of the email piece by piece over a one to two hour period. The other Board members could check for messages in the chat room, and they generally preferred to do this automatically with a programme which sifted the bits of email out from the "noise" of the chat as and when each bit came through. They believed that electronic eavesdroppers would have little chance of ever working out their messages, particularly as they used at least three chat rooms at any one time and changed them regularly. They used standard radio conventions, e.g. "Roger" was an affirmative and "over and out" embedded somewhere signified that there was no more email to come.

There were euphemisms. The current president of the United States was "JFK" which would be accompanied by a misleading reference to flying, so that it would be confused with the airport. Terrorist attacks were "strikes" and accompanied by a misleading reference to ten-pin bowling. Finally, any sensitive word could be sent as an anagram, after having been run through an anagram programme, listing all possible words from this combination of letters to protect against ambiguity. The letters of the anagram would then be dropped in individually as single stand-alone letters (double in the case of "i" and "a") as if they resulted simply from a key being pressed by accident, hardly perceptible during two hours of chat. The last letter would be followed by a dot to signify the end of the anagram. The recipient of the email would then run the letters through his anagram machine and all possible words would be placed in the position of the third letter of the anagram, representing the correct position of the word in the email. The only part of this process that was not automated by Ferdie's programmes was the recipient's choice of word from the list of words from the anagram, but the context would make this clear.

In summary, the real email was simply mixed in with vast quantities of verbal junk on transmission and sifted through on receipt to be assembled for the recipient. The process was as simple as throwing iron filings into the garbage and then retrieving them with a magnet.

Having logged on as *Blue Dolphin*, it took Ferdie just two minutes to set the process in motion. He then went through to Sue in the lounge. Sue was sitting very upright on a beige sofa. As he entered, she said, " Please, sit, Ferdie, I have something important to say." He sat down opposite her, a glass coffee table separating them, satisfied with the achievements of the day.

"There is no point in beating around the bush. There is only one way to say this, and in your language this in non-negotiable. I am leaving you Ferdie. I am going tonight."

Ferdie was quite simply shocked. After the elation of the evening, he fell with a crunch back to earth. "I don't understand." He said.

"Ferdie, that is exactly it. You don't understand. You are not the Ferdie I married seven years ago. The charming, lively Yale lawyer."

"So…" he began, but she interrupted.

"I think that the real Ferdie is still in there, but the Ferdie opposite me now is acting a part: he is brash, he is loud, he swears, he tells vile jokes. This in not the man I married. Are you trying to be someone else? You act like that guy Brewster who was on TV last night. Do you admire his kind? Is that it?" Ferdie thought of that meeting with Brewster in Michigan when he had berated Zenap for running Brewster down. Now he thought of this evening's meeting, and any illusions he may have had about Brewster being the driving force behind Constexo evaporated.

"Have you anything to say, Ferdie?"

"What can I say? Except what I mean. Please stay, Sue."

"It's worse, Ferdie. Consider this to be my last gift to you, a truth, hurtful but true. You should know, and that is my gift to you, to let you know. If I were a religious person, which I am not, I would say that you have been touched by evil, but I don't think you know it consciously."

"What do you mean, Sue?" Where is this leading now, he thought?

"These people you work with, Ferdie. What do they do?"

"Business, Sue, commerce. OK, I admit that I set things up for them, structures that permit them to sail very close to the wind, but they're not the only ones to do this, and we do it particularly well. We're good sailors, first class seamen."

"You, don't understand me, Ferdie. There is something troubling you. You talk in your sleep. You toss and turn at night. Are they your demons, Ferdie? What are their real aims, what do they really do?"

"I've never thought, Sue."

"I think you have, Ferdie, but you do not want to admit it to yourself. I think this is why the real Ferdie has been buried under the rubble of who he was and hidden behind the façade of who he is. You are very efficient at what you do, Ferdie, but it is possible to be very efficient at doing the wrong thing. That is no good. The Nazis were very efficient with their gas chambers. If you want to find your way to grace, Ferdie, you must find out the truth of these people, of what it is that you do for them. You must confront it and seek absolution, your absolution. There is no chance for *us* now, Ferdie, *you and me*. Perhaps there will be one day, if you handle this, but I promise nothing. I have no one else, Ferdie, but I am going. I must leave now, right now. Goodbye, Ferdie." She stood, and even as he rose, she was across the hall and out of the apartment. Gone. In that one moment Sue was gone, from his life.

Ferdie dropped back into the seat and sat there, devastated. It had been so quick. How could it all have ended in minutes, or even that actual second when she left the apartment, after seven years? He sat there, thoughts spinning through his head in all directions, getting nowhere, thoughts like shooting stars scattering through the night sky, every bit as focused as Ronald Reagan's star wars defence technology, spinning free of rational thought. Slowly he emerged from his personal misery and thought of what Sue had said. Was there something about Suleiman and Co? It was true that he did not know the agenda of the Board, but he had his suspicions. After an hour he rose and left the flat. He needed company, so he decided to go around the corner to the bar he frequented. As he walked, the irony struck him that Walter, the barman, was generally known as the Father Confessor. He entered the bar, which was emptying out by this time of night and took a stool at the end of the counter. Walter poured him his usual.

"You got time to chat, Walter?"

"Hang on." Walter went across to refill the glasses of a group of five at the other end of the bar. Elvis oozed out of the music machine. Walter returned.

"Sue has left me."

"You surprise me, Ferdie. Why?"

"I don't think she likes me anymore. Says I've changed," Ferdie said.

"I've known you these last five years, and you know what? She's right. I used to like you Ferdie. Now I think you're a jerk." The television behind the counter was showing some archive footage of the President denying impropriety with his young female intern.

"You know who you remind me of Ferdie, what with your cigars and all, that guy there." Walter pointed at the television, at the President. Ferdie was not sure if this was a joke, but it did not matter. The fact was that Ferdie did see a reality behind these words. By the time he returned to the apartment he had taken his wife's message to heart. He wished it were not too late. Somehow he would have to find a way, but one thing was clear to him: he had just conducted his last assignment for the Board.

***

By this time Zenap was already high over the Atlantic heading for London. She had to work out how to handle Nathan. They had to take action to protect certain of the accounts he managed that would be linked to the Constexo collapse, maybe very quickly, too quickly. On the face of it, nothing she told Nathan would necessarily incriminate her, but there was the possibility that he would put all the facts together and make an intelligent guess. She did not like this, but she could see no way around taking this risk. She would simply have to deal with any fallout when the time came. Would she be able to? I am putting myself in the hands of the uninitiated, she thought. I am taking a personal risk, but if I do not do it, Nathan and his bank hit scandal big time and that has its consequences. You think too much, Zenap, she said to herself. Just do it.

OK, problem one set. Decision taken. Now for problem two, she thought. I have to get Vermouth to attend a meeting in London, a meeting he cannot refuse. Instantly she saw how she could tie this into the situation with Nathan's accounts. She smiled with satisfaction, as the plan formed.

Finally, she thought about the Board. The truth was that they were at the far end of the scale. Irrespective of race, nationality or religion, only a fraction of the population would support the extreme measures for which they provided finance. Even those who sympathised with the same causes would not support the devastation these people wrought. She knew she was the only person privy to this knowledge other than the members of the Board, and she wondered whether she had been right to turn a blind eye. The scale had seemed so small, almost irrelevant once. Now it was not. One thing was clear to her: the path she had chosen to tread now was the right one.

CHAPTER FIFTEEN - ZURICH

Zurich, 31 July 2001

Vanesh was waiting in the lobby of the hotel in Zurich when she entered. He moved across rapidly to greet her.

"Zuri, Zuri," she said, using her private name for him, "you are smiling you have succeeded with your plan."

"Our plan," he said.

"You planned it."

"Yes, yes," he said, "my plan for us, our plan."

"Is the money here, Zuri?"

"It is here. We will visit the Bahnhofstrasse together. We will add your signature at each bank. I would hate to think of these Swiss inheriting if anything happened to me."

"How did you get the money here," she asked, smiling with admiration, as they entered the lift.

"I didn't. It's not the same money. I thought I could do this only once, so I decided to reserve the scheme I had available for myself rather than the Board. To simplify, the Board lent the money to a company, though it does not know that yet. The company deposited these funds and borrowed against them. The loan was disbursed via a circuitous route to our accounts here. The funds held as security were accidentally transferred to the Cayman Islands on the same day, an engineered bank error, I'm afraid. The bank loan was then repaid out of Cayman. The loan is unfortunately not recorded at either the bank or the company, so investigations will follow the transfer to Cayman and stop there. I don't believe the fundsflow out of Cayman could be reconstructed, but even then it would stop at the lending bank which has no record of the loan."

"You had someone in the bank in Cayman," she asked, knowing the answer, having guessed his plan long before. She had not fully understood his explanation, which was convoluted, but she had got the gist of it, and after all, she knew who the bent banker was, having set him up herself.

"I needed a bit of help in the lending bank to fly this kite," he went on, as they left the lift and walked along the hotel corridor to their rooms, "which is why I thought it should only be done once. Our friend from the bank has just become a rich man. He decided yesterday that he would give up his salaried job and go abroad. He's publicity shy," he said euphemistically, "so he probably used the passport I gave him, rather than his real identity. I think the Board will stop making their charitable contributions."

"Zuri this is a very sumptuous suite," she said, as she opened the door and preceded him into the room. "Are you sure we can afford it?" and she smiled at him.

The Bahnhofstrasse is a somewhat more welcoming place than the name, Station Road, implies. The station is there, and so are all the main Swiss banks. Perhaps it is no coincidence that the banks are so close to the station, so convenient in the days of rail for European travellers wishing to deposit their wealth quickly and discreetly. However, if it is just a few travellers cheques you plan to cash, you will not receive the same welcome as the traveller who is just popping into the main branch to effect transactions worth a few hundred million dollars. In the case of Zenap and Zuri there were quite a number of branches to visit. Until a couple of days ago the Board had become a very wealthy charity. That wealth had now changed allegiance, but, coincidentally, there was no net effect on the deposit base of the Swiss banks.

It took the full morning for them to complete the rounds of the banks. It was a wonderful experience for Vanesh, not by reason of the charm of the bankers; rather it was the solicitous attention Zenap paid him, her good nature, her sense of fun. She talked about his hometown in south India and could not contain her surprise when he told her that was where *he* came from. By the end of the morning, Vanesh and Zenap were each sole signatories of bank accounts which, taken together, added up to more money than the two of them, for all practical purposes, would ever be able to spend, or at least that was what Vanesh thought. He had been foolish to think twice about whether or not he should take her with him. Even if they split up later it would not matter; there was more than enough to share; he would let her go her own way if that was what she wanted.

After they had completed filling in the forms at the last bank, Vanesh decided to change some dollars. This was his stash of five thousand dollars in notes, which he had carried on him, in case anything had gone wrong over the last two days and a fast exit without a credit card trail would have been prudent. He chose to do this at the foreign exchange counter of a local bank. Zenap waited outside. When he came out he was surprised to see her speaking on a mobile phone as he knew she never used one. She clicked it off as he approached her, and a second later he had forgotten the incident. The phone was hired and the call had been put through to Bangalore.

Flushed with success, Vanesh was a very different man from the punctilious board member he had been until so recently: lavish with tips, desperate to hit the most extravagant spots, and draw attention to himself. If Zenap had had any doubts, which she did not, they would have been dispelled. She was not going to have him running around town tonight. How much he had given, in return for so little. How gullible. Such a short time to enjoy such immense wealth. But I suppose he was the type, she mused, suggesting they go back to the hotel and change for the evening.

***

Peter Arbakhov's flight arrived in Zurich early in the morning of the next day and Farah was there to meet him. He gave her his usual hug, tears flowing. To an onlooker it would have seemed an emotional reunion of husband and wife, or mistress, a reasonable assumption, given that Peter, married to his business, was unlikely to commit adultery with anyone, but if he had come close to an adulterous betrayal of his true love, the business, it would have been with Farah.

They took a taxi from the airport to drop Peter's bag at the hotel – she had moved from yesterday's hotel the previous evening. In the taxi, they had talked about Bangalore and how the albinos were managing the business. Now in her room they sat opposite one another at an oval glass coffee table. She had booked Peter's flight from Bangalore earlier and had yesterday put through a call from her hired mobile, which she had since returned, to confirm he should come. She had wanted to complete the formalities at the banks with Vanesh before giving the green light to Peter to fly over.

The plan for this morning was to take Peter around the Swiss banks, in order that he should become a signatory on accounts she had established. These were, she said, to support the new business division he was now in charge of. He did not ask where the funds came from. He trusted her and she did not tell him. Neither did she inform him of the elaborate scheme she had devised to transfer funds under her signature from the Vanesh accounts to these new accounts, accounts over which Peter would have control, containing sums of money beyond the imagination of an ordinary man, such as he was.

It has become difficult to move funds between banks for illegitimate purposes these days, even through Swiss banks. However, it is not in the tradition of Swiss banking to question the private purposes of bank clients. As long as you play by the rules, and quite often if you do not, you are unlikely to attract attention. Farah always played by the rules of the jurisdiction in which she found herself, so she had full confidence in her financial plan. For the first time in her life, she had been obliged to break the rules yesterday evening, to deal with the Vanesh situation. She hoped it would never happen again; this was not her style, it was not *what she did.* Still, she might use Switzerland to bank the money, but she was not planning to spend any time here. In fact, she felt that, in a legal technical sense, she was not here anyway: it was only her alias paying a visit. And this particular alias, whatever happened, would within a couple of weeks be consigned to the same evolutionary dead-end as the dodo, to paraphrase a popular expression.

She wanted to spend some time with Peter, so once they had completed the banking formalities, they checked out of the Zurich hotel, and the two of them had a car take them to Lausanne, on

Lake Geneva. She knew a family hotel just above the lake, where they would stay until Peter returned to Bangalore the next day, picking up a plane from Geneva.

They walked along the lake promenade. To their right green hills, and to their left the lake, shimmering in the evening light. A few boats were out on the lake, others were anchored just offshore.

"How is this compared to Bangalore, Peter?"

"This is wonderful, Farah. I will move here, when I have finished." By which he meant retire after he had completed his business plans, which he would never do – there would always be new plans.

"We are so different, Peter. I love India. I fly to Geneva. I am allowed to walk through immigration without twenty people hassling me. Crowds do not surround me offering to carry my baggage, bring me taxis. Instead, I walk to the Hertz desk and pick up my car keys, which I have ordered. They say to me, *follow this direction through the terminal, take the lift down, follow the signs to car park 3, take the stairs to level three, your car is parked in bay 12c.* Peter, in all this time I do not see a soul. And then I am in my one litre Opel, with air-conditioning and CD player, I need not worry in my cocoon, if the traffic snarls and I am stuck. No problem, I have my in-car entertainment. Peter, this is not me. Give me Bangalore any day."

"Farah, I know you called me here to talk about business, my new business division based on the mobile phone. Betsy, or was it Linda, asked you why you don't have a mobile."

"I don't need one, Peter: I meet people. I am here with you now. Why would I want to send text messages to other people, when I am with you, or send a text message to you now, when I am with you, which is what I gather they do these days? Why would I want to answer calls or make them to others? This is our time, Peter, you and me."

"That's why you're different, Farah. You live so many lives at once. Let's say, to take number, six lives. Each of those six lives is competing for a place in your one space/time dimension. Your physical reality."

"You spent too much time on physics in Moscow, Peter, of the Einstein variety."

"Untrue," he protested. "I'm at the other end of the scale with quantum theory, which is why I do information technology, and love the nano-world. I'm serious, Farah. Since I've been in India, I have learnt of reincarnation. We experience something similar in Russia, also, when we have emptied the first vodka bottle and reach for the second. For us it is like meditation, as it is for the guru. You smile, but let me be serious. The rest of us, people like me, we live our lives and must fill them. Sometimes we manage to fill half our life, like me with my business and nothing else, so we are bored in the other half of our life. We go to the cinema, we watch videos, we text message our friends. When did you last go to the cinema?"

"I don't do that."

"So you see! Most of us are living half a life. You are living six lives at once. You run a business in Bangalore, Farah, but I never see you. I am 10% of one of your six, or more, lives."

"From an Indian perspective, you have collapsed the next couple of centuries of reincarnation into one life, yours, and you're not even Indian. You have no time for text messages, Farah."

"Peter, I admire your insight. I can see how your university professors in Russia put Gagarin into orbit, while JFK was laid low by a simple base metal, lead, which proved more powerful than his brain, when the two were in direct confrontation, *complex molecules v. Pb*. But let's talk business, since you have appreciated that we are here for business, and at immense cost, the cost of your ticket from Bangalore and two rooms in this hotel in Lausanne."

Peter realised that he had gone way over the top. Was it the influence of Lausanne, the lake, which had made him question her existential soul? He was mortified, and backtracked straight into business.

"My research has led me to the epicentre of the problem," he started.

But she interrupted, as always reading his thoughts, just as she read the thoughts of anyone he had ever seen her interact with, "Peter, I understand that you are Russian and a businessman, and so Switzerland is your ideal. I want you to be here, once you have finished your project for me, for us. But now listen. I trust you. I believe you can do what I have asked you to do. I cannot do this myself. I do not understand why if you pump individual electrons through two discrete holes to a screen behind you get a wave formation on the screen and not two spots. Quantum physicists have told me that they do not understand this either, and if a colleague told them he did, they would deem him unworthy of his post at the university. This is not the point. You may wish to live in a world you do not understand. I do not."

"And so?" Peter asked.

"And so," she said, "I trust in your make-believe world of electrons and microchips in which I cannot believe. And since I cannot believe in it, you must be in control. Peter, I herewith contract myself to work for you for the next five years. Whatever the project needs, you tell me to get it. If I do not live up to your expectations, you tell me. I will not ask for your word on this; I know you and take it as given."

Peter continued with the "epicentre". "The nub of the whole thing is about effective use of time, he told her. If the human eye sees the tail of a mouse disappearing down a hole, the human's brain, whose eye has seen this tail, also visualises a mouse. But that human did not see a mouse: it saw a tail. Humans do not realise this, because they *see* what they think they see. The brain constructs what you think you see. The eye perceives light, but the brain does not process each and every reaction of each and every cone and rod in the eye. It sees what it expects, what it has learnt. It projects itself on the surrounding environment, in order to make sense of that environment."

"I'm getting bored, Peter," she said. "I work for you now. Tell me what to do."

"Just so that you understand. Our electronic handset will be programmed like the brain, and like the brain, it will learn. At the moment your mobile phone, or in your case someone else's mobile phone, receives vast amounts of binary data. Our device will spend much of its time cutting off the flow, once it's got what it wants. We did a test on the complete works of Shakespeare (the albinos chose this, by the way) and reduced the time on-line by 90%, compared to conventional data transfer."

Farah had perked up, "So that means, we get around a lot of the issues to do with transferring images both static and moving."

"You've got it," Peter said. "It's early days, so our efficiency will improve, but I would say that, even now, before we really start, we are several lengths, or maybe light-years, ahead of the rest of the field."

"Peter, I look forward to my new role. If it does not fulfil all of my six lives, I will be utterly conventional and find a man to marry. For the right person, I would willingly give up five of the six lives you attribute to me."

"I cannot imagine who such a man could possibly be," he said.

A vision of Nathan swaying from side to side, as he descended the piste in Méribel on skis, came unbidden into her mind, and then cleared.

"Peter, I have one last thing to say to you. I have done this in Switzerland with the banks, today, so that if anything happened to me, you can do our thing. You have the accounts."

"I can sign on the accounts. And?"

"Peter, you don't want to know what I have done. Yesterday I have done the only thing I have ever done in my life that I truly did not wish to do. I had to, and I hope never so to do ever again. I have to complete what I have to do, now. I will see you in Bangalore next week. If I do not, please, Peter, please, do not ask after me. Please, Peter, please, do what we wanted, create your dream, your dream and my dream."

She hugged him, and he realised that she was serious. He always hugged her when he met her. She had never hugged him before this moment.

***

Suleiman had convened an emergency board meeting by phone.

"Gentleman, this is an open telephone line. We have never done this before, but I think you will realise I have no choice. The agenda is that I ask the questions and you answer, if you have an answer."

Silence.

"Why do we have no funds in our charity accounts?"

Silence.

"Why was Vanesh found dead in a Swiss hotel?"

Silence.

"Do you have any pertinent information?"

Silence.
"Thank you, gentlemen. I will assemble a task force."

CHAPTER SIXTEEN – TASK FORCE

London, 2 August 2001

Vermouth was surprised by the composition of the task force. It was himself, Suleiman and Zenap. It must be for reasons of confidentiality, he thought, but he was still surprised not to see Jamal. On the other hand Jamal had been unusually silent these last couple of months. For reasons of face, decorum or whatever, Suleiman had determined to hold a full discussion without Zenap before bringing her in. Maybe he wanted her for implementation and did not want to disclose certain details. So they had spent three hours going over every angle they could think of and rummaging through Vanesh's files before Suleiman brought Zenap in.

"Zenap, what do you think?" Suleiman asked.

"Vanesh did not share our religious beliefs, but for a man like him, that cannot be it, and it is definitely not greed. It has to be a woman, *cherchez la femme*."

Incredibly, this was not a conclusion they had reached.

"The only seductive woman in our circle is you, Zenap," said Suleiman.

She smiled at him. "That may be the case as far as you and I are concerned, but I can assure you 100% that Vanesh holds no amorous intentions towards me."

"I know," said Suleiman. "He's dead."

"I'm sorry. It was an accident. I didn't realise." She had not been fully briefed, thought Vermouth.

Suleiman: "It was no accident, Zenap."

"My analysis stands," she said, "without reservation."

Suleiman proceeded with a review of the options and concluded that there was no choice. The scope of the investigation would require the services of a friendly intelligence agency, as they did not have sufficient resources themselves to extract the real information on Vanesh, especially when it came to breaching bank secrecy. He, Suleiman would deal with this. Otherwise, it was imperative that they keep all projects running. Scotched were Vermouth's plans of exiting the "powder" business.

Zenap was glad to be in the meeting. The "friendly intelligence agency" would have to be paid, and she knew it would not be a Saudi agency. If she could just find out who this was and overlay a political construction on a modicum of evidence, she could have them baying for Suleiman, guilty until proved innocent, especially if she could track the payment to the agency. This was one more term of the equation close to being resolved. She had secured the money for her venture, and now she just had to have someone tie up the loose ends, deflect, no prevent, any investigation that might incriminate her. It had become unavoidable to silence Vanesh in Zurich, but it was not the type of risk she liked to take: it fell way outside her preferred scope of activities. There had simply not been time for anything else. What counted now was that everything move very, very fast.

Suleiman asked Vermouth to take over the Board's finances. He asked Zenap to work closely with Vermouth. For the time being he wanted her to concentrate on carrying out any executive matters relating to the task force. Vermouth cringed at the thought of working closely with Zenap. True their work to date had often been connected, but they had always operated completely independent of one another. The meeting broke up, leaving just Suleiman and Vermouth in the room to go over some other matters.

As she waited outside for a taxi, Zenap pondered what she was should do. What was the task force really capable of establishing? What threats did she face from this task force, before she could close it down? Her keen senses told her that speed was of the essence, so why not go back and catch Vermouth now, agree some first steps, how they should work together, be practical, and something might turn up. She went back to the fourth floor of the offices, where they had met. As she stepped out of the lift the door of the neighbouring lift was closing, but she heard Suleiman: "They're your friends, Julian. Find out if they will see me." Neither Suleiman nor Vermouth saw her. There was something out of context about this, she thought. Suleiman did not get contacts from Julian. Who could "your friends" be?

In the taxi on the way back to the hotel she ran this strange comment through her mind. She would have to ask Julian. But how? She had the feeling that this was a very important part of the pattern and worth laying out high stakes to find out what was happening. She had time to think, the traffic along the Strand was heavy. Why was it called the Strand, beach in German? Had it really been a beach once, along the side of the Thames? She returned to the problem in hand. By the time she reached the hotel she had first, a very good idea of the answer, and secondly a plan of action. This is very unsavoury, she thought, but it should be very effective.

She had a splendid room, traditionally furnished, and a large bathroom with black and white tiles on the floor. Suleiman was on a floor above and Vermouth was in the room next door, which should be convenient for working together over the next couple of days while they stayed in London. It was also very convenient to her plan that there was a connecting door to Vermouth's room.

After showering, she dressed in formal business attire, a white blouse and matching Bordeaux skirt and jacket, and she called housekeeping. She and her colleague were about to have a business meeting and could housekeeping open the connecting door, as they would wish to break out into group meetings in the second room from time to time. Housekeeping, in the shape of a twenty-five year old Romanian girl as experienced in the ways of the business world as the rest of housekeeping staff, did as instructed. Zenap did what she had to do in Vermouth's room and then bolted the connecting door from her side. She knew Vermouth would be out on business for the rest of the day, followed by dinner. He would not be back before midnight.

***

Vermouth sat up in bed with a start as the door clicked open, a chink of light from outside growing as the door swung into the room. Then she stepped into the frame made by the open door, silhouetted against the light. He could see she was wearing one of his shirts, hanging loose, open at the front, and nothing else. The vision disappeared as the door swung closed behind her excluding the light, but he could sense her presence as she crossed to the bed, and then she was in bed beside him and the bedside light clicked on. She eased the shirt off her shoulders and pressed herself to him, pulling him down to lie beneath her. Her hair cascading around him.

"I want to do this, Julian." And he felt himself slide into her, his body coming alive.

"You hate me, Julian." It was true. He said nothing.

"That I understand, Julian, but why are you setting the Jews on to me?"

"I am not." She was moving with growing excitement.

"You've been talking to them, Julian." Julian knew that she was aware of his connections in Israel. How would he react to the question?

"That's not for you." As he spoke, he was asking himself why he was revealing this to her, but then it would not matter, if she knew, would it? "That's to protect Suleiman."

She had what she wanted to know. The Israelis were to be engaged to investigate Vanesh's murder and the misappropriated funds.

"I'm controlling you now, Julian. Can you feel it?" He could feel it.

"Not yet, Julian."

He gasped.

"I've changed my mind." She slipped from him and stood up from the bed, where he lay, prostrate and erect. He lay there seething. She picked up the shirt, walked to the door and looked back at his naked form.

"Nowhere to go," she said with taunt in her voice.

As she spoke, she asked herself, why am I doing this? This is not what I do. I do not make enemies. She threw aside the shirt, moved back to the bed and drew him into her, rolling over so that he was now above.

"I don't know why I did that, Julian. I have never disliked you. I have always admired you. Just pretend that I only did that, so that when I came back I would give you the best value you have ever had in your life." He held her against him.

"I admit I have never liked you, Zenap, but I have always given you credit for doing what you do better than anyone else...this...this is no exception."

"I am not used to this, Julian... right now...I am experiencing...the most wonderful sensation I have ever felt...in my whole life...I know that it is just going to get better. It is...it..."

As she stood at the door to leave, they both knew that nothing had changed between them, except that they would do this whenever they could.

"I will be back before breakfast, say, around six." She reached for the door handle, bethought herself. "But before I go..." She crossed the room and returned him.

***

Suleiman wanted Zenap to join him at breakfast. Zenap descended to the foyer, turned left and took the few steps up to a raised circular area to the rear of the foyer where breakfast was being served. Suleiman was already there, as she knew he would be.

"I have to ask something very unusual of you Zenap. I simply don't have any time to do otherwise than ask for your help. I have to meet someone at eleven very briefly in one of the courtyards of the Inns of Court just over the road from here. I'll take you there and show you exactly where after breakfast. There is one point from which you can achieve full surveillance of my contact and me. I want to position you there. All I want you to do is watch for anyone with a camera. I don't want to be photographed. If you see anyone pointing a camera in our direction, I want you to get to them quickly and grab the camera. For your and my protection shout "Suleiman", if you have to do this. They will realise they have been caught out, and simply leave." Suleiman did not tell her any more, nor did she expect him to. But she did begin to believe that everything was falling into her lap.

Suleiman and Zenap walked past the Royal Courts of Justice and proceeded along Fleet Street, past sandwich bars and small shops and then turned right into an alleyway that led them into the Inns of Court. They weaved their way through various courtyards, up and down steps, through arches, doubled back, having gone wrong, and then they were in a quadrangle. The buildings had white painted sash windows and in one corner was a pub. Suleiman showed her where he wanted her to stand, and reiterated the plan to her.

Zenap suggested she lead on the way back and she took them straight back to Fleet Street. Suleiman turned right to walk to the City. Zenap turned left for the hotel. On the way she stopped in a camera store and bought two identical Olympus cameras with a zoom lens. She then took a taxi to the West End, had the taxi wait outside a shop while she picked up the necessary materials to develop photographs in black and white, and then she returned to the hotel. She had figured out how to get away with using a flash, which would be needed to make out detail under the stone archway.

***

Suleiman needed no more than two minutes with his contact to satisfy himself that the plan Vermouth had proposed was accepted. As they shook hands to depart the contact swung round.

"Who's photographing?" he barked out, and in that moment a female voice shouted, "Suleiman", and Zenap appeared from around the corner, brandishing a camera.

"It's OK, she's mine," Suleiman said.

"It was only a Japanese tourist," Zenap said. "I don't think it was even pointed at you, but I didn't want to take the chance. I stuffed five hundred bucks in his hands, whispered, "security", and he took off as fast as he could."

Suleiman reached for the camera, and the Israeli said, "I shall take that."

"Gentlemen," Zenap said, stepping back as she opened the camera and pulled out the film. "I have a more equitable solution."

She unrolled the film, exposing it, and said to the mystery contact, as she handed it to him, "With my compliments, but the camera I have bought four five hundred bucks from its Japanese owner and am keeping." Suleiman smiled.

On the way back to the hotel she had ditched the camera in a rubbish bin. In her bathroom, temporarily doubling as a darkroom, she took the film from the second camera, the camera that had taken the shot, and developed it. Later she would give the camera to Suleiman and ask for five hundred dollars of expenses. He would not recognise that it was not the camera he had seen at the "crime" scene; for that he would have to have checked the serial number to distinguish the identical models.

While the developing process continued in her improvised darkroom, she hooked up to the Internet and assembled a package of information. Anyone could have assembled this package of lies, but pulled together in the manner she had employed, and accompanied by a photograph, it would be very persuasive. She thought it might even stand up in the Royal Courts of Justice, which she had just walked past, but that was not where it would be used. She addressed two envelopes to two different addresses in Riyadh. One would contain the package, the other instructions of where to deliver the package together with a code word, which when spoken over the telephone would be the green light to go ahead and deliver the package. Her mailbox, and local courier, was a Pakistani banker on contract in Saudi Arabia. He would never have an inkling of the contents of the package. He was just returning a well-earned favour, for a particularly attractive friend.

Zenap sat back in her hotel room armchair and regarded the photograph. It was perfect. She had caught the handshake, and in black and white it did look very clandestine. She had no idea who the Israeli was, and her whole plan hinged on the recipients being able to establish that, but she had little doubt that they could. He would have to be an above-board diplomat or businessman. They would not risk an undercover operative for a meeting as speculative as this one with Suleiman must have seemed to them. She would never know how Vermouth had engineered this, what he had told them, or how he would get them to investigate the Zurich situation.

But then she did not need to know. As of right now the endgame was underway, and it was all going her way.

Later that day two packages left London with DHL for Riyadh. Coincidentally, that same day British Intelligence retrieved from a computer, which they had been hacking into for some months, a very intriguing file on a Gulf based banker whom they had under observation. It was the perfect opportunity to pull Vermouth in for questioning. They just had to work out how best to do it.

Zenap reflected on how it had all come to this. The Board were in over their heads, she thought. They were like little boys, playing with water pistols in the scrap yard, who come across a case of Kalashnikovs, ammunition and a box of grenades. They decide to hand them out to their friends. These boys' friends were not up to handling the weapons any more than Suleiman's "charity" friends were up to handling the vast sums of money which Suleiman was intending to disburse to them. Absurd. She could not fault Vermouth's logic of how to get the money, a brilliant scheme, but surely he should have understood that you cannot employ sums on that scale for the purposes Suleiman had in mind. In her mind, the "charities" could be supported, though in truth she deplored some of their methods, but like all else, only within a reasonable context, within a reasonable framework. And that was not two billion dollars.

CHAPTER SEVENTEEN - ENDGAME

London, 9 August 2001

Nathan waited for Bill Robinson at Arrivals, Heathrow Terminal Two. The instructions were clear: act naturally, take him to the car, open the nearside rear door for him, take his bag as if you are putting it in the boot, slam the door as soon as he's in, and they'll be off. They had said that this was imperative, as they could not risk interception at immigration for his own safety against prying eyes (nor did they care to risk an arrest on the public concourse, but this they did not disclose to Nathan). No one should be alerted until they had had a chance to question Robinson, they said, for his own good. As far as Nathan knew they would question Bill as a matter of formality, but it had to be discreet. Presumably, they would then let Bill go, a bit shocked, nothing worse.

They had set up arrangements, they had told Nathan, for a meeting under circumstances which fitted Nathan's meeting Robinson at the airport. Sure enough, Robinson appeared through the frosted glass doors, raising his hand to indicate he had seen Nathan. I'm Judas, Nathan thought with a pang. Well, at least I won't have to kiss the guy. Bill reached out to shake his hand.

"I've gotta change some cash, Nathan."

Christ, thought Nathan, doesn't this guy know about ATMs? He was, of course, unaware that the only credit cards on Bill Robinson that would operate teller machines were in the name of Julian Vermouth, just as Nathan was unaware that the vicar had matched up the two identities through the phone number Nathan had given him. His nerves prickled as Bill joined the queue at the foreign exchange booth. It moved slowly. The teller seemed not to know how to use a calculator, but then Bill picked up the cash and they were away, down the stairs, moving towards the exit and through the doors to come out of the terminal building. The limo was exactly where it should be. Bill stopped and turned.

"For a second I though I saw a familiar face over there," he said. Nathan could hardly calm himself. Bill turned back and they moved across the taxi and bus lanes to the limo. As planned, it was over in seconds. Nathan watched the limo glide away.

***

She had landed at Heathrow half an hour ahead of Vermouth. She had to see this for herself, make sure it really happened, and then she would set the rest of the endgame in motion. She was standing just aside from the main corridor when she saw him striding towards immigration, carrying a light travel bag. She thought they would probably intercept Vermouth in immigration, so she followed, twenty metres and group of three businessmen separating them. Then she saw that he was waived straight through immigration and she had to quicken her pace to catch up; this did not look good.

She had been sure that they would haul him in on arrival, given the information that she had allowed the mystery hacker to retrieve: this had to be their opportunity; they could not afford to miss it. He disappeared through the automatic doors to the arrivals concourse. She stepped through the doors, still maintaining a safe ten metres. Through the doors she turned left towards the exit and quickly sidestepped behind a group of Italians – he was being met by Nathan. This was very strange. She moved forward slowly and saw them stop at a foreign exchange booth. The concourse was crowded, so she took the opportunity to pass them, and decided to take up a strategic position near the walkway to short-term parking. This would allow her to follow, if that were their route, or move in behind them if they took the more likely exit through to the taxis on the level below.

She was not disguised. She never was, despite her many aliases. Her principle was that the best way not to look suspicious was to be yourself. It held the risk of someone recognising you in the wrong identity, but that had never happened to her so far. Now she was not sure of how she was going to manage to follow two people who knew her, and she began to think she had mismanaged this whole situation. Then she saw them head for the exit on the lower level and moved fast. Outside there was little opportunity to blend into the background and for a moment she thought Vermouth had seen her, before she slipped between two buses on the first pedestrian island outside the terminal.

She saw them cross the bus and taxi lanes and go up to a limo, standing behind a light blue Jaguar. Next second Vermouth was in and the limo pulled away, leaving Nathan standing there, watching it leave. Instantly she thought, this must be the snatch. They had used Nathan. No way would Nathan have a limo, but they wanted a big secure vehicle that did not look out of place at an airport. It probably had a couple of armed guards inside. Vermouth was a fool to get in. He should have realised it was a set-up as soon as he saw the limo. So they must have pulled Nathan back into the loop for this part of the operation. What would they have disclosed to him to do a Judas exercise on Bill Robinson, she wondered. She knew that Nathan had the greatest respect for Bill. Surely he could not have been so calm if he knew the truth. She remembered his utter inability to dissimulate the first time she had met him in the wine bar in London. My intuition tells me, she thought, that I should confront Nathan directly, confuse his wits out of him, and see where we go from there.

"Hello, Nathan." He turned.

"Zelda!"

"I had to see it, Nathan, and you know for a moment I thought he saw me over there."

"How did you know?"

"Nathan, who else do you think could have set him up? You know who that was?"

"Bill Robinson." Nathan responded without doubt in his voice.

"There is no Bill Robinson, Nathan. There never was. That was Julian Vermouth."

"You mean…" Nathan started, and seeing his confusion, Zelda took a gamble.

"Yes, partner. You were simply not supposed to know that we were on the same side, for your own safety. Let's go."

As the cab headed into town along the M4, Zelda knew she was on the home straight. Vanesh had fulfilled his role and was dead. It had been his choice to betray the Board, and everyone else. He had fully deserved his end, although she was still unhappy that she had been forced to take such extreme action. Now she had shopped Vermouth. He would never open his mouth, but fight extradition, probably successfully, for years, and in the end he would be freed. She knew Vermouth would never do a deal with them here in London. She had guessed that they would hope for him to do a deal and talk, to get the big fish, which was why they had not arrested him yet but wanted to question him. They simply did not know enough of the facts, she thought, having simply relied on my bogus leaks to the hacker. Vermouth is a big fish, and therefore he cannot talk.

The other risk in London was Frank Chardonnay, but she felt confident that Frank, being Frank, would do everything he could to hang on to the illegal Constexo share trade she had deliberately leaked to him, and anyway he would have little credibility. As to Suleiman, she had the dossier with sufficient paper evidence and the supporting photograph. She would release this to the Saudis with a phone call and that would be the end of the Board. Jamal would run for cover once he realised that, with the October target for his plan, he had missed the boat. Maybe he would make a move on the businesses, wrest control of them for himself, and in the back of her mind she wondered if that is what he had been doing these last two months. Maybe he had just intended to bring her in for the big kill at the centre, which he must forego now that circumstances had overtaken him. That just left Nathan of those who knew too much, and he was secretly in love with her. Now he believed she was a British agent.

But the more she considered it, the weaker her original plan for Nathan seemed. Was she being sentimental? She had been intending to explain to him that private banking was over for him after all of this. He would be offered counselling, which he should refuse on the grounds that the best for him was to find a new job, maybe abroad. She would tell him that she, Zelda, felt they should see more of one another, that she saw something there, which was true – she did. She would say she had some inherited money that would tide them over for a while. Nathan would believe her. Why should he not? Then she would see how the wind blew. After all, none of them even knew her nationality, let alone her name.

No, this plan really was too weak. There was not enough time, the risks were high and there was too much at stake. Too much money for any of them to let it rest here. They might call Nathan in tonight. He might perceive her duplicity and fail to understand it. The vicar might check in, unlikely, but he might. Her mind was spinning. She was not able to focus. I have never balked before, she told herself. She leaned across to Nathan. "Do you mind if we go back to your place, Nathan?"

In the flat in Beaufort Street they sipped red wine, an Australian Shiraz a touch to young. They had ordered pizza, and the meal had helped Nathan to relax after the tension of the day. Their mood became amorous. She was in his arms, stretched out on the red sofa. Her head lay back and her hair covered his chest.

"Nathan, in all these months together I have felt so good with you. I have wanted this. I have not dared." Nathan smiled dreamily. She echoed his feelings. He bent towards her and their lips met. They slid to the floor, rolling onto the soft flokati carpet, letting their intimacy grow. Nathan felt himself slip into a dream world as his wishes were met. As she lowered herself upon him she whispered to him, that he was the one she loved. They were entwined and moving towards a Nirvana Nathan had only ever imagined. As they entered this Nirvana, she whispered again, "Nathan, please know that whatever may be, I do love you."

After eight seconds he gave a slight gasp at the pressure on the carotid artery in his neck, and by ten seconds his consciousness had slipped away. It took Zelda just one more second to ensure he would never breathe again. Zelda rose and looked down at him.

"I did not want this Nathan. I truly did not. Of them all, you were the one who did not deserve this. But what could I do? You would always believe you must do what is right, your flaw, Nathan. You were too principled for my world. You should have agreed to work for Suleiman and become a powerful man. But you could not do that. Suleiman could have; just as he had his grand cause. In his work he always claimed it was the "end" justifying the "means". But it wasn't. The "means" were simply the game they wanted to play, and the "end" just defined which side they were on. But for you it was different, Nathan. You had a noble spirit. In the end you would have turned me in. You would not have understood me. You would have had to sacrifice me for your principles. You could not have lived with that guilt after you had done that, Nathan. So I have done what I have done. I shall not forget this, but I have no guilt. Guilt implies choice, and I had none. Enough, I am speaking to myself, she thought. I must be practical.

With a towel and a belt she constructed a makeshift nappy for the corpse of Nathan. She hoisted the corpse onto her back, piggy back style, lowered it to a chair and then propped up the limbs in the piggy back position, so that she would be able to carry it in rigor mortis. She found a trolley bag for aircraft hand luggage and two luggage padlocks, which she slipped into her pocket for use in attaching the bag later. She found a steam iron and a cast iron Le Creuset saucepan, both of which she loaded into the trolley bag. Around the waist of the corpse she wound Nathan's thirty-six inch bicycle anti-theft cable of wire clad in blue plastic, snapped the lock shut and spun the combination. This would later be used to attach the trolley bag. And now I wait, she thought.

Who was likely to accost a female at three in the morning, carrying her almost naked boyfriend and pulling a trolley bag? She did not believe for a moment that anyone would offer to assist her. The scene was too grotesque. Even a suspicious call to the police would still be on the emergency line by the time she had made away - it was only two hundred yards to the Thames. In the unlikely event that anyone saw the drop, she would be long gone before the police arrived on the scene. At eleven the phone rang and went to the answer phone. She heard the voice of the vicar: " Call me." So she had done the right thing.

And so it was that Nathan left home with his mistress at 3 a.m., sat for a moment on the parapet of Battersea Bridge and slipped into his watery grave, less than three minutes after leaving his front door.

REMINISCENCE

French Riviera, January 2009 – Nine Years Later

I retired to the South of France a couple of years ago, still in my forties. I could have bailed out of the City earlier, after the financial killing I made on the Constexo Energy shares; but petrified of an insider trading investigation, I decided it was safer to stay put for a few years. In the end the various committees investigating Constexo took seven years, and no one ever came around to looking at small fry like me. But I am still haunted by the events of that time. It seems that the twin sins of ignorance and greed contrived an unwitting role for me, a role in a pattern of events that I could never have imagined. What could I have done? For months afterwards I lived in fear of a knock on the door from our authorities to lock me up or from others seeking private retribution, against me, outside the legal process. That knock never came.

I think of the others I knew who were involved. Julian Vermouth was the first of several to be extradited to the US after years of legal battles. There had been a huge controversy at the time. I remember the demonstrations in London and then the final decision. And what of Suleiman, whom I hardly met? He was put to death for political conspiracy in Saudi Arabia; the full story was never made public. Then there was Nathan, poor Nathan, his corpse dragged from the Thames, gruesomely weighed down by, of all things, a cast iron saucepan. This was in the week following Vermouth's disappearance, which we later found out was his arrest. The only time I had met Nathan was that one superb day in Méribel with Zara, when we skied together, an impressive young banker. For weeks he was the subject of the Sunday papers' investigative reporting. Some claimed he was an innocent dupe of MI5. Others that he was party to some financial scandal. It was thrilling stuff, linked to a murder in a top Swiss hotel. I could not see Nathan in a financial scandal, but no one ever asked me. The Swiss hotel murder sounded to me more likely to be connected to the Constexo Energy fiasco, which blew up at the time, and was, thanks to Zara, the source of my own wealth.

But most of all, sitting in a café on the Riviera, I wonder what became of Zara. She simply vanished. When I see a redhead in the street, I always walk ahead of her, and turn to check the face, but I know of no one who has seen or heard of her since that fateful time. I'm brought back to the present by the beep of my communicator, the ubiquitous Zelda Three. I press a button to see the result of a share sale programmed into the Zelda, which manages my money. We all use them now, for everything. The Zelda is the cornerstone of a huge international concern which came from nowhere, five years ago, and threw the technology, communications and media markets into turmoil. Its products trounced the third generation mobile phones and consigned the PC to the grave, a few years a head of schedule. It is apparently run by a reclusive entrepreneur, a lady they say – strange, this media silence from a firm that leads the world's media.

I stand and walk wistfully back up the hill to my apartment overlooking the seafront. As I walk, I ponder. For me things just happened: I moved from one scene to the next, and then the next, and now I am in the South of France. And what of the others? They were in control of their destinies, especially Zara. They knew what they wanted, they made plans, they had designs, and they enacted them. But they have all trodden their own individual roads to hell, paved with their own good intentions. I cannot remember having had a good intention in my life. Is that why I'm still here? Where are they now?

JAMAL

Mayfair, London, July 2003 – Six Years Earlier

Jamal Ali had purchased a house in Mayfair, a few steps from Grosvenor Square, just a house so far, but if this were Monopoly he would be well on his way to a hotel. The house doubled as his office. He had applied his organisational and administrative skills, silently derided by Zenap on the Malaysian islands, to consolidate and develop the businesses he had "inherited" from Suleiman.

He had not taken on the narcotics business for the same reason as he had withdrawn from his politico-religious activities: the war in Afghanistan. The gem trade had, however, been phenomenal. Adding this cash flow to his family wealth he had immediately launched into the retail side of the business. He had engaged three investment banks to seek out private and public jewellers for acquisition. His only condition was that there should be an active stock market on which they could be floated. Wherever possible he planned to use other people's money.

His first coup had been in the first quarter of 2002 when he had been able to acquire a public company in the UK. This had become his vehicle into which he had reversed the upstream businesses as far a possible and which acted as a holding company for the retail jewellers. Strategy and execution was in the hands of his professional team, substantially the same as the group who had met in Malaysia. He was no longer a gem smuggler, but a trader and retailer, a very respectable chairman of a public limited company.

Jamal prided himself on the Italian décor in his conference room;

however, it is unlikely that many Italians would have shared his taste. The ceiling was royal blue with traditional stucco mouldings set off in gold and silver. Full-length mirrors glittered in their frames where they hung on pastel green walls, interspersed with works of modern art in differing styles. The conference table was of smoked glass on a steel frame with fourteen matching chairs. In each corner of the room stood a titanium halogen uplight. At each end of the room was a rosewood almeira, carved with patterns of long legged birds, storks and herons. Finely knotted silk rugs lay on a grey marble floor and depicted traditional Mogul hunting scenes. Perched by the window were two hunting falcons, of the real live variety, retired from active life since their move to London. Jamal had not employed an interior designer, preferring to put his own talents to use. This was out of character compared to his use of professionals in business life, but the result was, well, let's just say unique.

Jamal sat with his old friend from Karachi, David the jeweller, who had accepted the position of head of the purchasing division of Jamal's company. David's side of the business was the key to its success: this was where the money was made. In Jamal's highly unconventional business model, stone setting and the craftsmanship were subcontracted out, and the retail stores were required only to cover their costs. This gave the ladies of the world (and the gentlemen buying for them) a truly amazing deal. The result had been a dramatic rise in the turnover of every jewellery shop Jamal had acquired, huge power on the buying side and a clamour of cries of "foul" from his competitors.

Jamal closed the presentation deck in front of him.

"Thank you, David. These are excellent results. More tea?" Jamal asked.

"Yes, I will, thanks." David assented to the tea and poured them both a second cup.

"I have a meeting now with the owner of some Swiss company. They are an introduction from the venture capital people. You remember I said that we should diversify into some unrelated businesses."

"You did and I agree. We are in an upcycle now but it won't go on forever. Let's get some of the cash put away, though I would prefer the stock market. It's liquid: you can get the money when you want," David replied.

"That kind of investment is too far removed for me, David. You have no control. You don't know when the Chairman starts to hit the bottle too hard or the financial man decides he's cleverer than he is and sticks the company's money into duff financial instruments. I'd like you to stay for the meeting. They're here waiting. I'll have them sent in." He bleeped his doorman-cum-secretary.

The door to the conference room opened. "They" which was a "she" in this case entered wearing a classical blue dress with red hair flowing over her shoulders.

"Hello, Jamal Ali." Jamal was stunned, eyeing her in sheer disbelief, and for five seconds he simply sat there, in turn prompting amazement on David's part, amazement at Jamal's reaction.

"David, I would prefer to take this meeting alone. Hello, Zenap."

David stood and left the room, somewhat confused but also intrigued by Jamal's relationship to this stunning looker, who truly had stunned Jamal.

"May I take a seat?" she asked.

"In the lion's den? Why not?" He offered her a chair.

"I am no Christian here for the lions, Jamal."

"In the wolf's lair then, for you. After what happened to the rest of them, I guessed that it was you who took the money. You betrayed me," Jamal said.

"I did not take the money, Jamal. Vanesh did. I took it from Vanesh. If you had done the same you would not have given it to me. You were too late with your plan, Jamal. Vanesh pipped you at the post. I thought he would and moved in. That's all. As I said, I am no Christian and saw no need for Christian charity with you as beneficiary." She smiled, leaning towards him, and he could not dispute her logic.

"So why are you here?" Jamal asked, believing as ever in the direct approach.

"First, I am not Zenap nor ever have been, as you probably knew. Here. Have my card." She passed a business card across to him. "It is simple. I have a Swiss company which has spent just over two billion dollars to create a product that we will give the brand name of *Zelda Three.*"

"That is much money, Farah," he said, laying emphasis on *Farah,* a new name for him.

"It is all the money I have, or had, which is why I am here. I need money to bring the Zelda Three to market. It's a personal communicator which, in my assessment, is several incarnations ahead of its rivals, or let's say it's what Homo sapiens is to the chimp."

"As always you are very precise," he said.

"I shall be more precise. I am offering you 25% of the company. Just taking the money we have spent that would be worth five hundred million. I believe that if we were to take into account the future cash flows the value would be many times that. We need two hundred million from you, so think of the difference as being my little gift to you to ask forgiveness. Am I forgiven?" And that was Farah's proposition.

Jamal called David back in and introduced them. He watched as David and Farah clicked instantly. Jamal outlined the proposition to David and then the two of them went through the presentation that Farah had brought, grilling her in detail for three hours. They went through the technology, the markets, the financial projections and the proposed corporate structure. At the end David turned to Jamal and made his proposal.

"Jamal, everything about this stacks up. If someone had come to me with plans for a DVD player, I would have done it. I say we do this."

"I agree. Terms? Should we retire for a private discussion?" Jamal suggested.

"Not necessary, Jamal. Farah will take whatever we offer. I don't see her as having a real choice, unless she wants to shop around which would be dumb." David smiled at Farah.

"I could stand up and leave," she said.

"Why would you? You want to hear what I have to say," he continued. "We have up to four hundred million dollars that we could invest today, if this deal were the only thing we did. I say we do it. Shelve our other plans for the time being. This is the big one. The only change I would make to Farah's plan is that we spend twice as much as she proposes on marketing in the interests of speed, of getting this thing to market. I expect you would have asked for four hundred, Farah, if you had known we had it, and you could only have found that out by hacking into our computers." Farah gave him a little smile.

"And the equity?" Jamal asked.

"I accept that Farah's partner, Arbakhov, should have 24%, as he's the brains, and that she wants control with 51%," David responded.

"So how do we give Farah four hundred million?" Jamal would not want to double the price for the same amount of equity, and she had offered it to them for two hundred million.

"We'll take 25% for two hundred and lend two hundred to be repaid out of free cash flows, and Farah, we want your personal guarantee on the loan as well as your husband's if you've got one," David said, and he was quite interested to find out her response on the last part, about the husband.

Farah's response probably contributed to the two outcomes of the meeting: first, that the investment was agreed; and secondly, that she and David left together for dinner. Somehow they omitted to invite Jamal to join them. He did not mind. His smile was almost fatherly as he watched them leave. Downstairs they waved down a taxi and Farah gave the driver instructions. She told David that she had to conduct a brief mercy mission before going to eat, and he may as well join her. They headed for Holland Park.

***

It had been an unhappy time for Sue after she had left Ferdie. She had decided to make a clean break; a job opportunity had come up in London and she had taken it. In her drawing room she was occupying a Queen Anne armchair as she watched life passing on the street outside. Immediately opposite was a police station, and a couple of hundred yards to the right was Holland Park. She saw a taxi pull up in front of her building. A tall blonde man stepped out onto the pavement, accompanied by a red haired lady. A few seconds later her doorbell rang.

"Do you mind if we come in for a moment?" the lady asked Sue as she opened the door to them. The lady handed Sue a visiting card with a company name on it and an address in Lausanne. They seemed respectable and no doubt they would explain what this was about so she let them in. Once in the hall it seemed courteous to take them through, so she took them into the drawing room.

"I love these traditional London buildings," the lady said, "and you have furnished it so beautifully. Please do feel free to call me Farah, and this is my friend, David." Sue invited them to take a seat and they chose the Queen Anne leather armchairs.

"I should explain why I am here. May I call you, Sue," she continued. "I know your husband very well."

Sue was visibly shocked, the colour draining from her face.

"My *ex-husband*," Sue corrected.

"I understood you were not divorced," Farah responded.

"That is true, but he is still *ex* to me," Sue asserted, biting her lip, tears not far from her eyes as a vision of Ferdie drifted into the foreground. It was always lurking somewhere. Farah's blue-grey eyes looked deep into Sue and held her for a few seconds before Farah continued.

"He does not wish to be your ex. That is why I am here."

Farah paused as if working out how to put this

"If there were a place of spirituality in this world it would be Tibet. But the Chinese have usurped Tibet. Perhaps that place is now Nepal. It is a place of mountains, a place of monasteries, a place of meditation – somewhere to search for and find inner peace."

"What has this to do with Ferdie, or me for that matter?" Sue asked.

"Sue," Farah replied, "Ferdie is in Nepal. He has asked me to give you a message. He wanted me to tell you in person. The day you left was the last day of his work for the Board. I am to tell you from him that he has understood you now and that he hopes it is not too late, that he hopes you will accept that he understands."

She looked at Sue and the pain in Sue's eyes told her that it was not too late, but she also saw that it would take much to convince Sue, so she held Sue's gaze and continued.

"I worked with Ferdie, Sue. I knew our employers for what they were and you can despise me for that. Ferdie did not know, Sue, and he had no proof for any suspicions he may have entertained. I know that, and I ask you to believe me. I do not know you, Sue, but I truly believe that you will take the right decision now." David had no idea of what this was about, but he was deeply moved by the scene he was witnessing. Farah drew a packet from her bag and placed it on the marble table. She stood, and without a word she and David retreated to the street.

Sue remained seated in her grand drawing room. She saw them walk off towards Holland Park, but still she did not move. She was reliving that last night in Manhattan: the strains of music coming from Ferdie's study while she made her final decision; her announcement to him which followed; and then her devastation as she descended in the elevator with that one impossible desire which she had resisted, to return to him. She opened the packet. It contained air tickets and the name of a hotel in Kathmandu and another in Pokhara. She felt the red haired lady had reached deep into her and plucked out any indecision she may have had.

***

"There is a layer of mist over the airport, which we expect to clear in thirty minutes, so you are lucky," the accented voice of the pilot announced. "I will take you on a free tour of the Himalayas, courtesy of the airline so tell your friends, while we wait for permission to land. Watch out for Everest on the left." Sue was sitting at the very front of the plane, the only passenger in first class. She had a steward and a hostess all to her herself and they had had great fun during the flight, consuming several glasses of Champagne. It had helped her take her mind off the reason for being here. Through the porthole she could see white peaks beside them, delicious bites of ice cream, and sure enough, there was the unmistakable shape of Everest, no mountaineers visible on the summit today. The plane banked smoothly, unlike the tourist planes that would be buffeted by mountain gales.

Sue picked up a visa on arrival and was met by a young man holding her name on a signboard. He suggested he take her to the hotel, and then he would take her on a tour in the afternoon if she wished. Tomorrow he would pick her up to catch the plane to Pokhara. She preferred to simply register at the hotel, drop her bag and the go straight out on his tour. The glimpse of the mountains from the plane had exerted its irresistible attraction.

The striking thing about the architecture in Kathmandu is its lack of respect for the plumb line. Not even by accident did any of the beams in the buildings Sue could see achieve verticality. The second striking thing is that everything that has been restored has been restored by other nations, and every aspect of the modern world, be it a road or a hospital, seems to have been the offering of a competing power bloc. It was no surprise that unrest had been fomented among the local population at the turn of the millennium.

They left the city and headed up to a viewing point for the mountains. Beside the road rice terraces had been cut into the slopes. Every last tiny space of every plot had been terraced; right down to individual terraces the size of the palm of a hand. The boy driver was a source of information as they drove, the perfect guide. The power of the mountains impressed Sue deeply. She could understand why monasteries had grown up here and why meditation was imbued in the culture. From the viewing point she absorbed the magnificence of the mountains, gazing in fascination and awe at the Himalayan splendour. It struck her that her husband had chosen this venue astutely. She was beginning to lose the edge of her tension by the time they returned to the hotel in the evening.

***

Even the most pleasant of touristic experiences is easily eclipsed by terror, the sort of terror that can be inspired by flying a jet aircraft straight at a cliff face. And this seemed to be exactly what they were doing as they approached Pokhara. The pilot's door was flapping open, and through the cockpit windshield all Sue could see was a cliff face directly ahead, looming ever closer, and still they did not land. Then it appeared that the pilot had taken a split second decision to snatch them from the jaws of certain death and they were on the ground. Inexplicably the cliff face had retreated to a respectable distance.

"I've got give it to this guy," she said to her neighbour, a young American. "He sure knows how to scare the pants off you, panties in my case."

"I guess he just wants a good tip, so he demonstrates his flying skill," the young man answered. "Once we got up in those clouds, I thought no way was he going to get us back down. All I could think of was the mountains on the left and the mountains on the right, both higher than us. No way would he find the valley down below through all that thick cloud."

"You got it. I think I'll drive back." She said.

"I've tried that too," he replied. "You want my advice? Forget it."

Ferdie was not there to meet her at the airfield, but another sign with her name was. She felt this was turning into a treasure hunt. On arrival at the hotel she registered at the reception and went up to her room. There was an envelope with her name on it on the table. She did not open it. She needed to relax, to think.

So this really is it, she thought. I am here and the contents of this envelope will lead me to my husband whom I have not seen for three years. Why am I doing this? I am a mature woman, and I have let myself be led here like an adolescent girl, a girl blinded by hope and dreams that later curdle into regret. Is this what I want? No, you are listening to the voices of long- dead devils, she told herself. I am here *because* I am a mature woman and *because* I have faith that what I have lost may be recovered.

She walked onto her balcony and gazed out at the lake of Pokhara, gleaming beneath the peaks which rose up behind. Far off she saw a solitary figure standing beside the lake and she knew she need not open her envelope. Serene of spirit she left the hotel and followed the lakeside path to join him.

THE END

OTHER BOOKS AVAILABLE FROM TWENTY FIRST CENTURY PUBLISHERS LTD

THE SIGNATURE OF A VOICE

The Signature of a Voice is a cat-and-mouse game between a violent trio, led by a psychopathic killer, and a police officer on suspension. Move and countermove in this chess game is planned and enacted. The reader, in the position of god, knows who is guilty and who plans what, but just as in chess, the opponents' plans thwart one another. The outcomes twist and turn to the final curtain fall.

The Signature of a Voice by Johnny John Heinz
ISBN 1-904433-00-6

RAMONA

How did a little girl come to be abandoned in the orange scented square of the Andalusian City of Seville? Find out, when the course of her life is resumed at age seventeen.

"Ramona" is a literary work that deals with Europe in transition and the relationships that form an ususual life.

Ramona by Johnny John Heinz
ISBN: 1-904433-01-4

TARNISHED COPPER

Tarnished Copper is a story of greed, deception and corruption in one of the most volatile of financial markets. The author, Geoffrey Sambrook, has been a metal trader for 20 years, seeing the collapse of the International Tin Council, the Sumitomo Affair and numerous other market shenanigans, and brings an insider's unique insight into the way markets can be manipulated for profit. The fictional characters of Tarnished Copper seem horrifyingly real as they follow their dance of deception, culminating in untold riches for some, and death for another. A new, cerebral voice in financial fiction.

Tarnished Copper by Geoffrey Sambrook
ISBN 1-904433-02-2

Visit our website: www.twentyfirstcenturypublishers.com

www.ingramcontent.com/pod-product-compliance
Lightning Source LLC
Chambersburg PA
CBHW020321260626
47156CB00004B/1321

* 9 7 8 1 8 4 3 7 5 0 0 8 6 *